The Best Ghost Stories
1800-1849

A Classic Ghost Anthology

Edited and Introduced
by
Andrew Barger

For Maeve, my young literary spirit.

Fiction by Andrew Barger

Mailboxes – Mansions – Memphistopheles
A Collection of Dark Tales

Coffee with Poe
A Novel of Edgar Allan Poe's Life

Edited by Andrew Barger

The Best Horror Short Stories 1800-1849
A Classic Horror Anthology

The Best Werewolf Short Stories 1800-1849
A Classic Werewolf Anthology

Edgar Allan Poe
Annotated and Illustrated Entire Stories and Poems

Leo Tolstoy's 20 Greatest Short Stories
Annotated

Orion
An Epic English Poem

Website:
AndrewBarger.com

Blog:
AndrewBarger.blogspot.com

The Best Ghost Stories 1800-1849
A Classic Ghost Anthology

Edited and Introduced by
Andrew Barger

First Edition
Manufactured in the United States or United Kingdom
ISBN: 978-1-933747-33-0

Printed on 100% recycled paper in both
the United States and United Kingdom
(20% Post Consumer Waste)

Fonts: Bookman Old Style & Chiller

CONTENTS

All Ghosts are Gray

ALL CATS ARE GRAY in the dark. This sly phrase dates back to 1596 when John Heywood recounted in his popular *Proverbs* that "when all candles be out all cats be grey." Benjamin Franklin—who got around in his day—turned the phrase to mean that all women look the same in the dark. Modern books contain the phrase as their title and The Cure released a song on their *Faith* album called "All Cats Are Grey"; lyrics inspired by Mervyn Peake's groundbreaking *Gormenghast Trilogy*.

But what about ghosts? Don't they all look the same in the dark, too? When all candles be out, all ghost be gray? From folklore to poetry to short stories to novels—literature has mysteriously evolved to assert that all ghosts are void of color.

For reasons unknown, ghosts have been solidified in our collective minds as being pale or lacking color. In the bloodletting Romantic and Victorian ages, this may have been the result of the bloodless skin of corpses or the thick powder applied to the dead before funeral viewings. The ashen pallor of the terminally ill may be another instance why ghosts are thought to lack color. The graying hair of the elderly comes to mind. Perhaps it is the white light cast off by Biblical angelic hosts that led to all spirits not of this realm missing color.

To find out, I conducted an experiment (using the wealth of data provided by the keyword searchable publications on Google Books) that compared usages of "white ghost" versus "pale ghost." I was surprised to learn that through the Victorian age the later term won out by a large margin.

Throughout the ages ghosts have been represented in many stories as being white, as are a number in this collection. In *The Tragedy of Albertus Wallenstein* by Henry Glapthorne published in 1639 we have "a pure white ghost...." The term "white ghost" is found twice in the English language between 1200 and 1699. From 1700 to 1799 it is not used and for the period in review the term is found in nearly 150 publications.

A much more common association is the pale ghost. The colorless ghost. The *gray* ghost. Reference to ghosts being pale took hold in the eighteenth century where it became commonly used in poetry and stories. And then in the first half of the nineteenth century, which is the central focus of this anthology, the "pale ghost" phraseology saw a fourfold increase over the prior hundred years; while the "white ghost" was used about one fourth as much during the same half century.

Consider these stats on the term "pale ghost": It is found twice in English between 1200 and 1699. From 1700 to 1799 it is used over 200 times and from 1800 to 1849 it is found in almost 900 instances. Google Books does not contain as many searchable books from 1200-1699 as in more modern periods, but there were also much less written then, too, given the arduous task of publishing and lack of mass market printing devices.

Ghost stories are readily accessible. We've grown up on them, hearing them around campfires and at church alike. The *Bible* includes many ghost stories. One of the holy trinity is the Holy Ghost. The very name implies that there are *other* ghosts. I Samuel 28 tells of the woman at Endor who conjures the spirit of Samuel. The recently deceased king of Israel appears out of the earth to both her and Saul. He is old looking, dressed in a robe and is perturbed at having been "disquieted." Jesus Christ himself, when He arose from the tomb, chided His apostles for believing He was a ghost after rising from the dead. Doubting Thomas went so far as to touch His pierced side.

Ghost stories are perhaps one of the oldest stories known to human kind. They are everywhere; woven into the very fabric of our being, in every language and culture. With a few keystrokes we can now pull up an inexhaustible number of them on our computer screens.

Transparent. Gray. Colorless. Pale.

Speaking of gray, you will find that the Ghost of a Gray Tadpole (Thomas Dunn English's derogatory term for Edgar Allan Poe) only has one story in this collection and Ernst T. A. Hoffmann (considered the grandfather of the weird ghost story) has none. This may be surprising to some. While Edgar Allan Poe is the undisputed king of the short horror story for the first half of the nineteenth century, he wrote very few ghost stories.

The five possible Poe stories that may contain a ghost are: "The Fall of the House of Usher," "The Mask of the Red Death," "Morella," "Ligeia," and "The Oval Portrait." All are extremely well written, yet none are frightening enough to make the cut. In *The Best Horror Short Stories 1800-1849* I picked "The Fall of the House of Usher" as the very best horror story for the period in question. There has been much scholarly debate over the appearance of Madeline Usher, the cataleptic twin sister of Roderick Usher, in the story. In my view she was laid to rest while still alive and with her brother being uncertain if she was actually dead, which leaves him in a state of nervousness. Therefore, her reappearance does not foster a ghost sighting.

The second story, "The Mask of the Red Death," is clearly a ghost story. Consider this haunting passage: "The figure was tall and gaunt, and shrouded from head to foot in the habiliments of the grave. The mask which concealed the visage was made so nearly to resemble the countenance of a stiffened corpse that the closest scrutiny must have had difficulty in detecting the cheat."

That leaves the final three Poe stories listed above. I am a true believe that in any genre if a person has to work hard to figure out if the story belongs in that genre, then probably it does not. The last three—if for the sake of argument they are ghost stories—though written extremely well, do not rise to the level of terror needed for this collection.

Much more than Poe, Nathaniel Hawthorne and Washington Irving did much to elevate the American ghost story. The underlying meaning of Hawthorne's ghost stories, many of which address puritanical social issues of the day, brought a new dimension to the modern ghost story. Hawthorne's excellent "The Old Maid in the Winding Sheet" is included here.

Washington Irving had his moments of brilliance in the short ghost story space. His constant infusion of humor in his horror and ghost stories, however, leaves terror *wanting*, and for all but a handful of stories, does not leave us *wanting* more. H. P. Lovecraft took it one step further when he only mentioned "Adventure of the German Student" in his *Supernatural Horror in Literature* and no other Irving story:

"Washington Irving is another famous figure not unconnected with the weird; for though most of his ghosts are too whimsical and humorous to form genuinely spectral literature, a distinct inclination in this direction is to be noted in many of his productions."

But to then not mention "The Legend of Sleepy Hollow" as an exception, given its horrific moments of terror, is to rend the very fabric that clothes all excellent ghost stories—great characters—the second leg of the great story tripod (the other two being originality and fine writing). Well developed characters are essential for a high fright factor in any ghost story. When an author has a reader caring about a character, the reader is at the author's mercy, like we all do when Ichabod Crane and his broken-down horse Gunpowder see a large shadow from the bridge.

In Europe, Ernst T. A. Hoffmann was a frontrunner of the weird ghost story. He influenced many throughout Europe and America. Sparse translations from German to English inhibited widespread reading of this supernatural tales. Some of his ghost stories were a mishmash of styles and storylines like "Automata" and "The Elementary Spirit." Some were novellas and not considered for this collection. His most frightening short ghost story is "The Mines of Falun," yet its tremulous light from the deep mineshaft does not shine as brightly when compared to the other ghost stories found here.

Another writer highly influential in this genre was Sir Walter Scott. During the first half of the nineteenth century Sir Walter Scott was perhaps the chief architect in promoting supernatural tales throughout Britain. He backed the horror and ghost story publishing efforts of fellow Scotsmen: James Hogg and Allan Cunningham. Scott also found great merit in the works of Washington Irving and was instrumental in getting the American's publishing career started in London. Posthumously, Scott influenced *The C'ock and Anchor*, which was the first novel of Joseph Sheridan le Fanu, father of the Victorian ghost story.

The literature, especially for the period under review, gives us ghosts that are gray in personality, too, and at once limited in their ability to interact with the living world. The muted ghosts created by Edgar Allan Poe and Joseph Sheridan le Fanu impart very few words to the living, and no wisdom when they do. In Washington Irving's shortest story the ghost speaks at length, but gives no wisdom and is lost in this world. We see the aftermath of Joseph Sheridan le Fanu's specters through the base destruction of lives, yet we never see them slit the throat or tie a knot in the noose or push the protagonist off the railing. The ghost crew that mans the doomed ship of the Flying Dutchman hopelessly tries to get a message home to their loved ones.

Colorless. Pale. Gray. The terms are synonymous when ghosts appear in the dark, as they almost always do in the literature. Whether they are called specters, phantasms, spirits, or ghouls, in the literature:

all ghosts *are* gray.

Andrew Barger
May 22, 2011

WASHINGTON IRVING
(1783-1859)

Introduction
to
Adventure of the German Student

The first ghost story in this collection is the oldest and its shortest. No inferiority is implied because of its age or small size any more than Leonardo Da Vinci's compact "Mona Lisa," is inferior because it measures 77 cm x 53 cm.

The comparison does not assume that this ghost story is the "Mona Lisa" of literature. To be certain, the "Adventure of the German Student" has its faults. It's first sentence is poorly written ("On a stormy night, in the tempestuous times of the French revolution . . ..") and the machinations of the story are unoriginal.

Washington Irving admitted the lack of complete novelty in *Tales of a Traveller*, where he first published the story. "As the public is apt to be curious about the sources from whence an author draws his stories, doubtless that it may know how far to put faith in them, I would observe, that the *Adventure of the German Student*, or rather the latter part of it, is founded on an anecdote related to me as existing somewhere in French; and, indeed, I have been told, since writing it, that an ingenious tale has been

founded on it by an English writer; but I have never met
with either the former or the latter in print."

The story is but one in a collection that Edgar Allan
Poe applauded in the April 1842 issue of *Graham's
Magazine* while lamenting the poor state of the American
short story. "With rare exception — in the case of Mr.
Irving's 'Tales of a Traveller' and a few other works of a like
cast — we have had no American tales of high merit."

For those anthologists who believe that the greatest
short stories are the longest, I beg to differ. The
"Adventure of the German Student" is head of its class; an
apt pupil of the ghost story school that is one of the most
likely to succeed from the graduating class for the 50 year
period in review.

The revered H. P. Lovecraft, in his *Supernatural Horror
in Literature,* agreed: "'The German Student' in *Tales of a
Traveller* (1824) is a slyly concise and effective
presentation of the old legends of the dead bride."

Adventure of the German Student
(1824)

ON A STORMY NIGHT, in the tempestuous times of the French Revolution,[1] a young German was returning to his lodgings, at a late hour, across the old part of Paris. The lightning gleamed, and the loud claps of thunder rattled through the lofty narrow streets—but I should first tell you something about this young German.

Gottfried Wolfgang was a young man of good family. He had studied for some time at Gottingen, but being of a visionary and enthusiastic character, he had wandered into those wild and speculative doctrines which have so often bewildered German students. His secluded life, his intense application, and the singular nature of his studies, had an effect on both mind and body. His health was impaired; his imagination diseased. He had been indulging in fanciful speculations on spiritual essences, until, like Swedenborg, he had an ideal world of his own around him. He took up a notion, I do not know from what cause, that there was an evil influence hanging over him; an evil genius or spirit seeking to ensnare him and ensure his perdition. Such an idea working on his melancholy temperament, produced the most gloomy effects. He became haggard and desponding. His friends discovered the mental malady preying upon him, and determined that the best cure was a change of scene; he was sent, therefore, to finish his studies amidst the splendors and gayeties of Paris.

Wolfgang arrived at Paris at the breaking out of the revolution. The popular delirium at first caught his enthusiastic mind, and he was captivated by the political and philosophical theories of the day: but the scenes of blood which followed shocked his sensitive nature, disgusted him with society and the world, and made him more than ever a recluse. He shut himself up in a solitary apartment in the *Pays Latin*,[2] the quarter of students. There, in a gloomy street not far from the monastic walls

---

[1] French Revolution (1789-1799)
[2] Latin quarter

of the Sorbonne,[3] he pursued his favorite speculations. Sometimes he spent hours together in the great libraries of Paris, those catacombs of departed authors, rummaging among their hoards of dusty and obsolete works in quest of food for his unhealthy appetite. He was, in a manner, a literary ghoul, feeding in the charnel-house of decayed literature.

Wolfgang, though solitary and recluse, was of an ardent temperament, but for a time it operated merely upon his imagination. He was too shy and ignorant of the world to make any advances to the fair, but he was a passionate admirer of female beauty, and in his lonely chamber would often lose himself in reveries on forms and faces which he had seen, and his fancy would deck out images of loveliness far surpassing the reality.

While his mind was in this excited and sublimated state, a dream produced an extraordinary effect upon him. It was of a female face of transcendent beauty. So strong was the impression made, that he dreamt of it again and again. It haunted his thoughts by day, his slumbers by night; in fine, he became passionately enamoured of this shadow of a dream. This lasted so long that it became one of those fixed ideas which haunt the minds of melancholy men, and are at times mistaken for madness.

Such was Gottfried Wolfgang, and such his situation at the time I mentioned. He was returning home late one stormy night, through some of the old and gloomy streets of the Marais, the ancient part of Paris. The loud claps of thunder rattled among the high houses of the narrow streets. He came to the Place de Greve, the square where public executions are performed. The lightning quivered about the pinnacles of the ancient Hotel de Ville,[4] and shed flickering gleams over the open space in front. As Wolfgang was crossing the square, he shrank back with horror at finding himself close by the guillotine. It was the height of the reign of terror, when this dreadful instrument of death stood ever ready, and its scaffold was continually running with the blood of the virtuous and the brave. It had that very day been actively employed in the work of carnage, and there it stood in grim array, amidst a silent and sleeping city, waiting for fresh victims.

---

[3] House of the University of Paris near the *Pays Latin*
[4] Houses the municipality offices of Paris

Wolfgang's heart sickened within him, and he was turning shuddering from the horrible engine, when he beheld a shadowy form, cowering as it were at the foot of the steps which led up to the scaffold. A succession of vivid flashes of lightning revealed it more distinctly. It was a female figure, dressed in black. She was seated on one of the lower steps of the scaffold, leaning forward, her face hid in her lap; and her long dishevelled tresses hanging to the ground, streaming with the rain which fell in torrents. Wolfgang paused. There was something awful in this solitary monument of woe. The female had the appearance of being above the common order. He knew the times to be full of vicissitude, and that many a fair head, which had once been pillowed on down, now wandered houseless. Perhaps this was some poor mourner whom the dreadful axe had rendered desolate, and who sat here heart-broken on the strand of existence, from which all that was dear to her had been launched into eternity.

He approached, and addressed her in the accents of sympathy. She raised her head and gazed wildly at him. What was his astonishment at beholding, by the bright glare of the lightning, the very face which had haunted him in his dreams. It was pale and disconsolate, but ravishingly beautiful.

Trembling with violent and conflicting emotions, Wolfgang again accosted her. He spoke something of her being exposed at such an hour of the night, and to the fury of such a storm, and offered to conduct her to her friends. She pointed to the guillotine with a gesture of dreadful signification.

"I have no friend on earth!" said she.

"But you have a home," said Wolfgang.

"Yes—in the grave!"

The heart of the student melted at the words.

"If a stranger dare make an offer," said he, "without danger of being misunderstood, I would offer my humble dwelling as a shelter; myself as a devoted friend. I am friendless myself in Paris, and a stranger in the land; but if my life could be of service, it is at your disposal, and should be sacrificed before harm or indignity should come to you."

There was an honest earnestness in the young man's manner that had its effect. His foreign accent, too, was in his favor; it showed him not to be a hackneyed inhabitant of Paris. Indeed, there is an eloquence in true enthusiasm that is not to be doubted. The homeless stranger confided herself implicitly to the protection of the student.

He supported her faltering steps across the Pont Neuf,[5] and by the place where the statue of Henry the Fourth[6] had been overthrown by the populace. The storm had abated, and the thunder rumbled at a distance. All Paris was quiet; that great volcano of human passion slumbered for a while, to gather fresh strength for the next day's eruption. The student conducted his charge through the ancient streets of the Pays Latin, and by the dusky walls of the Sorbonne, to the great dingy hotel which he inhabited. The old portress who admitted them stared with surprise at the unusual sight of the melancholy Wolfgang with a female companion.

On entering his apartment, the student, for the first time, blushed at the scantiness and indifference of his dwelling. He had but one chamber — an old-fashioned saloon — heavily carved, and fantastically furnished with the remains of former magnificence, for it was one of those hotels in the quarter of the Luxembourg palace, which had once belonged to nobility. It was lumbered with books and papers, and all the usual apparatus of a student, and his bed stood in a recess at one end.

When lights were brought, and Wolfgang had a better opportunity of contemplating the stranger, he was more than ever intoxicated by her beauty. Her face was pale, but of a dazzling fairness, set off by a profusion of raven hair that hung clustering about it. Her eyes were large and brilliant, with a singular expression approaching almost to wildness. As far as her black dress permitted her shape to be seen, it was of perfect symmetry. Her whole appearance was highly striking, though she was dressed in the simplest style. The only thing approaching to an ornament which she wore, was a broad black band round her neck, clasped by diamonds.

The perplexity now commenced with the student how to dispose of the helpless being thus thrown upon his protection. He thought of abandoning his chamber to her, and seeking shelter for himself elsewhere. Still he was so fascinated by her charms, there seemed to be such a spell upon his thoughts and senses, that he could not tear himself from her presence. Her manner, too, was singular

---

[5] Oldest standing bridge that spans the Seine River in Paris
[6] King of France (1553-1610)

and unaccountable. She spoke no more of the guillotine. Her grief had abated. The attentions of the student had first won her confidence, and then, apparently, her heart. She was evidently an enthusiast like himself, and enthusiasts soon understand each other.

In the infatuation of the moment, Wolfgang avowed his passion for her. He told her the story of his mysterious dream, and how she had possessed his heart before he had even seen her. She was strangely affected by his recital, and acknowledged to have felt an impulse towards him equally unaccountable. It was the time for wild theory and wild actions. Old prejudices and superstitions were done away; every thing was under the sway of the "Goddess of Reason." Among other rubbish of the old times, the forms and ceremonies of marriage began to be considered superfluous bonds for honorable minds. Social compacts were the vogue. Wolfgang was too much of a theorist not to be tainted by the liberal doctrines of the day.

"Why should we separate?" said he: "our hearts are united; in the eye of reason and honor we are as one. What need is there of sordid forms to bind high souls together?"

The stranger listened with emotion: she had evidently received illumination at the same school.

"You have no home nor family," continued he; "let me be every thing to you, or rather let us be every thing to one another. If form is necessary, form shall be observed — there is my hand. I pledge myself to you for ever."

"For ever?" said the stranger, solemnly.

"For ever!" repeated Wolfgang.

The stranger clasped the hand extended to her: "then I am yours," murmured she, and sank upon his bosom.

The next morning the student left his bride sleeping, and sallied forth at an early hour to seek more spacious apartments suitable to the change in his situation. When he returned, he found the stranger lying with her head hanging over the bed, and one arm thrown over it. He spoke to her, but received no reply. He advanced to awaken her from her uneasy posture. On taking her hand, it was cold—there was no pulsation—her face was pallid and ghastly.—In a word she was a corpse.

Horrified and frantic, he alarmed the house. A scene of confusion ensued. The police was summoned. As the officer of police entered the room, he started back on beholding the corpse.

"Great heaven!" cried he, "how did this woman come here?"

"Do you know any thing about her?" said Wolfgang, eagerly.

"Do I?" exclaimed the officer: "she was guillotined yesterday."

He stepped forward, undid the black collar round the neck of the corpse, and the head rolled on the floor!

The student burst into a frenzy. "The fiend! the fiend has gained possession of me!" shrieked he: "I am lost for ever."

They tried to soothe him, but in vain. He was possessed with the frightful belief that an evil spirit had reanimated the dead body to ensnare him. He went distracted, and died in a mad-house.

NATHANIEL HAWTHORNE
(1804-1864)

Introduction
to
The Old Maid in the Winding Sheet

The modern concept of ghosts being clothed in sheets can be traced back to "The Old Maid in the Winding Sheet." The story also furthers the perpetuation of the pale and gliding (or hovering) ghost.

"The Old Maid in the Winding Sheet" was widely reprinted as were most of Hawthorne's short stories and novels. The story was first published in the July 1835 edition of the *New England Magazine* along with "The White Old Maid." Hawthorne subsequently included it in his 1837 collection *Twice-Told Tales*.

Edgar Allan Poe felt national pride in the collection as he pointed out a number of times, the last of which was published in *Works* of 1850. "Of Mr. Hawthorne's Tales we would say, emphatically, that they belong to the highest region of Art — an Art subservient to genius of a very lofty order. We had supposed, with good reason for so supposing, that he had been thrust into his present position by one of the impudent *cliques* which beset our literature, and whose pretensions it is our full purpose to expose at the earliest opportunity; but we have been most agreeably mistaken. We know of few compositions which the critic can more honestly commend then these 'Twice-Told Tales.' As Americans, we feel proud of the book."

The Old English turns of phrase are an annoyance in "The Old Maid in the Winding Sheet," and at times make a person feel they are reading *The King James Bible.* Still, this is the finest example of Nathaniel Hawthorne's literary prowess in the supernatural realm.

His power of suggestion throughout is surpassed only by his creepy story "The Minister's Black Veil" included in *The Best Horror Short Stories 1800-1849.*

The Old Maid in the Winding Sheet
(1835)

THE MOON-BEAMS CAME through two deep and narrow windows, and showed a spacious chamber, richly furnished in an antique fashion. From one lattice, the shadow of the diamond panes was thrown upon the floor; the ghostly light through the other slept upon a bed, falling between the heavy silken curtains, and illuminating the face of a young man. But, how quietly the slumberer lay; how pale his features; and how like a shroud the sheet was wound about his frame! Yes, it was a corpse in its burial clothes.

Suddenly, the fixed features seemed to move with dark emotion. Strange fantasy! It was but the shadow of the fringed curtain, waving betwixt the dead face and the moonlight, as the door of the chamber opened, and a girl stole softly to the bedside. Was there delusion in the moonbeams, or did her gesture and her eye betray a gleam of triumph, as she bent over the pale corpse—pale as itself—and pressed her living lips to the cold ones of the dead? As she drew back from that long kiss, her features writhed as if a proud heart were fighting with its anguish. Again it seemed that the features of the corpse had moved, responsive to her own. Still an illusion! The silken curtain had waved, a second time, betwixt the dead face and the moonlight, as another fair young girl unclosed the door, and glided ghost-like to the bedside. There the two maidens stood, both beautiful, with the pale beauty of the dead between them. But she who had first entered was proud and stately, and the other a soft and fragile thing.

"Away!" cried the lofty one. "Thou hadst him living! The dead is mine!"

"Thine!" returned the other, shuddering. "Well hast thou spoken! The dead is thine!"

The proud girl started, and stared into her face with a ghastly look. But a wild and mournful expression passed across the features of the gentle one; and, weak and helpless, she sank down on the bed, her head pillowed beside that of the corpse, and her hair mingling with his dark locks. A creature of hope and joy, the first draught of sorrow had bewildered her.

"Patience!" cried her rival.

Patience groaned, as with a sudden compression of the heart; and removing her cheek from the dead youth's pillow, she stood upright, fearfully encountering the eyes of the lofty girl.

"Wilt thou betray me?" said the latter calmly.

"Till the dead bid me speak, I will be silent," answered Patience. "Leave us alone together! Go, and live many years, and then return and tell me of thy life. He, too, will be here! Then, if thou tellest of sufferings more than death, we will both forgive thee!"

"And what shall be the token?" asked the proud girl, as if her heart acknowledged a meaning in these wild words.

"This lock of hair," said Patience, lifting one of the dark clustering curls that lay heavily on the dead man's brow.

The two maidens joined their hands over the bosom of the corpse, and appointed a day and hour, far, far in time to come, for their next meeting in that chamber. The statelier girl gave one deep look at the motionless countenance, and departed—yet turned again and trembled, ere she closed the door, almost believing that her dead lover frowned upon her. And Patience, too! Was not her white form fading into the moonlight? Scorning her own weakness, she went forth and perceived that a negro slave was waiting in the passage with a wax-light, which he held between her face and his own, and regarded her, as she thought, with an ugly expression of merriment. Lifting his torch on high, the slave lighted her down the staircase, and undid the portal of the mansion. The young clergyman of the town had just ascended the steps, and bowing to the lady, passed in without a word.

Years, many years rolled on; the world seemed new again, so much older was it grown, since the night when those pale girls had clasped their hands across the bosom of the corpse. In the interval, a lonely woman had passed from youth to extreme age, and was known by all the town, as the "Old Maid in the Winding Sheet." A taint of insanity had affected her whole life, but so quiet, sad, and gentle, so utterly free from violence, that she was suffered to pursue her harmless fantasies, unmolested by the world, with whose business or pleasures she had nought to do.

She dwelt alone, and never came into the daylight, except to follow funerals. Whenever a corpse was borne along the street, in sunshine, rain, or snow, whether a pompous train of the rich and proud thronged after it, or few and humble were the mourners, behind them came the lonely woman, in a long white garment, which the people called her shroud. She took no place among the kindred or the friends, but stood at the door to hear the funeral prayer, and walked in the rear of the procession, as one whose earthly charge it was to haunt the house of mourning, and be the shadow of affliction, and see that the dead were duly buried. So long had this been her custom, that the inhabitants of the town deemed her a part of every funeral, as much as the coffin-pall,[1] or the very corpse itself, and augured ill of the sinner's destiny, unless the "Old Maid in the Winding Sheet" came gliding, like a ghost, behind. Once, it is said, she affrighted a bridal party with her pale presence, appearing suddenly in the illuminated hall, just as the priest was uniting a false maid to a wealthy man, before her lover had been dead a year. Evil was the omen to that marriage! Sometimes she stole forth by moonlight, and visited the graves of venerable integrity, and wedded love, and virgin innocence, and every spot where the ashes of a kind and faithful heart were mouldering.

Over the hillocks of those favoured dead would she stretch out her arms, with a gesture, as if she were scattering seeds; and many believed that she sought them from the garden of Paradise; for the graves which she had visited were green beneath the snow, and covered with sweet flowers from April to November. Her blessing was better than a holy verse upon the tomb-stone. Thus wore away her long, sad, peaceful, and fantastic life, till few were so old as she, and the people of later generations wondered how the dead had ever been buried, or mourners had endured their grief, without the "Old Maid in the Winding Sheet."

Still, years went on, and still she followed funerals, and was not yet summoned to her own festival of death. One afternoon, the great street of the town was all alive with business and bustle, though the sun now gilded only the upper half of the church-spire, having left the house-tops and loftiest trees in shadow. The scene was cheerful and animated, in spite of the sombre shade between the high brick buildings. Here were pompous merchants, in

---

[1] Thin cloth that covers a casket

white wigs and laced velvet; the bronzed faces of sea-captains; the foreign garb and air of Spanish creoles; and the disdainful port of natives of Old England; all contrasted with the rough aspect of one or two backsettlers, negotiating sales of timber, from forests where axe had never sounded. Sometimes a lady passed, swelling roundly forth in an embroidered petticoat, balancing her steps in high-heeled shoes, and courtesying, with lofty grace, to the punctilious obeisances of the gentlemen.

The life of the town seemed to have its very centre not far from an old mansion, that stood somewhat back from the pavement, surrounded by neglected grass, with a strange air of loneliness, rather deepened than dispelled by the throng so near it. Its site would have been suitably occupied by a magnificent exchange, or a brick-block, lettered all over with various signs; or the large house itself might have made a noble tavern, with the "King's Arms" swinging before it; and guests in every chamber, instead of the present solitude. But, owing to some dispute about the right of inheritance, the mansion had been long without a tenant, decaying from year to year, and throwing the stately gloom of its shadow over the busiest part of the town. Such was the scene, and such the time, when a figure, unlike any that have been described, was observed at a distance down the street.

"I espy a strange sail, yonder," remarked a Liverpool captain; "that woman in the long white garment!"

The sailor seemed much struck by the object, as were several others, who at the same moment caught a glimpse of the figure that had attracted his notice. Almost immediately, the various topics of conversation gave place to speculations, in an under tone, on this unwonted occurrence.

"Can there be a funeral so late this afternoon?" inquired some.

They looked for the signs of death at every door—the sexton,[2] the hearse, the assemblage of black-clad relatives—all that makes up the woeful pomp of funerals. They raised their eyes, also, to the sun-gilt spire of the church, and wondered that no clang proceeded from its bell, which had always tolled till now, when this figure

---

[2] Person in charge of maintaining the church and surrounding grounds

appeared in the light of day. But none had heard that a corpse was to be borne to its home that afternoon, nor was there any token of a funeral, except the apparition of the "Old Maid in the Winding Sheet."

"What may this portend?" asked each man of his neighbour.

All smiled as they put the question, yet with a certain trouble in their eyes, as if pestilence, or some other wide calamity, were prognosticated by the untimely intrusion, among the living, of one whose presence had always been associated with death and woe. What a comet is to the earth, was that sad woman to the town. Still she moved on, while the hum of surprise was hushed at her approach, and the proud and the humble stood aside that her white garment might not wave against them. It was a long, loose robe, of spotless purity. Its wearer appeared very old, pale, emaciated, and feeble, yet glided onward, without the unsteady pace of extreme age.

At one point of her course, a little rosy boy burst forth from a door, and ran, with open arms, towards the ghostly woman, seeming to expect a kiss from her bloodless lips. She made a slight pause, fixing her eye upon him with an expression of no earthly sweetness, so that the child shivered and stood awe-struck, rather than affrighted, while the Old Maid passed on. Perhaps her garment might have been polluted, even by an infant's touch; perhaps her kiss would have been death to the sweet boy, within the year.

"She is but a shadow!" whispered the superstitious. "The child put forth his arms, and could not grasp her robe!"

The wonder was increased, when the Old Maid passed beneath the porch of the deserted mansion, ascended the moss-covered steps, lifted the iron knocker, and gave three raps. The people could only conjecture, that some old remembrance, troubling her bewildered brain, had impelled the poor woman hither to visit the friends of her youth; all gone from their home, long since and for ever, unless their ghosts still haunted it—fit company for the "Old Maid in the Winding Sheet." An elderly man approached the steps, and reverently uncovering his gray locks, essayed to explain the matter.

"None, Madam," said he, "have dwelt in this house these fifteen years agone—no, not since the death of old Colonel Fenwicke, whose funeral you may have remembered to have followed.—His heirs, being ill agreed among themselves, have let the mansion-house go to ruin."

The Old Maid looked slowly round, with a slight gesture of one hand, and a finger of the other upon her lip, appeared more shadow-like than ever, in the obscurity of the porch. But, again she lifted the hammer, and gave, this time, a single rap. Could it be, that a foot-step was now heard, coming down the staircase of the old mansion, which all conceived to have been so long untenanted? Slowly, feebly, yet heavily, like the pace of an aged and infirm person, the step approached, more distinct on every downward stair, till it reached the portal. The bar fell on the inside; the door was opened. One upward glance, towards the church-spire, whence the sunshine had just faded, was the last the people saw of the "Old Maid in the Winding Sheet."

"Who undid the door?" asked many.

This question, owing to the depth of shadow beneath the porch, no one could satisfactorily answer. Two or three aged men, while protesting against an inference which might be drawn, affirmed that the person within was a negro, and bore a singular resemblance to old Caesar, formerly a slave in the house, but freed by death some thirty years before.

"Her summons has waked up a servant of the old family," said one, half seriously.

"Let us wait here," replied another. "More guests will knock at the door anon. But the gate of the grave-yard should be thrown open!"

Twilight had overspread the town, before the crowd began to separate, or the comments on this incident were exhausted. One after another was wending his way homeward, when a coach—no common spectacle in those days—drove slowly into the street. It was an old-fashioned equipage, hanging close to the ground, with arms on the pannels,[3] a footman behind, and a grave, corpulent[4] coachman, seated high in front, the whole giving an idea of solemn state and dignity. There was something awful in the heavy rumbling of the wheels. The coach rolled down the street, till, coming to the gateway of the deserted

---

[3] Coat of arms mounted on the side pannels
[4] Fat

mansion, it drew up, and the footman sprang to the ground.

"Whose grand coach is this?" asked a very inquisitive body.

The footman made no reply, but ascended the steps of the old house, gave three raps with the iron hammer, and returned to open the coach-door. An old man, possessed of the heraldic lore[5] so common in that day, examined the shield of arms on the pannel.

"Azure, lion's head erased, between three flower de luces," said he; then whispered the name of the family to whom these bearings belonged. The last inheritor of its honours was recently dead, after a long residence amid the splendour of the British court, where his birth and wealth had given him no mean station. "He left no child," continued the herald, "and these arms, being in a lozenge, betoken that the coach appertains to his widow."

Further disclosures, perhaps, might have been made, had not the speaker suddenly been struck dumb, by the stern eye of an ancient lady, who thrust forth her head from the coach, preparing to descend. As she emerged, the people saw that her dress was magnificent, and her figure dignified, in spite of age and infirmity—a stately ruin, but with a look, at once, of pride and wretchedness. Her strong and rigid features had an awe about them, unlike that of the white Old Maid, but as of something evil.

She passed up the steps, leaning on a gold-headed cane; the door swung open, as she ascended—and the light of a torch glittered on the embroidery of her dress, and gleamed on the pillars of the porch. After a momentary pause—a glance backwards—and then a desperate effort—she went in. The decypherer of the coat of arms had ventured up the lowest step, and shrinking back immediately, pale and tremulous, affirmed that the torch was held by the very image of old Caesar.

"But, such a hideous grin," added he, "was never seen on the face of mortal man, black or white! It will haunt me till my dying day."

Meantime the coach had wheeled round, with a prodigious clatter on the pavement, and rumbled up the street, disappearing in the twilight, while the ear still tracked its course. Scarcely was it gone, when the people began to question, whether the coach and attendants, the

---

[5] Expert in deciphering coat of arms

ancient lady, the spectre of old Caesar, and the Old Maid herself, were not all a strangely combined delusion with some dark purport in its mystery.

The whole town was astir, so that, instead of dispersing, the crowd continually increased, and stood gazing up at the windows of the mansion, now silvered by the brightening moon. The elders, glad to indulge the narrative propensity of age, told of the long faded splendour of the family, the entertainments they had given, and the guests, the greatest of the land, and even titled and noble ones from abroad, who had passed beneath that portal.

These graphic reminiscences seemed to call up the ghosts of those to whom they referred. So strong was the impression, on some of the more imaginative hearers, that two or three were seized with trembling fits, at one and the same moment, protesting that they had distinctly heard three other raps of the iron knocker.

"Impossible!" exclaimed others. "See! The moon shines beneath the porch, and shows every part of it, except in the narrow shade of that pillar. There is no one there!" "Did not the door open?" whispered one of these fanciful persons. "Didst thou see it, too?" said his companion, in a startled tone. But the general sentiment was opposed to the idea, that a third visitant had made application at the door of the deserted house. A few, however, adhered to this new marvel, and even declared that a red gleam, like that of a torch, had shone through the great front window, as if the negro were lighting a guest up the staircase. This, too, was pronounced a mere fantasy. But, at once, the whole multitude started, and each man beheld his own terror painted in the faces of all the rest. "What an awful thing is this!" cried they.

A shriek, too fearfully distinct for doubt, had been heard within the mansion, breaking forth suddenly, and succeeded by a deep stillness, as if a heart had burst in giving it utterance. The people knew not whether to fly from the very sight of the house, or to rush trembling in, and search out the strange mystery. Amid their confusion and affright, they were somewhat reassured by the appearance of their clergyman, a venerable patriarch, and equally a saint, who had taught them and their fathers the way to heaven, for more than the space of an ordinary lifetime.

He was a reverend figure, with long, white hair upon his shoulders, a white beard upon his breast, and a back so bent over his staff, that ho seemed to be looking downward, continually, as if to choose a proper grave for his weary frame. It was sometime before the good old man, being deaf and of impaired intellect, could be made to comprehend such portions of the affair as were comprehensible at all. But, when possessed of the facts, his energies assumed unexpected vigour.

"Verily," said the old gentleman, "it will be fitting that I enter the mansion house of the worthy Colonel Fenwicke, lest any harm should have befallen that true Christian woman, whom ye call the 'Old Maid in the Winding Sheet.'"

Behold, then, the venerable clergyman ascended the steps of the mansion, with a torch-bearer behind him. It was the elderly man who had spoken to the Old Maid, and the same who had afterwards explained the shield of arms, and recognised the features of the negro. Like their predecessors, they gave three raps with the iron hammer. "Old Caesar cometh not," observed the priest. "Well I wot, he no longer doth service in this mansion."

"Assuredly, then, it was something worse, in old Caesar's likeness!" said the other adventurer.

"Be it as God wills," answered the clergyman. "See! my strength, though it be much decayed, hath sufficient to open this heavy door. Let us enter, and pass up the staircase."

Here occurred a singular exemplification of the dreamy state of a very old man's mind. As they ascended the wide flight of stairs, the aged clergyman appeared to move with caution, occasionally standing aside and oftener bending his head as it were in salutation, thus practising all the gestures of one who makes his way through a throng. Reaching the head of the staircase, he looked around with sad and solemn benignity, laid aside his staff, bared his hoary[6] locks, and was evidently on the point of commencing a prayer.

"Reverend sir," said his attendant, who conceived this a very suitable prelude to their further search, "would it not be well that the people join with us in prayer?"

"Well-a-day!" cried the old gentleman, staring strangely around him. "Art thou here with me, and none other?

---

[6] Old or ancient

Verily, past times were present to me, and I deemed that I was to make a funeral prayer, as many a time heretofore, from the head of this staircase. Of a truth, I saw the shades of many that are gone. Yea, I have prayed at their burials, one after another, and the 'Old Maid in the Winding Sheet' hath seen them to their graves!"

Being now more thoroughly awake to their present purpose, he took his staff, and struck forcibly on the floor, till there came an echo from each deserted chamber, but no menial, to answer their summons. They therefore walked along the passage, and again paused, opposite to the great front window, through which was seen the crowd, in the shadow and partial moonlight of the street beneath. On their right was the open door of a chamber, and a closed one on their left. The clergyman pointed his cane to the carved oak pannel of the latter.

"Within that chamber," observed he, "a whole lifetime since, did I sit by the death-bed of a goodly young man, who, being now at the last gasp"—

Apparently, there was some powerful excitement in the ideas which had now flashed across his mind. He snatched the torch from his companion's hand, and threw open the door with such sudden violence, that the flame was extinguished, leaving them no other light than the moonbeams which fell through two windows into the spacious chamber. It was sufficient to discover all that could be known.

In a high-backed, oaken arm chair, upright, with her hands clasped across her breast, and her head thrown back, sat the "Old Maid in the Winding Sheet." The stately dame had fallen on her knees, with her forehead on the holy knees of the Old Maid, one hand upon the floor, and the other pressed convulsively against her heart. It clutched a lock of hair, once sable,[7] now discoloured with a greenish mould. As the priest and layman advanced into the chamber, the Old Maid's features assumed such a semblance of shifting expression, that they trusted to hear the whole mystery explained by a single word. But it was only the shadow of a tattered curtain, waving betwixt the dead face and the moonlight.

"Both dead!" said the venerable man. "Then who shall divulge the secret? Methinks it glimmers to-and-fro in my

---

[7] Black

mind, like the light and shadow across the Old Maid's face. And now, 'tis gone!"

ANONYMOUS

Introduction
to
A Night in a Haunted House

The contagion that became anonymous publishing in the romantic age of short literature and poetry served at least one important purpose: It freed writers from the tight bonds of the shakers and puritans and religious dogmas that were holding supernatural literature back. Edgar Allan Poe didn't care about any of it and he transformed the short story because of it. The story before you is a prime example, which vaulted the ghost story to new heights.

In the May 1848 issue of *The Dublin University Magazine* one of the most terrifying ghost stories from the first half of the nineteenth century was published. James F. Waller, an Irish poet, was editor of the magazine from 1846-1854 and published a number of Joseph Sheridan le Fanu's early stories including "The Watcher" (1846), "The Mysterious Lodger" (1850), "Ghost Stories of Chapelizod" (1851), and "An Account of Some Strange Disturbances in an Old House in Aungier Street" (1853).

This only makes me wonder if Fanu had a hand in writing "A Night in a Haunted House." Fanu's association with *The Dublin University Magazine* and Waller is clear. What's more, he did not publish any stories between 1846 "The Watcher" and 1850 "The Mysterious Lodger." This is one of the longest droughts of his adult writing career. Is it coincidence that the story at hand was published in 1848, right in the middle of Fanu's four year abeyance from writing? Fanu's ghost stories were *long* short stories, too. "A Night in a Haunted House" weighs in at 30 single-spaced pages. It was described beneath the title as "being a passage in the life of Mr. Midas Oldwyche." In a similar fashion Fanu published a number of tales in *The Dublin University Magazine* as being an "extract from the legacy of the late Francis Purcell FP, of Drumcoolagh."

Yet the style is different from Fanu's. It is oddly more flowing and somehow less calculating in it's design. In places the story lacks the tightness of a Fanu tale. It is presented in the first person, which is unlike Fanu. He also did not republish it in any of his subsequent collections, which is strange given the high merit of this ghost story. The story is not mentioned in the remaining letters of Fanu, either. For those reasons if he did have a hand in this story it was likely a collaboration with another writer.

Due to its length, it was anthologized only a few times and each were published as abridged versions. The first was in the *Weird Irish Tales* series of 1888 and subsequently in the June 1889 issue of *Current Literature* as "The Club-Footed Lady." I am unable to find it any anthology in the past 120 years.

The lack of an anthology run and name of the author fails to diminish what is one of the best ghost stories of its time. It is a force unanswered in early nineteenth century literature.

A Night in a Haunted House
(1848)

THE FESTIVAL WE LATELY celebrated (I mean All-fools'-day[1]), always brings to my mind a most singular adventure which happened to me in 1837, while staying for the Easter holidays at Bleaklawns, my old schoolfellow Harry Fenwick's place in the north of England. The way it came about was this.

It was a rude evening in the end of March (Easter, it will be recollected, fell early that year); half a score of neighbours, including the clergyman of the parish and his wife, had dined at Bleaklawns, and we were sitting in a close-drawn circle about the great, old-fashioned parlour chimney, and listening to the wind as it roared in the leafless trees, and wailed and sobbed at the windows of the house, almost like a human being.

To such an accompaniment it is not wonderful that the conversation ran on shipwrecks and perils of the deep, and that from this subject it passed, by an easy transition, to that of murders. Hence, at the instance of a fair member of our conclave, whose tongue bore the slightest touch of the music of Minister, and who voted murders common-place, it was on the point of leaping the grave, and going headlong into the chapter of ghost-stories, when two of the company entered a protest.

I was one. I objected to ghost stories, on the ground of their manifest antagonism to the spirit of an enlightened nineteenth century. The other protesting party went on opposite grounds. This was a young lady who had come from a greater distance than the other guests, and was to sleep at Bleaklawns, and who declared that if she were to hear a ghost-story in an old house like that, where it was impossible not to believe in such things, she would not be able to close an eye for terror the whole night.

Our hostess, upon this, observed, for the encouragement of her young guests, that at Bleaklawns there was happily no occasion for fears of the kind; since, ancient as the house certainly was, it had never had the reputation of being haunted, nor had either its present,

---

[1] April 1st, also called "April Fools' Day"

nor, as far as she knew, any former occupants, ever experienced any disturbances in it which they were tempted to refer to supernatural causes.

"Well, do you know," said another of the party (a rather forward young fellow, who was but lately come to the neighbourhood), "I think that almost a pity. Such a house as this *ought* to be haunted. We must try and conjure a ghost into it, Harry, out of the old Fenwick vault under the church. Perhaps Mr. Hammond would lend us a helping hand. What would you think, sir, of reading the burial-service backwards?"

The clergyman looked grave, and said Mr. Fenwick should be very thankful that his house was free from all intrusions of the world beyond the tomb; and that the subject was by no means one to be treated in a light and jesting spirit. To this our host agreed; and added, that Mr. Emerson (that was the forward man's name) himself would adopt a very different tone with respect to such matters, if he were to spend a short time in some houses to which he (Harry Fenwick) could give him an introduction.

"Harry," said I, "I'm not quite so sure that I understand you. Do you mean to say that there are houses in England, or, indeed, anywhere else, in which such things as Mr. Emerson—jestingly, I am sure—just now spoke of, are really to be met with?"

"Fifty," answered Fenwick, "to my own knowledge."

"Haunted houses!" said I.

"Houses," replied he, "which the people who live in them believe to be haunted; houses in which things are heard and seen, which there is no explaining, but on the supposition that they *are* haunted."

"But the nineteenth century—" began I.

"My dear fellow," interrupted Fenwick, "if you can get the other world to believe in the nineteenth century, your business is done; but the misfortune is, you can't; and so, in spite of the nineteenth century, the houses I tell you of are haunted."

"But what kind of houses?—houses belonging to what class of people?" demanded Mr. Emerson, "for a great deal depends upon that."

"Parsonage-houses,"[2] answered Harry, "some of them; and some, houses like this; and some, houses belonging to

---

[2] House provided to the clergy, often located near the church

respectable people in the middle class, people quite as well able to form a judgment upon the subject as any one here."

"I should be glad," said I, "to have an opportunity of passing some time in one of these houses. I shrewdly suspect I should find a clue to the mystery: an unprejudiced person, whose mind is previously made up on the subject of investigation, is not so easily put on a false scent."

"Then you would like to spend a night in a haunted house?" cried my old schoolfellow.

"In a house having the reputation of being haunted," answered I, "by all means."

"Then, by all means, you shall," said he; "there is a house not five miles off that will just suit you. I have no doubt that I can get you leave to pass a night in it; and if you come out of it in the morning, and talk to us of the nineteenth century, I give you up."

"Mr. Fenwick," said the clergyman, "I must express my hope that you will reflect very seriously on what you are about to do, before you determine on sending your friend to that awful house. And you, my dear sir," added he, turning to me, "would also do well not to play with things, the dark and terrible nature of which you are far from being aware of."

I was astonished. "What! reverend sir," I exclaimed, "am I to understand that you, a clergyman, and, as I can afford my humble testimony from having listened to your most excellent, most edifying, and most logical discourse on Sunday last, a clergyman of no ordinary amount of talent, of erudition, and of sound good sense—am I, I would ask, to understand that *you* attach credit to the exploded tales handed down to us from an age groping in the darkness of an unreasonable superstition?—that you, in fact, believe in what are called ghosts?"

"I am sorry to say," was the clergyman's answer, "that I have had proof—proof most unwelcome—that the tales of which you speak are not so idle as the present age is too generally disposed to believe."

"That you have seen ghosts!"

"No, not seen; but I have certainly had indications of the proximity of a being no longer of this earth. I have heard sounds which could not otherwise be accounted for; and Mrs. Hammond, and other members of our household, have not only heard, but have actually seen the being in question."

"Bless my soul!" said I; "this is a most surprising circumstance. And a gentleman *so* collected in the pulpit. May I, reverend sir, pray you to put me in possession of the circumstances of this very extraordinary case of what you will pardon me for calling mental hallucination. It will be of advantage to *all* the company to hear them explained."

"I must begin, then," commenced the clergyman, "by mentioning, that, before my being appointed to the living which I now hold, I was for a short time curate at Wester Hilton, a market-town between four and five miles from this place.

"When I first went to that curacy, which was about fifteen years ago, strange reports were current about a house in the outskirts of the town, which was said to be haunted; and although I laughed at these things when they first came to my ears, yet, finding that the whole town believed them, that sober, business-like people—the last I could suppose to be given to anything like romancing or flights of fancy—spoke of them as undoubted facts, and that the owner of the house (a gentleman of the name of Greenborn) could neither live in it himself, nor get any one to take it off his hands—so that it had now for some years past stood empty—I felt myself compelled to believe that there was something very extraordinary in the matter, although I was still very far from going the length of supposing that there was anything preternatural.

"To come to particulars—it was said that all kinds of inexplicable noises were continually heard in the house, chiefly at night, but sometimes even in the day-time; that the most frequent sound was that of a person walking through the rooms, or up and down the stairs; and, what was most curious, that the steps were like those of a club-footed person—that, in fact, it was not so much a walking as an uncouth kind of stumping that was heard, and which could not be listened to without feelings of the most strangely disagreeable kind.

"It was said that the doors would often open and shut of themselves, as the footsteps went into or out of the rooms, and that, still oftener, the *sound* of the opening or shutting of a door would be heard, while to the eye the door remained unmoved. Frequently sighs were heard;

sometimes, though not often, a slight laugh, and sometimes a low whispering that would continue for hours together, as if the being that made all these noises were talking to itself as it stumped along.

"It was not often that anything had been actually seen, though this had occurred too, the form of a woman having appeared to more than one person, at different times, when the club-feet were distinctly to be remarked. But it was observed that when the form was seen, the steps were inaudible, the spirit never manifesting itself to more than one sense at the same time. However, if two persons were together, it would sometimes be heard but not seen by the one, while it would be seen but not heard by the other.

"A circumstance that most painfully spoke for the authenticity of these stories was this: the apparition had been seen by the maiden sister of Mr. Greenborn, and the shock had been so great as to derange her mind. This lady had the misfortune to have distorted feet, and the spectre appeared to her a perfect duplicate of herself; her insanity took the horrible form of fancying herself the spectre, and she was living in retirement and under restraint, in another house of her brother's, at the opposite side of the town.

"I was unmarried at this time, but an engagement already subsisted between me and the lady who is now my wife; and our union was delayed only till I should have got properly settled in my curacy, and be in possession of a suitable dwelling to bring my bride to. On first arriving at Wester Hilton, I had taken a small lodging sufficient for a single man, and then proceeded to make inquiries about a house, intending to see everything that was to be disposed of in the little town, and to choose the most agreeable.

"However, a month passed over, and I had met with nothing that would answer; another month, and I was no nearer to the object of my quest; a third month had begun, still no prospect of settlement, and all the impatience of an engaged man chafing in my breast! All at once I thought of Mr. Greenhorn's house. It was a good house, and agreeably situated, had a nice garden, was out of the noise of the town —in fact it was the very place a new married lady would like to come home to. Why not take it at once? To be sure, there was all that talk about its being haunted, but how absurd it would be to suffer myself to be influenced by such nonsense! What rational being, in these days, believed in a haunted house? No, I would show the Wester Hiltonians that they had an enlightened man among them; I would make them ashamed of their superstition; I would put down the foolish tale which had so long frighted their town from its propriety : in short, my dear sir, I was extremely impatient to marry, and I wrote to Mr. Greenborn, proposing to become his tenant for the haunted house.

"Mr. Greenborn was glad to get a tenant, and let me have the house on reasonable terms. He wrote to his man of business at Wester Hilton, to put me in possession, and, next day, the town talked of nothing but the curate's impiety, and how shocking it was to have to listen to the sermons of a man who did not believe in the other world. It was not long before I had proofs that my acceptableness among the Hiltonians had received a serious shock; my pastoral visits seemed scarcely welcome—fewer hats were lifted as I passed through the streets—and some of the more zealous parishioners walked out of church when I ascended the pulpit. I believe the people would have broken my windows if they had not been afraid that it might be taken amiss by the ghost. However, I comforted myself by thinking all this would pass off, and pushed forward the preparations for bringing home my bride. Meantime, I retained my lodging, feeling a sort of repugnance which I did not care too curiously to analyze, to sleep in my new house alone. At length all was ready, and, leaving the house in charge of a rough, fearless fellow, whom Mr. Greenborn had already had in it as a caretaker, I went my ways, married, and brought home *that* lady"—with a smile and a nod towards Mrs. Hammond—"as my wife."

"I must confess that I did not act quite fairly towards her—I told her nothing about the ghost. The motive I assigned to myself for this concealment was fear of making her uneasy; but I am afraid, at bottom, there lurked another fear—that of its leading to a delay of our marriage. Well, as I said, we came home; my wife's mother accompanied us, and we brought with us a man and a maid servant, whom I had engaged in another place, besides a maid of my wife's mother's, a Frenchwoman, who neither spoke nor understood a word of English.

"The morning after our arrival, my mother-in-law said, at breakfast, that she had been disturbed, she did not know how, during the night. She had fallen asleep soon after lying down, and slept, she thought, some hours, very soundly, when, on a sudden, she had awoke all at once, and though she could not say she had heard anything, she had had, in the most distinct manner possible, the feeling of having been called and awakened, as if by some person come for the purpose to her bedside. She always slept with a light in her room, and on awaking in this singular way, she had sat up in the bed, and looked with great anxiety about her; all was still, however, in the chamber, but an oppressive sense of fear, which she could not account for, continued to disquiet her for some hours, and she had not fallen asleep again till towards daybreak.

"At hearing this, I confess I was not without some stirrings of conscience; however, I put them down, and told my mother-in-law she had, no doubt, had an attack of nightmare, occasioned, probably, by the fatigue of the journey, and that I hoped she would rest better the next night. It happened that that day was very wet and stormy, and nobody left the house. In the evening I heard our man-servant asking the maid what was the matter with 'Mamzell,' that she had been *walking about all day on her heels.* The maid replied that she knew nothing about it, but supposed it was some of her popery. Now, I knew very well that 'Mamzell' had *not* been walking about on her heels, having spent the day in reading some French book—I remember it was 'Florian's[3] Tales'—to her mistress. I confess the man's expression brought the *club-feet* to my mind in an unpleasant manner; however, I had made an irrevocable determination not to believe in the ghost, and to hold the rats responsible for all unaccountable noises I might hear, or hear of, in the house. I therefore continued to keep my own counsel, and was glad to observe, at bedtime, that my mother-in-law's thoughts did not seem at all to be running on her disturbance of the preceding night.

"The next morning my wife awoke in a state of singular agitation of spirits, for which she could assign no cause. She felt, she said, as if something had been related to her, which was at the same time very melancholy and very absurd, and which had exited in her mind emotions of pity and horror, so startlingly mixed up with a sense of the ridiculous, that the most painful conflict of feelings was the result. I asked her if she had had any dream, the

---

3 Jean-Pierre Claris (1755-1794) "Chevalier de Florian" French author of plays, fables and comedic novels

recollection of which affected her in this disagreeable way; but she answered, that, although she had some vague consciousness of having dreamed during the night, no trace of what the dream had been about remained in her memory—only the feeling she had described rested on her like a load which she could not shake off, and filled her with an uneasiness unlike anything she had ever before experienced. This disturbed me, I will not deny, seriously. If the ghost (supposing it to exist) could extend its influence into the region of sleep—could approach the soul in her dreams—could inspire dark terrors, of which the mind could give no account to itself—could act directly upon the feelings, and depress and agitate them at its pleasure, without affording any clue to its mode of operation, any notice of the moment of its assault—what could exceed the horror of our situation?—what was to hinder madness, as in poor Miss Greenhorn's case, from being the end of it? But then, I thought again, all this was supposition. Who could say that any preternatural influence had had a share in producing my wife's state of feeling? Supposing she had had a frightful dream, which had faded from her memory, but left its effect upon her nerves, what reason had I to conclude that she would not have had the same dream anywhere else as here? The probability was that she was not well—that she was nervous, perhaps feverish; and I resolved that I would call on the doctor in the course of the morning, and ask him to see her.

"Well, at breakfast we met my mother-in-law, who, as I saw at a glance, had had another disturbed night. She looked worn and unrefreshed, and told us she had been awakened, just as the first night, suddenly, out of a profound sleep; had felt the same indefinable dread, which lasted some hours, and then passed off all at once; and had again lain awake, until towards the approach of morning.

"'Nightmare, my dear madam, again,' said I; 'the effect of your having been confined to the house all day yesterday.'

"'But I'm not subject to nightmare,' pleaded the good lady; 'I never had nightmare in my life.'

"'No doubt, the strange bed,' said I, 'had something to do with it. Emma herself did not sleep well last night, and I think, my dear madam, the doctor must have a little conversation with both you and her by-and-bye.'

"Indeed, my wife's looks told as plainly as her mother's, though in a different way, of the effects of a disturbed rest. She was pensive, preoccupied, had a peculiar expression of perplexity in her countenance, like that of one to whom some illusion is presenting itself with all the vividness of a reality, and who, half conscious of the cheat, is struggling either to be quite alluded or quite undeceived. To her mother she gave the same account of her feelings as to me: an impression, she said, of having come to the knowledge of something extremely sad, and at the same time extremely ludicrous, had got possession of her in such a way, that, although she knew how groundless it was, she could not get rid of it. Whence this impression came—from a dream, or from what other source—she knew not; but there it was, and, spite of all she did to reason it away, there it remained, weighing her down with a sense of inquietude which she in vain struggled to cast off, and so drawing her thoughts in its own direction, that it was not without an effort she turned them to other subjects.

"She begged, however, and her mother joined in the request, that I would not think of sending for the doctor that day; the weather was fine, she would go out, the air would revive her, a walk would do good both to her and mamma, and things would get right again without the help of physic; or should these means fail, she would not object to the doctor's being called in on the morrow.

"The house, as I mentioned before, was situated in the outskirts of the town, and there were green lanes, and footpaths leading over stiles and under hedgerows, from one field to another, in its neighbourhood. By these pleasant ways I led my wife and her mother a stroll of some hours, and, when we came back, Mrs. Hammond was really so much cheered up, and altogether so different from what she had been in the morning, that I began to think we should, after all, be able to do without the doctor.

"But, on coming home, I found new perplexities awaiting me. No sooner had I entered the house, than John (our man-servant), with a face of great mystery, begged I would let him speak to me in private. I gave him an audience, and he told me a sufficiently curious story.

"He had been brushing my clothes, he said, in the hall, and, he confessed, making a great dust, when he heard, as he thought, the French *mamzell* coming down stairs,

walking in a sort of popish way she had lately taken to —
on her heels. He stopped brushing, that she might not be
incommoded by the dust as she passed; however, there
was still quite a cloud of it in the hall and up the stairs,
and he was not at all surprised to hear her sneeze once or
twice on her way down. But when she came, as he judged
by the sound of the steps, to the landing-place at the top
of the last flight of stairs, leading down into the hall, and
which was full in his view, he *teas* surprised, for he saw
nobody! The steps, nevertheless, continued audibly
coming down towards him—stump-stump, stump-
stump—till they reached the bottom of the stairs, came on
directly for the spot where he was standing, passed, not
by, but, as it were, *through* him, as if he had been so
much air, and the next moment were heard behind him,
going along the hall towards the street door. After the
lapse of about a minute, they were heard as if coming
back; again they seemed to go through him (he, however,
not *feeling* anything as he was thus permeated), and
finally they went up stairs in the same stumping manner
as they had come down, leaving John in a state of
amazement to which no words could do justice.

"He had said nothing, John added, of all this to the
maid, as he saw no use in frightening her, and perhaps
making her unwilling to stay in the house. As for him, he
was not afraid; he had a good conscience, and besides,
with a clergyman in the house, he thought there could not
be much danger. He had considered it his duty to tell me,
both *as* a clergyman and as his master; but, if he might
venture to speak, he would say, in his humble judgment,
it was better *mamzell* and the other females should hear
nothing about it.

"It is curious that at this very time, Betsy, our maid-
servant, was making a communication to her mistress,
not less startling and mysterious than John's to me.
Several times that forenoon, as she was alone in her
kitchen, she had plainly felt something brush by her, or
had found herself jostled, as if some person whose footing
was not steady had staggered against her in passing.
There was no sound accompanying this, and poor Betsy
could not tell what to think of it. She had observed silence
respecting it to her fellow-servant, lest he should laugh at
her.

"Thus, John and Betsy had each a secret from the
other, and the same was the case between my wife and

me, for she feared to tease me with the maid's story, and I feared to frighten her with the man's.

"The night came, and the morning in due time followed. My wife was in the very same state as the morning previous; had had she knew not what dream, of which no trace remained at awaking but in the tone it had given to her spirits; if possible, her agitation and distress were greater on this than the preceding day, and I saw that the matter would not brook being trifled with. At breakfast I learned that my mother-in-law had had her usual night's unrest, and no sooner was the meal dispatched, than I went to look for the doctor, accompanied by whom, I speedily came back to my two invalids.

"The doctor was one of the few Hiltonians who did not believe in our ghost, and who continued my good friend after the scandal I had given by becoming the tenant of the haunted house. Having been informed that my wife was troubled with unpleasant dreams at night, and consequent agitation of mind during the day, he felt her pulse, told her that she was nervous, but he would soon have her herself again, and then began to chat on general subjects.

"In the course of conversation, he came on the subject of our house, and asked me if I had ever heard the history of its first possessor. On my replying in the negative, he said, that the house had been built, about ninety years before, by a lady of the Greenborn family, who was said to have been a great beauty, as far as the face and upper part of the figure were concerned, but who unfortunately had clubfeet.

"A young gentleman, who saw this lady in her box at the theatre one evening, fell in love with her; met her next day in an open carriage in the park, and a mutual acquaintance being by good luck at hand, got introduced to her on the spot, rode two hours at the side of her carriage, called the next morning to hope she had caught no cold, and, in short, made such good use of his time, that in less than a month they were a betrothed couple, and their wedding-day fixed. All this time the gentleman had never, except on that one occasion in the theatre, seen the lady anywhere out of her own house, but in the open carriage; and at home he always found her sitting on a particularly low sofa, her hooped petticoat spreading in such a wide waste of satin over the floor all round her, that not only were her feet invisible, but it was impossible to guess whereabouts they were.

"Thus he remained without a suspicion of the truth, until, on the very morning of the day that was to make her his own for ever, fate willed that a boy carrying a green bag should come up just at the moment that he was knocking at the door. The door opened, the gentleman was stepping in, when the boy took a pair of nondescript objects out of his bag, and handed them to the servant with the words, 'Miss Greenhorn's shoes.' The bridegroom's eye rested on them. 'Are those Miss Greenhorn's shoes?' he asked, in an accent of horror. The servant looked confused, but the boy answered ingenuously, 'Yes, sir.' 'And,' faltered the unhappy gentleman, his gaze riveted on the dreadful tell-tales, 'they fit her?' 'Oh, bless you, to be sure,' replied the boy, in a cheerful tone; 'all the ladies and gentlemen as has got them kind of feet in Lunnun, deals with master, and he have the knack of fitting of 'em, just as if they was regular Christians.'

"The gentleman did not say another word: he stared wildly a moment at the boy, then turning about, ran down the steps, climbed into the carriage that had brought him to the place, drove to the nearest hotel, took post-horses down to Dover, and embarked by that night's packet for the Continent. The lady never saw him again, and the servant's report of what had happened left no doubt of the cause of his sudden disappearance. She left town, and shut herself up in her house at Wester Hilton, where, some say, she died of a broken heart, others, of the influenza, and others, again, maintain that she banged herself in her garters.

"While the doctor related this story, my wife looked like a person on whose mind the solution of a great riddle is dawning, and as he pronounced the concluding words, she exclaimed, 'That is what I have dreamed these two nights past. I remember it all now.' She then told us that this very story had been related to her, both the last night and the night preceding, by the unfortunate lady herself; and though it had till this moment so entirely eluded her waking memory, the lively feelings of sympathy with which she had listened to it in her sleep had continued to tingle on, even when she could not recall their origin. The lady, she added, by her own account, had not hanged herself, but really died of a broken heart, which the people about her mistook for the influenza.

"It was very remarkable that, from the time my wife was able to tell her dream, its effects on her spirits went off, and her composure and cheerfulness returned. In fact, the change was so obvious, that the doctor gave up all idea of prescribing for her, and expressed a desire to see his other patient, for my mother-in-law had not been present at the conversation. My wife went to look for her, and when the doctor found himself alone with me, he could not help expressing his wonder at the circumstance, that the history of Miss Greenborn should have been the subject of a dream to a person who had never heard of it. With true medical scepticism, however, he resolved the difficulty by supposing either that my wife *had* heard the story before, and forgotten it, or that she did but fancy now that it had been the subject of her forgotten dream. I was not quite satisfied by his solution, and told him of the stumping and sneezing which had been heard by John the day before. But he had a very ready explanation for this: the rogue, he said, had certainly heard all about the club-footed ghost from some one in the town, and he had trumped up his story, merely for the sake of being listened to by his master.

"After a few minutes, my wife returned, accompanied by her mother. On hearing what the good lady complained of, the doctor said, the only thing he would prescribe for her was an attendant to sleep in her room. She was quite well, he assured her, and to give her anything to make her sleep would be to do her a great injury; a few nights more would accustom her to her new bed; she should go out, too, every day, and she would soon sleep as well as ever she had done in her life. In the meantime, as long as watchfulness did continue to trouble her, the presence of another person in the room would prevent her feeling it dreary.

"The doctor now took his departure, leaving us all in much better spirits than he had found us, and the day passed without anything remarkable occurring. We walked out, as the day before; and the air, the sunshine, and the face of the earth and waters, put to flight all lingering shadows which the night had left in our souls. A bed was put in my mother-in-law's room for her own maid, Annette, and at the end of this day we retired to rest in a more tranquil and cheerful mood than we had done since our first night in the haunted house.

"Yet this night was the last we were to spend in it. The horror became too great to be endured, and the next morning I removed my whole household to a lodging which yielded far inferior accommodation in many respects, but where, at least, whatever inconveniences we had to submit to arose from earthly causes. But you shall hear how the night was passed.

"I might have slept about an hour, when I was awoke by my wife, who, in a voice that expressed an agony of terror, asked me if I heard nothing. I listened—and it is impossible to describe to you the icy feel that crept over me, as I distinctly heard a low wailing and sobbing, as if of a person in the bitterest grief, and which it was impossible to doubt for a moment was in the room. Never did human tones meet my ear that gave such an impression of utter and desperate sorrow as that crying did: my own heart was wrung, even to weeping, as I listened to it, in the midst of all the horror which I felt at the thought that a being was near me whose life was not of the earth—for in the character of the tones I felt there was something *not* earthly. Shrill, and wild, and yet not rising above a kind of sighing whisper, they were like shrieks heard from a great distance, or like the faint cries of a dreaming man, who tries to shout.

"It was some moments before I could collect resolution to ask who was there: when I did so, there was no answer, nor were the sounds of woe interrupted. I got up and struck a light, but there was no one to be seen in the room but ourselves, and still the wailing continued. I approached the part of the room from which the tones proceeded, till it seemed to me that the invisible mourner was close to my face; I put out my hand, but no substance encountered its touch. I made a step in advance, and felt that I was standing on the same spot—filling the same space—with a being whom I could not see, but whose voice I still heard distinctly, and now as if coming out of my own breast! Seized with insupportable horror, I sprang forward, and the sounds of lamentation were behind me. I thought now of what had been told me by John; this mysterious being had passed through him, or he through it, as if he had been air; and so had I now passed through the space occupied by it. And yet this being, to which body was no obstacle, and which was itself no obstacle to body, was no unsubstantial shadow, for John had heard its footsteps, and I was at this moment listening to its voice. Such things, told me three days before, I would have scouted, as contradicting the laws which govern the universe; but this night taught me to suspect that there were 'more things in heaven and earth than—'[4] you know the rest of the quotation.

"Ah! hope of sleep was gone: I lay down in bed, but left the light burning: and now my wife told me, in broken whispers, what had happened the maid the day before; a confidence which I requited in kind, by imparting to her, in the came suppressed accents, all about John and the footsteps.

"'This is a dreadful house,' said my wife: 'I never believed in such things before, but you may depend on it, it is haunted by the club-footed lady.'

"Scarcely had she spoken these words, when stumping footsteps were heard approaching the bed. Our hearts beat aloud with terror; but at the moment that the steps reached the bedside, all was still, and an air, as of the charnel, seemed to float around us, for perhaps half a minute, and then passed gradually away.

"That, I may say, was the drop that made the cup overflow. My wife lay more dead than alive, and it was only the necessity of supporting her that enabled me to preserve some remains of composure. As soon as she had in some degree recovered herself, I promised her that we should leave the house at as early an hour as possible next morning, and rather submit to be lodged less roomily, for a while, than once more encounter what we had been this night exposed to. But the terrors of the night were not yet at an end.

"My mother-in-law slept in the room over ours, and, as I have mentioned, her maid Annette, on this night, shared-her bedchamber. While my wife and I were talking over our designs for the morrow, we suddenly heard the good lady's voice overhead, in a loud and anxious tone, calling 'Annette!'—a piercing shriek from the maid succeeded. We were both on our feet in a moment, and hastily wrapping ourselves in whatever lay nearest, we flew up stairs.

---

4 Quote from William Shakespeare's (1564-1616) *Hamlet*, Act I. Sc. v, "There are more things in heaven and earth, Horatio, Than are dreampt of in your philosophy."

"On entering the room, we found the girl sitting up in her bed, her face white, her eyes dilated, pointing with frantic terror towards my mother-in-law, who lay in her own bed, apparently awake, but motionless, and with an indescribable character of anxiety and indefinable distress stamped on her features, like one suffering under an attack of nightmare. 'There, there,' cried the girl, in her own language, 'don't you see it? It lies where *madame* lay but this moment. Ah! *mon Dieu,* I see them both lying in the same place!'

"I followed the direction of her finger, but saw only my mother-in-law, lying in the state I have already described; but my wife clung almost fainting to my arm, and whispered, scarce audibly, 'I see it!' I asked what she saw, but she could only say, 'take my mother out of the bed—I will help you.'

"Wrapping the good lady in the bedclothes, we lifted her up, though not without difficulty, for she was perfectly cataleptic, every muscle rigid as iron, and her body weighing like a mass of lead. But the moment we had succeeded in drawing her aside a little, both the rigidity and the preternatural weight all at once disappeared, the haggard look passed from her countenance, and she came to herself in a way that I can only give you an idea of, by saying that it seemed as if a spell had been broken.

"However, we brought her down stairs, followed by Annette, whom no power on earth could induce to remain in the room a moment by herself, and who trembled and sobbed hysterically, as she collected her mistress's and her own clothes; for it was determined that all should dress, and that there should be no talk of going to bed again in the house. Leaving the good lady and her maid with my wife, therefore, to put themselves in a condition to stay up, I went to call the other servants, that we might have fires lighted, and pass the night with as little discomfort as circumstances would permit.

"John was awake, and seemed very glad when I told him to get up and dress himself. He had heard *the heels,* he said, stumping about the house, more than once during the night, and the doors of different rooms opening and shutting, and had not been able to close an eye for uneasiness; though he had a good conscience, he said, too—to say nothing of the encouragement he found in thinking that his master was a clergyman.

"Betsy I found not only awake, but up and dressed: she had been afraid to go to bed, and was sitting at the window of her room, which she had opened for the sake of company. The poor soul had had a dreadful fright, and was crying bitterly: her candle had been blown out, and her foot trod on by she could not tell what strange animal in the dark, and she hoped I would not take it amiss, but she was going tomorrow. She knew she must forfeit her wages, but gold would not pay for what she endured in that house: and her only regret was, in leaving without giving missez time to suit herself. I told her we were all going tomorrow, so that there would be no need of parting; and comforted her much by the intelligence that all in the house were up, and that she would find John in the kitchen.

"On meeting in the breakfast-room, in which a good fire was soon blazing, my wife and I on one side, and my mother-in-law and her maid on the other, compared notes on the night's disturbances. My mother-in-law said she had awakened as usual, with the impression of having been called, and, feeling the same vague inquietude as on former nights, had waked Annette for company; that, presently after, the sense of suffocating oppression and nameless dread, the approaches of which she now knew so well, had come over her, and from that time she had lain, conscious, but deprived of all power of speech and motion, until my wife and I removed her from the place she was lying in, when it had seemed to her as if she had been taken out of an atmosphere in which she could not breathe, into the pure air, and her faculties had returned to her at once.

"Annette's account was this:—On awaking at her mistress's call, she saw a woman, with frightfully misshapen feet, in the act of stepping up on the bed of the good lady. Her first thought was, that it was a crazy person, who, by some accident, had got into the house; but what was her horror when she saw the woman lie down, not *beside* her mistress, but in the very place where the latter was already lying! This was what had drawn from her the shriek which had reached our ears. At first, the woman's figure had, as it were, seemed to obliterate that of her mistress; but as her eyes dwelt longer on the horrid object, the lineaments of both forms were plainly visible to her, each filling the place, yet neither displacing the other, as if two transparent pictures were laid together, and held up between the beholder and the light!

"Something of the same kind had been seen by my wife. As she looked at her mother lying on the bed, the uncertain contour of another shape had seemed to her to blend dimly with that of the known one, bewildering her eye in the manner which is experienced when *two shapes of the same object* illude the vision, the one *almost* covering the other, but the baffling outlines refusing to merge into singleness, and to give to the sense the impression of that unity which the understanding is convinced of.

"The next morning, as I said, we left the house, to the great triumph of the Wester Hiltonians, to whom I had the satisfaction of perceiving that my ministry now became more acceptable than ever. I was a convert to their way of thinking, and they set more store by me than by ninety-and-nine who had never been in the wrong about the haunted house, and had no need to be converted.

"That's the end of my story, my dear sir, and I have to apologize to you, and indeed to all our friends here, for making it so long."

I will not relate the conversation which ensued on the end of the clergyman's narrative. Suffice it to say, that I was not brought over, by anything it contained, to the side of the superstitious party. I explained all that he and his family had experienced—or seemed to themselves to have experienced—in Mr. Greenhorn's house, by the well-known agency of the imagination; and on his asking me, with the air of a man who thinks himself armed with a real poser, how could so many people imagine the same thing, I replied that nothing was more easily accounted for, this being nothing more than a curious—and I would not deny it to *be* a curious—coincidence. I believe the clergyman felt that I was too many for him, for, after this answer, he did not try me again.

However, what I had heard added to the liveliness of my wish to pass a night in the house of which such absurd stories were related. What Mr. Hammond had failed in, I would accomplish: I felt that it was an achievement reserved for me, to disenchant the Wester Hiltonians, to slay their dragons, and enable them to call their town their own—for surely it was not their own, so long as they abandoned one house that it contained to the possession of a pretended denizen of the other world.

Harry Fenwick was as anxious as I, that I should pass a night in the "haunted house," though his views, in desiring it, were different from mine. He wished to win me over to the dark ages; I, to gain him, and all his neighbourhood, for the nineteenth century. But my concern was not with his motives, and I thankfully accepted his offer of writing to Mr. Greenborn, to obtain me permission to undertake the enterprize I was bent on.

Mr. Greenhorn's consent was readily given. Indeed, there was nothing that he wished more than that somebody might get to the bottom of the mystery attaching to his house; and, from the way in which Harry Fenwick wrote (as I suppose he did) of me, no doubt he saw that I, if any one, was the person to fathom it.

It was on Saturday, the first of April, that my preparations for the exploit were completed, and, late in the evening, I sallied forth in Harry's gig,[5] with a man-servant of his from a distant part of the country to drive me, for Wester Hilton. In the gig was a basket, containing a bottle of Madeira,[6] and other materials for a cold supper, besides a couple of books, and a brace of pistols. For fire and light, I reckoned upon the caretaker (the same Mr. Hammond had found there), an Irishman, as I was informed, of the name of Leary, to whom I had an order for admission from Mr. Greenborn.

Wester Hilton seemed a pretty, little, old-fashioned town, as well as I could judge by the twilight, which, as we drove into the main street, was fast changing into darkness. My guide knew no more than I where the house was, which was the place of my destination; all we knew was, that it was in the outskirts of the town, and, as most towns have outskirts all round them, this was too wide a direction to be practically useful. To meet the difficulty, I made him draw up as we were about passing a group of little boys, who were amusing themselves somewhat noisily about the town-fountain, and, calling to the one I saw nearest, I asked whereabouts was Mr. Greenhorn's house?

"Mr. Greenborn has two houses," was the urchin's reply.

"Yes; but I have a letter to a man named Leary, a caretaker. I want the house *he* has the care of."

---

[5] Small, two wheeled carriage pulled by a horse
[6] A fortified wine from Madeira Island off Portugal

"They are both in the care of Learys—Mat Leary takes care of one and Mick Leary of the other."

"Humph," said I, "my note is addressed 'M. Leary;' that may be either Mat or Mick; I don't know what to do."

"The gemman wants the house where the lady is, what makes a queer noise with her feet," said my guide, coming to my assistance in a very handsome manner.

"There are two ladies that make queer noises with their feet," was the baffling reply.

"The gemman wants to go to the house where the lady is what's dead, then," said the man, "and now you have it."

"And what does he want to do there?"

"He's a-going to spend the night there."

"That's rum, that is!—what's he going to do that for?"

"That's my business, my good boys," said I (for the whole party had collected about us during the colloquy); "all I request of you is, to be so obliging as to direct me to the house."

The boys whispered together, and I heard the word "Prime!" pronounced by several of them in tones of great approbation. Then the boys, one and all, vociferously proclaimed their readiness to act as my guides, and ran off in a troop, crying, "This way! this way!" the gig following at the cautious pace necessary in driving over the pavement of a town at dusk.

We passed through several streets, of various degrees of narrowness, and then came to a complicated knot of lanes, dark and steep, containing the habitations of the poorer people, and alive with children, who were snatching a brief hour's bliss among the puddles, before being called in to bed.

As my guides scoured along, whooping like wild Indians, stopping now and then at the corners to let the gig come up, they indulged in all sorts of tricks appropriate to the day—giving runaway knocks at hall-doors, whipping each other's caps off, and "shying" them in at open parlour windows, where quiet families were at tea; calling over half-doors into shops for pennyworths of all kinds of things that were never sold, and exclaiming, in the hearing of mothers who knew that their children were out, that a baby had just been run over by the gig, and was lying in two halves in the gutter!

To any of their own order whom they met, and who demanded where they were going, they stated that there was a great conjuror come to town for the purpose of laying the ghost; that I was he, that the other chap (meaning the servant) was the devil, and that they (the boys) were showing us the way to the haunted house. This announcement (to which I perceived that something very short was added in a whisper) was always received with expressions of enthusiastic delight, and produced the immediate accession of all who heard it, to the ranks of my escort.

At length we were out of the lanes, which had gradually conducted us to a height overlooking the greater part of Wester Hilton, and where the breath of the open country came upon us with a welcome freshness, after the close and dingy labyrinth through which we had just passed. One large, dark-looking house stood here alone. "That's it! There you are, sir! that's your address!" burst from my conductors in chorus. I thanked them for their obliging services, and they stood huddled together in a watchful group, at sonic distance from the dreaded mansion, while the gig drove up to the foot of the broad steps that led to its door.

I will not say that there was absolutely nothing queer in my sensations as I alighted, and walked up the steps, through the interstices of which, as I felt rather than saw, a rank growth of grass had found way. Nor will I be positive that the prevailing tone of my mind was liveliness, as I looked up at the house, with the consciousness in my mind of what had brought me there. It was a tall, black-looking, silent building, with a wide area on each side of the door-steps, to look down into which, at this hour, was like looking into bottomless gulf of darkness.

It seemed as if that murky chasm cut off the house from the living world—as if he who ascended those steps crossed a bridge that carried him from the pleasant earth into he knew not what doleful region, from which there might be no return. Even the windows, through which no glimmer of light came, to indicate that all the wide extent of the house was not abandoned to utter loneliness, seemed to survey me with a strange spectral look, as I stood still for a moment, when half-way up, and ran my eyes over the whole spacious front, in search of some token of the presence of anything within, that yet belonged to the fellowship of the living.

"There are no such things as ghosts," said I, encouragingly, to myself; "let me not forget in what century I live; these are not the dark ages. The house looks dreary, but so all uninhabited houses do; I was prepared for that—it is quite natural, and so is the grass on the steps—nothing more so."

It was, nevertheless, with some tumult about the heart that I lifted the huge knocker (for everything there was huge), and knocked at the door. The sound of the knock itself had something hollow and sepulchral, I thought, and seemed to awaken a hundred dim echoes in the vast space of the empty rooms and passages, which spoke of solitude and desolation with a gloomy eloquence not calculated to raise my spirits. I felt as if I had rashly uttered a spell—as if I had summoned a spirit—and, if I must tell the truth, the hope I was at that moment most disposed to take to my heart was, that he would not come. I don't think I should have felt a whit mortified at the slight personal estimation in which such disregard of my summons might have implied that I was held in the other world.

After knocking, I waited a long time, but there was no answer; and the silence impressed me with such a sense of I knew not what, that I felt half inclined to get into the gig again, drive back to Bleaklawns, and say I had not been able to get into the house.

I did not do that—I knew Harry Fenwick; and, after waiting about five times as long as one generally does, or as I would have done at any other door, I gave another knock. This time there was an answer. Heavy steps made themselves heard from within, not, as it seemed, in the hall, but in a room adjoining; then one of the windows overlooking the area was opened, and a gruff voice asked, "Who the devil was there?"

I said I had a note from Mr. Greenborn to the caretaker of the house; and if he, as I supposed, was that person, I would trouble him to come to the door.

Instead of doing this, he reached me a stick out of the window, and bid me "fix the letter in that." The end of the stick was split, and I placed the letter in it, marvelling, however, at the excessive reluctance the fellow showed to quit his solitude. I thought, if I were the inmate of such a dwelling, I should be glad at any time to come to the door, and hold a little converse with mortals yet in the body. But the man seemed to have got used to spiritual society, and had no wish to extend his acquaintance in an earthly direction. After a while, his steps were heard coming along the hall, then there was the moving of a chain, the drawing of bolts, the taking down (to judge by the sound) of a ponderous bar, and, lastly, the turning of the massive key, which grated in the lock as if it liked the work it was doing as little as he in whose hand it was held.

At last the door opened, grinding and growling on its hinges as if it had no more mind to be opened than the key and the porter had to open it: it did open, nevertheless, and the man of the window appeared, with a candle in his hand. He was rather a savage-looking fellow, strongly built, and with something peculiarly hard and determined in his look. I recollected what Mr. Hammond had said of him, and could not but confess that, had there been such a thing as a ghost, he was, to all appearance, the very man to keep house with it.

"This is a curious thing," said he, in a tone that did not express much liking or respect for my person: "what's the meaning of it at all?"

"Does not the note tell you what you are to do?" said I.

"What's the meaning of it, I say," repeated he; "or what do you want in the place?"

"I am the bearer of a note to you," replied I, "from the gentleman in whose employment you are. If I am not mistaken, he directs you to suffer me to pass a night in the house alone. I most remark, my good fellow, that I am surprised—much surprised—at the reception you give me, coming to you with such authority."

"It's a devil of a curious thing!" said the man, soliloquizingly, and not appearing to have heard my last words "it's a thing I don't know the meaning of, at all at all." Then eyeing me with great disfavour, and with a strong expression of suspicion in his features, he asked rudely, "And what do you want to pass a night in the house for?"

"I should think," answered I, "it may suffice you that Mr. Greenhorn places me at liberty to do so: if he is satisfied, I presume you may be so!"

"I'm not satisfied, then," said the fellow, with an oath. "This paper says—'Let the bearer take your place for one night, or more if he wishes—but he won't. Place everything at his disposal, and make him as comfortable as you can. You can go to the other house for the night, or to the Greenborn Arms if you like it better. Signed, Valentine Greenborn.' I say I'm not satisfied at all: I want no one to take my place."

"Why, what objection can you possibly have, when the gentleman who owns the house has none?" exclaimed I, more and more surprised at his demeanour.

"What objection, is it? Why wouldn't I have an objection? I'm to give you up my place for a night! And where would I be if you wouldn't give it back to me again in the morning?"

"Not give it back to you! Oh, upon that score, I assure you, you may be perfectly easy. One night is all I wish for. I am surprised you think I want to make a longer stay."

"But I do think it," persisted the man: "sure I see it plain enough"—and his voice grow hoarse with anger—"it's to supplant me is what you want to do."

"To supplant you!"

"Ay, to supplant me—to get the place. That's English, isn't it. You want to get the place. You'd take it a night on trial, and you'd take it tomorrow for good. And I'm to put everything at your disposal, and make you as comfortable as I can? The devil may make you comfortable (or warm, anyhow), and to him I pitch you."

I had never been treated with such rudeness in my life, and I felt inexpressibly shocked: it mortified me, too, to be taken for a person of the class likely to come on the errand he supposed. Did I look like a servant out of place? I could not utter a word.

"Go away," continued the fellow; "you're losing your time. They were looking for an April fool that sent you here. Go home with you, man. You're not fit for the place, I tell you, You haven't it in your eye. You have neither the constitution nor the courage for it. She'd frighten you out of your life in the first three days. She'd cow you,[7] man alive, and then where would you be? Under her feet. And pretty feet they would be to be under."

I confess that a thrill ran through my heart at these words, they conveyed so direct an allusion to the clubfooted lady. However, as soon as I could find utterance, I assured him that his suspicions were misplaced; that I had no ambition to supplant him in his place; that I was a person in his master's rank in life, and had a servant of my own, in London, where I lived when I was at home. That I was at this time on a visit at Mr. Fenwick's of Bleaklawns, in whose gig I had come, and

---

[7] To "cow" a person is to scare them into submission, to make them cower

whose servant was at that moment sitting in the said gig, with a basket for me, and would put up for the night at the Greenborn Arms, and come to fetch me in the morning.

"He shall give you a set down," said I, "if you like: you can go in the gig anywhere you fix on, to spend the night. That will convince you. Look, there is *the gig* in the street: I am sure you must perceive, *now,* that I am a respectable person."

By degrees, conviction appeared to dawn on his mind, and when I added the clinching argument of a guinea, that he might drink my health at the Greenborn Arms, the last shadow of a doubt fled: I had paid my footing, and was free of the haunted house. Well, I ran down to the gig, and received the basket from the servant's hand. It occurred to me that the young man might like to share my adventure, and I made him the offer, which was "declined with thanks."

I now entered the house, and found its internal aspect not such as to belie the external. A wide hall, wainscoted, and looking vaster than it was by the light of a single candle; a broad staircase, of a most forlorn aspect, with a massive wooden balustrade, that spoke of times when the old mansion was merrier; a long passage, along which the echoes of our own footsteps pursued us, and shot the thought into my brain, "What sort of footsteps shall I, perhaps, hear along this passage, when this man has left me alone in the house;" then another staircase—a back staircase, narrow, of stone, winding down into regions I could only guess at, and up to the second floor, to which we ascended by it: finally, a back-room on the second floor, into which my guide conducted me, and in which a fire was burning.

This was the room, he said, he generally kept in, and he thought I should be more comfortable there than anywhere else; there was his bedroom adjoining, in case I should feel inclined to take a stretch in the course of the night.

After making some arrangements for my accommodation, the man was going to take leave, when I thought I should like first to have a few words of conversation with him about the ghost. I therefore asked him, as he was about to quit the room, whether he ever *saw* the—the lady, in short, with the clubfeet?

"Did he ever see her?" repeated the man, in surprise: to be sure he saw her, every night of his life.

"Every *night!*" said I. "Then she doesn't appear in the day-time?"

"Not often," was his reply.

"And, do you think it likely, may I ask, that I shall see her to-night?" inquired I, somewhat taken aback by finding the man give such an unequivocal testimony to the reality of the apparition.

"Will you see her to-night? To be sure you will," answered he, with a look of surprise. "What would hinder you?"

"Then she appears *every* night?" said I, hoping perhaps to hear that now and then, at however long intervals, a night passed without the visitation.

"Every night, as sure as the night comes."

"And," I hesitatingly asked, "are you not at all afraid of her?"

"Faith I'm not," replied the fellow, with a hardened laugh. "It's little use I'd be here, if I was. It's she, poor soul, that's afraid of me."

I was thunderstruck.

"And you must make her afraid of you too," he pursued, "or faith she'll make you afraid of her, sure enough; and if she sees that, you're a lost man. I see you're a gentleman that has no notion or understanding of these kind of things, and I can't think, at all at all, what made you come here. But I tell you, you mustn't let her think you're afraid of her, or you're done for. It's *the eye* does it all: keep a steady eye, if you can, and you'll manage her easy. A child could manage them, if it would keep a steady eye."

"But, dear me," pleaded I, "surely if I am afraid, she will know it, in spite of any efforts I may make to keep from showing it in my countenance. Surely it is impossible to deceive such a being."

"It isn't easy," replied the man; "but it isn't impossible all out. Still, I don't think *you'll* do it, and upon my soul, sir, I'm sorry to leave you in this house to-night. If I was a gentleman of your meek temper, I wouldn't be a night in this house for a thousand pounds. Good night, sir."

With these encouraging words he withdrew. I went to the door of the room, listened to his footsteps along the passage, down the winding stair, and then along the passage on the first floor. In the deep and echoing silence of the old house, I could catch the reverberations of his heavy tread, until he reached the hall below, and then I heard the huge house-door open and shut, and, a few moments after, the gig rumble slowly away.

I now resolved to make myself as comfortable as circumstances would admit, and to think as little as possible of where I was, and for what purpose. It would be too much to say that my opinions on the subject of apparitions were changed: they rested on far too solid a substratum of argument to be easily shaken.

Still, the positive way in which the caretaker had spoken of seeing the club-footed lady made me feel odd, the more from the very easy way in which he had treated the matter, as if there were nothing at all in it to be wondered at. I could understand a fearful man's fancying that he saw ghosts, but this savage was not a bit afraid— nay, he boasted that the ghost was afraid of him. By what influence, then, could *his* imagination—a faculty seldom lively in people of his stamp—be worked up to the pitch necessary for such illusions? Did he, perhaps, drink? He looked not very unlike it. Yes; no doubt, he drank; that explained the mystery: the spirits by which he was haunted were not without but within him. A superstitious man—as all the lower order, and especially the Irish, were—and living in a house reputed to be haunted—what could be more natural, than that, when his senses were disordered by liquor, the confused impressions they gave him should assume the shapes with which the popular tradition taught him to believe himself surrounded, and that he should be ready to swear, when he came to himself again, that he had seen ghosts?

Besides, habitual indulgence in intoxicating liquors produced a disposition to see spectres even when sober, and this man might, for anything I know, be the victim of a chronic *delirium tremens.*[8] That would solve the riddle at once. I set it down, therefore, for a made-out thing, that Leary was a drinker, and felt considerably comforted in my mind by the establishment of the point.

Still more comforted did I feel after I had drawn a chair to the fire, thrown on a fresh shovelful of coals, unpacked my basket, drawn the cork of a bottle of Madeira, poured myself out a glass, tossed it off, poured out another, left that standing at my elbow, and then, snuffing my candles,

---

[8] Shaking and nervousness caused by alcohol withdrawal

and taking the last Maga[9] out of my pocket, threw myself back in my chair, and stretched out my legs for a luxurious read.

The fire was good, the Madeira better, Maga the best of all, and I basked, and sipped, and read, till really a very great tranquillity began to steal over my spirit, my pulse beat again in full unison with the pulse of my century, and I felt that I was doing a very enlightened thing, and dealing a heavy blow and a great discouragement to all superstitious and dark-age ideas, by being where I was, and doing what I did.

It is true, that the silence of the great house would at times drag away my thoughts from the page before me, and lead them through the lonesome rooms and deserted passages which, I knew, were below, and above, and around me; and show them that drearily-echoing staircase again, and that hall with its age-blackened panelling, which lay between me and the door that shut out all human life but my own; and remind them of the dark depth that seemed to insulate the house, and of that grass-grown bridge which it had vainly thrown across, to the world that repudiated it, to tempt men with warm blood in their veins into its woe-stricken solitude. But these feelings were momentary, and every glass of Madeira contributed to widen the intervals between them—to make them fewer and farther between. In short, I was getting on extremely well in the haunted house.

At last, what with the fire, and what with the wine, in spite of Anthony Poplar, I fell asleep. I dreamt I was at Bleaklawns, and giving the Fenwicks a triumphant account of my enterprise, and that a deputation of the Wester Hiltonians, with the mayor at its head, was come out to bring me the thanks and freedom of their town in a blue bandbox, when something, I don't know what, awaked me. For a moment I forgot where I was, but in a moment more I was fearfully reminded.

Standing not three paces from me was a lady, whose face was white and still as death, and whose eyes gleamed with a peculiar vague brightness, staring at me in silence, and with an unchanging, stony expression, that made my own heart feel as if suddenly turned into stone. I knew it was the ghost. At first I tried to believe that I was still asleep, but could not accomplish it. Then I said, "It's the

---

[9] Magazine

Madeira;" but I could not believe that rightly either. Then I looked down at the lady's feet—involuntarily, I must say; for I felt, the moment I had done it, that I had been guilty of a great breach of politeness. However, it was but a glance, and it was sufficient; there were the clubfeet, sure enough.

How I felt, words cannot tell. Amazement and desperate fear were, I think, the uppermost sensations—I call them sensations, for I had them in my nerves, and in my blood, as well as in my mind. I did not, for an instant, indulge the hope of making the ghost think I was not afraid of her, much less of making her afraid of me: I was conscious that it was out of the question, that it would be madness to think of it, and Leary's words, "She'll cow you, and then where will you be?—*under her feet!*" recurred to my mind with a terrible distinctness. I looked at her feet again.

"That's twice you've looked at them," said the ghost: "you'd better not do it a third time."

The voice was as unearthly as her aspect—a strange, shrieking whisper, which sounded as if she drew in her breath when she spoke, instead of letting it out.

I was confounded: I tried to articulate something about not meaning any offence, but my voice stuck in my throat.

"Of course you are aware," said the lady, in the same tone, and after a short pause, "that I am the ghost of poor Miss Greenhorn."

I was still voiceless, but, as she seemed to expect my answer, I bowed.

"There's a poor, foolish creature," proceeded she, "in Mr. Greenhorn's other house, who fancies that *she* is the ghost. But she is not, for I am."

I bowed again.

"She's out of her wits," continued the apparition: "I frightened her out of them."

I must observe, that the ghost's countenance never changed, let the subject she spoke of be what it might. It assumed no expression of passion—of pleasure or displeasure; but wore the same vague, troubled stare, that varied as little as if the features had been cast in marble.

"I have been expecting you long," resumed the spectre after another pause. "Indeed, ever since you died, I knew that sooner or later you would find your way to me. You are come, and we will part no more."

"God bless my soul!" murmured I, my voice beginning to return, but dying away again before I could say that I wasn't dead.

"No—in the world of which we are now both denizens," she pursued, "there are no partings: they who meet in this world are united for ever."

She paused again, and added, "We will haunt this house together—we shall be very happy."

Making a great effort, I now, in faltering accents, assured the lady that she was under a mistake, that I was not a ghost, not dead, but a gentleman residing in London, who, being on a visit in this neighbourhood, and hearing of the extraordinary things said in connexion with this house, had solicited and obtained Mr. Greenhorn's permission to pass a night in it, for the satisfaction of a philosophical curiosity. I added, that I had never believed in ghosts before, but that this did not leave me a word to say.

"You are one of those unhappy spirits, I perceive," began the apparition, when I had done, "who are in the dark as to their own identity. There are many such among the departed. They who have been faithless to their vows while living, are often punished by not knowing who they are when dead. This is your case. You have existed sixty years"

"I beg your pardon," interrupted I; "I'm not forty yet."

"You were not forty when you died," said she; "but you have been sixty years dead; and these sixty years you have passed in a dream, believing yourself alive, believing yourself another person—a person, who, if he be living at all, might be your grandson. It is time to undeceive you. You are he who broke this faithful heart—this heart which, in the grave, still beats but for you. You are he who won this heart, and then flung it from him, and left it to break in loneliness. And for what? For these feet!"

She put one forward as she spoke, and I felt as I looked at it, that the faithless gentleman had not been so very much to blame.

"Feet," she continued, "which in China would be considered particularly handsome![10] But you are come back, and the truant, lost and blighted, shall to this

---

[10] Reference to small feet being desirable in China, which practiced foot binding for nearly a thousand years

bosom be taken once more. All is forgotten. Are you," she added, "a good rider?"

"Pretty well," replied I, wondering what the drift of this question could be—"nothing very extraordinary."

"I am," said she, "and will take you up behind me. We are but twelve miles from the Scottish border, and, on a black cat which I have below stairs, we shall be there in three quarters of an hour."

"God bless my soul!" exclaimed I; "I never rode on a black cat in all my life."

"If you'd rather have a broomstick, say so," replied the ghost; "there's one in the house."

"I declare," said I, "I don't think I should make it out much better on the one than the other."

"Then a horse," said the ghost; "there's a horse in the stable which belongs to the live man, Leary. He will be unquiet under ghosts, but we shall manage to sit him, notwithstanding."

"But what are we to go to the Scottish border for?" asked I, feeling a horrid anxiety taking possession of me.

"To be married," answered the ghost.

"Oh, dear!" cried I, "I must really say"—and I stopped.

"What?" said the ghost.

"I am not the person you take me for," said I; "I am not, indeed! It's quite a mistake. I'm not dead—I never *was* dead in all my life; and—I don't at all feel that I am the sort of man—likely to make a ghost happy."

"Wait," said the ghost; "I perceive you are under an enchantment, and you will never know who you are till it is dissolved. Did you ever read the 'White Cat?'"[11]

I replied in the affirmative.

"Do you remember how the princess in the tale was disenchanted?"

"I think the prince cut off her head."

"He did; and you must be disenchanted in the same way. Just give me that knife you have in the basket there—will you?"

I protested strenuously against the proposed treatment. She then said perhaps a finger would do, or my nose; but I expressed an unchangeable determination to retain both.

"I have it," said she; "there's a live woman in the house, who is very much in my way. You shall cut off her

---

[11] Fairy tale called "The Story of the White Cat"

head, and we will fancy it yours; it will come to the same thing."

"I wouldn't do such a thing for the world," cried I, excessively horrified; "wouldn't the black cat's head do?"

"Mention such a thing again," said the ghost, "and see what will happen to you. No; I know another means. The live woman is a witch; she has a wand, by means of which she has often greatly tormented and controlled me. She is now asleep; I will go fetch her wand, and disenchant you with it."

She stumped gravely away, leaving me a prey to the most indescribable tumult of feelings. It occurred to me that the best thing I could do would be to start off before she came back; and putting on my hat and great coat, I proceeded to put my design into execution. Taking a candle in my hand, and hastily swallowing a couple of glasses of Madeira, I stole out of the room, and along the passage, reached the winding-stair, hurried along the passage on the first floor, and was near the great staircase, when I met the ghost.

It was my own fault; if I had not stopped to drink those two glasses of Madeira, I should have been out of the house before she knew anything about it.

She held her right hand behind her back, and without expressing any surprise at meeting me, bid me take off my big coat. Of course I did not dare to disobey. She then directed me to take off my coat; this I also did. Upon this she shewed the hand which she had held behind her back, and in which was a very neat riding-whip.

"Do you know what that is?" said the apparition.

"It's a horsewhip," said I, feeling very queer.

"No," replied she, "that's a wand; and I must conjure you with this wand until you are disenchanted, and know who you are."

Without another word, she rained a perfect deluge of blows, with the cursed cutting-whip, upon my shoulders and arms. I made a run for the stairs, but she was before me, and turned me back, laying on all the while with an energy that I should never have given a disembodied spirit credit for. From time to time she asked if I was disenchanted yet, and if I still fancied myself to be alive; but I made no answer, partly because I could do nothing but shout with the pain, and partly because I saw plainly that there is no use in arguing with a ghost, especially when it happens, besides, to be the ghost of a woman.

At last, making a fortunate plunge, I got at the stairs, and ran down. It was a happy circumstance for me that the ghost had club-feet, for it prevented her running quick enough to come up with me before I reached the door; and, although I did get a cut or two more while I was opening it, I scarcely felt them for the joy of being so nearly out of her clutches; nor did it in the least diminish the satisfaction with which I sprang down the steps that bridged the yawning area, to reflect that I had paid with my coat and hat for the curiosity which had led me to spend a night in a haunted house.

I went to the Greenborn Arms for that night, and set off nest morning for London, having left a note for Harry Fenwick at Hilton, to say that I gave up the nineteenth century.

Yet I don't know how it is—I sometimes suspect those little rascally boys made an April Fool of me, and brought me to the wrong house.

WILHELM HAUFF
(1802-1827)

Introduction
to
The Story of the Spectral Ship

This ghostly tale of the sea is a derivation of the story of The Flying Dutchman. In the legend, a Dutch captain is doomed to sail the seas forever while he and his crew try but repeatedly fail to get letters taken back to their loved ones. The first Flying Dutchman story was published in the May 1821 issue of *Blackwood's Edinburgh Magazine* and awkwardly titled "Vanderdecken's Message Home; or, the Tenacity of Natural Affection." In the following year the legend gained greater fame when Washington Irving published "The Storm Ship" in *Bracebridge Hall*.

Four years after "The Storm Ship" appeared, Wilhelm Hauff—the German author of a number of outstanding horror and ghost stories during his brief life—published "The Story of the Spectral Ship" in his 1826 collection *"Die Karavane"* ("The Caravan"). It is the best of the three Flying Dutchman stories.

During this important 50 year period in question, Hauff also penned "The Severed Hand," which is firmly planted in *The Best Horror Short Stories 1800-1849*. It is certainly worth your time as is "The Story of the Spectral Ship."

The Story of the Spectral Ship
(1.826)

MY FATHER OCCUPIED A little shop in Balsora. He was neither very poor, nor very rich, and was one of those persons who venture nothing, without great deliberation, for fear of losing the little they possess. He brought me up plainly and honestly, and it was not long before I was of considerable assistance to him. When I was eighteen years old, and just at the time when he had made his first really great speculation, he died, probably from anxiety at having entrusted so large a sum as a thousand gold-pieces to the treachery of the ocean. The result compelled me, not long after, to regard him as happy in his death; for a few weeks afterwards the news came that the ship in which my father ad ventured his goods, had gone to the bottom. But this misfortune could not break my youthful courage. I turned everything which my father had possessed into money, and set forth to try my fortune among strangers, accompanied by only one aged servant, who, from old associations, refused to separate himself from my destinies.

We embarked at Balsora, with favorable winds. The ship I had selected was bound for India. We had been sailing for fifteen days on the usual course, when the captain gave us notice of the approach of a tempest. He wore an air of great uneasiness, and confessed that, in this locality, he was not well enough acquainted with the true course to encounter a storm with indifference. He took in all the sails, and we ploughed along very slowly. The night had come on, clear and cold, and the captain was already beginning to think that he had been deceived in his anticipations, when suddenly a ship, which we had not seen till now, came on close by us with great speed. Wild shouts and frantic revelry sounded from her deck. The captain at my side was as pale as a ghost. "My ship is lost!" he cried; "for there sails Death!"

Before I had time to inquire the meaning of his strange exclamation, the ship's crew rushed up, shrieking and howling. "Did you see him?" they shouted. "Our end has come at last!"

The captain ordered passages from the Koran to be read aloud, and took the helm himself. In vain; the storm visibly increased, and, before an hour had passed, the ship began to settle in the waves. The boats were hoisted out, and scarcely had the last man time to quit the wreck, when the vessel sunk before our eyes, and I was floating beggared on the open sea. But our sufferings were not yet over. The tempest raged with increasing fury, and the boat soon became unmanageable. I flung my arms round my old servant, and we promised never to leave one another. Day broke at last.

But just as the earliest rays of morning shone in the east, the wind caught our boat, and we were overturned. I have never seen any of the ship's company since. The shock stunned me; and, when I awoke, I found myself in the arms of my old, faithful servant, who had saved himself on the overturned boat, and had drawn me up after him. The storm had subsided. Nothing was to be seen of our ship; but we discovered not far from us another vessel, towards which we were being driven by the waves.

As we came nearer, I recognized the same ship which had rushed by us the previous night, and which had filled our captain with such intense terror. I felt a strange horror at its sight. The captain's exclamation of foreboding, so fearfully verified; the decayed look of the ship itself, on which, near as we were, and loud as we shouted, no living thing was to be seen, terrified me. But it was our only means of rescue, and we glorified the Prophet, who had watched so wonderfully over our safety.

A long rope hung from the bow of the vessel. We guided our boat towards it with hands and feet, to bring it within reach, and at last succeeded. But, although I exerted my voice to its utmost pitch, everything remained profoundly silent aboard the ship. At length we resolved to climb on board,—I, as the younger, going first. But, 0 horror! what a sight met my eye when I stepped upon the deck! The floor was red with blood, and twenty or thirty corpses, in Turkish clothes, lay extended on the planks, while at the mainmast stood a man, richly dressed, and with a sabre in his hand; his face pale and distorted, and through his temples went a long nail, fastening him to the mast. He was stone dead. Such was my horror that I scarcely dared to breathe.

Meanwhile my old servant had succeeded in following me. He, too, stood aghast at the sight of the deck, peopled solely by so many frightful corpses. We ventured at last, after calming somewhat the anguish of our souls by prayers to the Prophet,[1] to advance further into the ship. At every step we looked for some fresh and more dreadful horror to present itself to our gaze. But there was no further change; far and wide, no living creatures but ourselves, and the restless sea. We dared not speak above our breaths, lest the dead and transfixed master should turn his staring eyes upon us, or one of the dead bodies lift its ghastly head. At length we came to the stairs leading to the cabin. We halted involuntarily, and looked long at each other in silence, neither of us daring to express his thoughts aloud.

"0, master!" at length said my old servant, "some horrible deed has been committed here. But should the ship below be filled with murderers, I would rather throw myself at once on their mercy, than remain a moment longer among these frightful dead!"

I shared his feelings, and, plucking up a little courage, we descended to the cabin. Here, too, all was silent, and our footsteps on the stairs were the only sounds we heard. We halted at the cabin door. I held my breath and listened; but no murmur came to our ears. I opened it. The room was in the greatest disorder. Clothes, weapons and other articles, lay scattered confusedly about. Nothing was in its place. The crew, or perhaps the captain, had been carousing, to judge from appearances, only a short time before the massacre.

We went on, from room to room, and everywhere we found scattered about vast stores of silks, pearls, sugars and other valuable goods. I was beside myself with joy at all this; for, as there was no one on board to claim them, I thought I might fairly appropriate them to myself; but Ibrahim called to my remembrance that we were still far from land, and that without assistance from others we must despair of reaching it.

We refreshed ourselves somewhat with the food and wine, which we found at hand in great abundance, and at length reascended to the deck. But here our flesh crawled at the frightful appearance of the dead men, and we resolved to throw them overboard, and relieve ourselves of

---

[1] Prophet Mohammed

their presence. But imagine our sensations when we found that not one of them could be lifted from his position! They adhered so firmly to the deck that we should have been obliged to tear up the planking to remove them, and instruments to do this were not at hand. Our attempts to release the captain from the mast were equally unsuccessful; nor could we even take away the sabre from his stark and rigid hand.

We spent the day in unhappy reflections over our situation, and on the approach of night I permitted Ibrahim to lie down to get some sleep; I myself remaining awake on deck, to keep a look-out for means of escape or rescue. But when the moon rose, and I had judged by the stars that it was about eleven o'clock, such an irresistible torpor overpowered me, that I fell involuntarily to the deck behind a cask which was standing near. Still my condition more nearly resembled a stupefaction than a sleep, for I could plainly hear the sea beating against the sides of the vessel, and the sails creaking and groaning in the wind.

Suddenly I thought I heard voices and men's footsteps on the deck. I tried to raise myself to look, but an invisible power held me motionless, and I could not move my eyes. Yet the voices came constantly plainer to my ears; and it seemed as if a jovial ship's company were hurrying to and fro about the deck. Now and then, too, I thought I heard a master's powerful voice, and the sound of ropes and sails drawn noisily up and down. Gradually, however, my senses left me, and I fell into a profound sleep, during which I thought I could hear the clash of arms; and I did not wake till the sun stood high in heaven, and was painfully burning my face. I looked about, confused and bewildered; the storm, the ship, the dead men, and the occurrences of the past night, coming before me like a dream. But, when I looked up, everything remained as it had been the previous day. Unmoved lay the bodies; the captain stood immovably at the mainmast. I laughed at my dream, and rose to seek my old servant.

I found him sitting sadly in the cabin. "O, master!" he exclaimed as I entered, "I would rather lie at the bottom of the ocean than spend another night on board this ship."

I inquired the cause of his distress, and he answered: "After sleeping some hours, I awoke, hearing people running up and down over my head. I thought at first it was you pacing the deck; but instantly perceived my mistake, for there were twenty or thirty moving over my head, and orders shouted in a stentorian voice struck hideously on my ear. At last heavy footsteps descended the stairs. I knew nothing further for some time; but, consciousness at length returning for a few moments, I saw the man who is nailed to the mast overhead sitting at this table, drinking and carousing, and him whose body, dressed in a suit of crimson, lies nearest to the captain, sitting here also, and sharing in his revels."

You may easily imagine, my friends, the effect this statement had on me. It had been, then, no vision of an excited fancy which had disturbed my slumbers, but a stern and terrible reality.

Meanwhile Ibrahim had been deep in thought. "I have it!" he exclaimed, at length. A stanza had occurred to his memory, which had been taught him by his grandfather, and which was of potent efficacy in exorcising apparitions; and he hoped by its aid, and by fervent prayers from the Koran, to keep away during the coming night the torpor which had overpowered our senses the evening before.

The old man's suggestion pleased me and we waited in gloomy expectation the approach of night. There was a little apartment, opening out of the cabin, in which we resolved to take refuge. We bored several holes in the door, large enough to enable us to overlook the whole cabin, and then fastened the door on the inside as well as we could, while Ibrahim wrote the name of the Prophet in the four corners. Thus prepared, we waited for the horrors of the coming night.

About eleven o'clock a strong inclination to sleep came over me; but my companion begged me to recite prayers from the Koran, and I did so, with marked effect. All at once everything over our heads became replete with life: the ropes creaked, steps moved up and down on deck, and several voices could be plainly heard. We sat several minutes in intense anxiety, when we heard some one descending the cabin stairs. Hearing this, my old servant commenced reciting the verse which his grandfather had given him as a protection against magic:

"Be ye spirits of upper air,
Or haunt ye the depths of the sea?
In loathsome tombs do ye have your lair,
Or come ye from fire to me?
Remember Allah, your God and Lord;
All wand'ring souls obey his word."

I am free to confess I felt little confidence in this
stanza; and, when the door opened, my hair stood on end.
The same tall, handsome man, whom I had seen nailed to
the mainmast, entered the cabin. The nail still pierced his
forehead, but he had returned his sword to its sheath; and
behind him came another man, less richly clad than his
leader, whom I had also seen lying dead on deck. The
captain, for such he undoubtedly was, had a livid face, a
large black beard, and a pair of fierce, rolling eyes, with
which he searched every corner of the cabin. I saw him
with great distinctness as he passed our little chamber;
but he seemed to take no notice of the door behind which
we were concealed.

Both took their seats at the table in the middle of the
cabin, and conversed with each other in loud, harsh
tones, and in an unknown tongue. Their voices grew
louder and harsher, until at last the captain brought down
his clenched fist on the table with such force that the
whole room shook. The other sprang up, with a wild burst
of laughter, and signed to the captain to follow him. The
latter rose from his seat, tore his sabre from its sheath,
and both left the apartment.

We breathed more freely after they had left us; but our
terror was far from being at an end. The uproar on deck
grew louder and louder. We could hear them running
rapidly to and fro overhead, shouting, laughing, and
yelling. At last a hellish noise was heard, mingled with
yells and the clash of arms; then came a sudden silence.

When we ventured to return to the deck, many
hours after, we found everything as we had left it the day
before. Not one of the bodies had changed its posture, and
all were as stiff as if carved in wood.

Thus passed many days on the ship. We drove
constantly towards the east, where, according to my
reckoning, land was surely to be reached at last. But
though by day we traversed many miles, we seemed to
return to our previous position during the night, for we
found ourselves, when the sun rose, invariably in the
same place. We could not explain this, otherwise than by
supposing that the dead men steered their ship back every
night with the trade wind. To prevent this we took in all
the sails before night, and secured them by the same
means we had employed with the cabin door: we wrote the
name of the Prophet on parchment, together with the

above-mentioned stanza, and fastened the talismans to the lowered sails.

We waited in our state-room for the result, in intense anxiety. That night, magic seemed to be working with increased fury; but, O, joy! the next morning the sails were still furled as we had left them the evening before. Henceforth, we spread during the day only so much sail as was needed to urge the ship moderately forward; and in this way in five days we advanced a considerable distance on our voyage.

At length, on the sixth day, we discovered land in the horizon, and gave thanks to Allah and his Prophet for our wonderful preservation. All this day and the following night we drove onward towards the coast, and on the seventh morning thought we discovered a city at no great distance. With great difficulty we hove over an anchor into the sea, and launching a small boat, which stood on the deck, rowed with all our strength towards the city.

In half an hour we ran into the mouth of a stream which discharged into the ocean, and landed on the shore. Proceeding on foot to the city, we inquired its name at the gates, and learned that it was an Indian city, at no great distance from my original place of destination. We took lodgings at a caravansary; and, after refreshing our strength, which had been exhausted by our perilous voyage, I made inquiries for a man of wisdom and learning, giving our landlord to understand that I should prefer one somewhat acquainted with magic. He took me to a retired street, and knocked at an obscure house, giving me directions to inquire for Muley.

As I entered, an old, diminutive man, with a gray beard and a long nose, came towards me, and demanded my business. On my replying that I was in search of Muley the Wise, he told me it was himself. I asked him for advice as to what I should do with the dead bodies, and what measures I should adopt to get them out of the ship. He replied, that the people in the vessel had probably been bewitched because of some great crime perpetrated on the sea.

He thought this witchcraft could be exorcised if they could be brought on shore; but that this was impossible, unless the planks on which they lay were taken up; that by all the laws of God and justice, the ship and all she contained belonged to me, but that I must keep profoundly silent in regard to it; and, if I would present to him a small portion of my surplus wealth, that he would bring his own slaves to help me in disposing of the bodies. I promised to reward him handsomely; and we set out for the ship, with five slaves, provided with saws and hatchets. While on our way, the magician could not sufficiently compliment the wisdom of our plan of guarding the sails with quotations from the Koran. He declared that this was the sole means by which we could have been saved.

It was still early in the morning when we reached the ship. We went zealously to work, and in an hour's time had placed four of the bodies in the skiff. Some of the slaves were ordered to row them ashore and bury them. They declared, when they came back, that the dead men had saved them the trouble of burial, for no sooner had they been laid on the ground than they had crumbled into dust.

We continued to remove the corpses, and before evening every one of them had been carried to the land. No one was left but the man whom we had found nailed to the mainmast. We tried in vain to draw out the nail. No exercise of strength seemed to start it a hair's breadth. I was at a loss what to do next; for it was out of the question to cut down the mast in order to take him ashore. But Muley helped us out of this embarrassment.

He directed a slave to row quickly to the shore, and bring away a basket of earth. When this had been done the magician uttered some mysterious words, and sprinkled the earth on the dead man's head. The latter instantly opened his eyes, drew a deep breath, and the wound made by the nail in his brow began to bleed. We now drew the spike out without difficulty, and the body fell into the arms of one of our slaves.

"Who has brought me here?" he asked. Muley pointed tome, and I stepped closer. "Thanks, unknown stranger," said he. "You have released me from long torments. For fifteen years my body has been sailing on these waters, and my soul been condemned to revisit it at night. But now earth has rested on my head, and I can go to my fathers, forgiven."

I begged him to let us know how he had merited this fearful punishment, and he went on:

"Fifteen years ago I was a powerful and distinguished man, and lived in Algiers. A thirst for gain induced me to fit out a ship and take to piracy. I had practised this mode of life for some time, when one day I took on board at Zante a dervish,[2] who wished to travel free of expense. I and my crew were fierce people, and paid no regard to the sanctity of our passenger, but, on the contrary, made him the object of our ridicule. But on one occasion, when, in his holy zeal, he had rebuked my sinful course of life, my anger, which was more easily excited as I had been drinking deeply, obtained complete mastery over me.

"Furious at hearing from a dervish what I would not have endured tamely from the sultan himself, I plunged my dagger in his heart. With his dying breath he cursed my crew and me, condemning us to an existence of neither life nor death till we had laid our heads upon the earth. The dervish died, and we threw him into the sea, laughing at his imprecations; but that very night his sentence was fulfilled. A part of my crew mutinied. We fought with dreadful fury till my adherents were all slain, and I nailed to the mast. But the mutineers also perished of their wounds, and soon my ship was merely one vast grave. My sight left me, my breath failed, and I awaited death. But it was only a torpor which had overpowered me. On the next night, at the same hour in which we had thrown the dervish into the sea, I and all my crew awoke to life; existence had returned to us again, but we could do nothing, say nothing, but what we had said and done that dreadful night.

"Thus we have sailed for fifteen years, unable to live, unable to die. We have spread every sail to the tempest with frantic joy, hoping to be dashed at last upon some friendly cliff, and lay our weary heads at rest on the bottom of the ocean. It was denied to us. But now I can die. Once more, my unknown savior, I thank you; and, if you value treasures, take my ship and its contents in token of my gratitude."

The captain let his head fall upon his breast, and, like his companions in suffering, crumbled into dust. We collected his ashes in a box, and buried them on the beach; and I obtained workmen from the city, who soon put my vessel in repair. After I had bartered away, at a great profit, the goods which I found on board, I hired seamen, remunerated richly my friend Muley, and sailed for my native country. I took a circuitous route, visiting many countries and islands, and disposing of my goods.

---

[2] Muslim monk

The Prophet blessed my undertaking. At the end of nine months I returned to Balsora twice as rich as the dying captain's bequest had made me. My fellow-citizens were surprised at my wealth and good fortune, and would not believe but that I had found the Valley of Diamonds of the famous voyager, Sindbad.[3] I left them to their belief; and my example tempted all the youths of Balsora to go out into the world, in order, like me, to make their fortunes.

I lived calmly and at peace, and have made, every five years since then, a journey to Mecca,[4] that I might thank God, in his holy place, for all his blessings, and pray for the captain and his crew, that He would receive them into Paradise.

---

[3] Fictional sailor who had seven adventurous journeys on the seas; in The Second Voyage of Sinbad, a valley of large snakes is discovered that slither over the ground covered with diamonds
[4] Holiest city in the Islamic religion

SIR WALTER SCOTT
(1771-1832)

Introduction
to
The Tapestried Chamber

During the first half of the nineteenth century Sir Walter Scott was perhaps the chief architect in promoting supernatural stories throughout Britain. Before you is his most famous ghost story.

In an 1831 introduction to "The Tapestried Chamber" Scott admitted that the origins of the story were not his own. They were told to him "many years ago, by the late Miss Anna Seward" who was a romantic English poet. She lived from 1747-1809 and Scott edited her collected poetical works published in 1810. The constructs of the story are attributed to her again within the introduction of the text.

Extending his love of the supernatural to his death, in 1830 Scott penned *Letters on Demonology and Witchcraft*. Two years prior he published "The Tapestried Chamber," one of only three stories he collected in *The Keepsake Stories*; the other two being "My Aunt Margaret's Mirror" and "Death of the Laird's Jock."

This is one of the first supernatural stories where the sins of a lifetime are shown in the horrific face of ghostly figure. It's moments of terror are not to be denied.

The Tapestried Chamber
(1828)

THE FOLLOWING NARRATIVE IS given from the pen, so far as
memory permits, in the same character in which it was
presented to the author's ear; nor has he claim to further
praise, or to be more deeply censured, than in proportion
to the good or bad judgment which he has employed in
selecting his materials, as he has studiously avoided any
attempt at ornament, which might interfere with the
simplicity of the tale.

At the same time, it must be admitted, that the
particular class of stories which turns on the marvellous,
possesses a stronger influence when told than when
committed to print. The volume taken up at noonday,
though rehearsing the same incidents, conveys a much
more feeble impression than is achieved by the voice of the
speaker on a circle of fireside auditors, who hang upon the
narrative as the narrator details the minute incidents
which serve to give it authenticity, and lowers his voice
with an affectation of mystery while he approaches the
fearful and wonderful part.

It was with such advantages that the present writer
heard the following events related, more than twenty years
since, by the celebrated Miss Seward,[1] of Litchfield, who to
her numerous accomplishments, added, in a remarkable
degree, the power of narrative in private conversation. In
its present form, the tale must necessarily lose all the
interest which was attached to it by the flexible voice and
intelligent features of the gifted narrator. Yet still, read
aloud, to an undoubting audience by the doubtful light of
the closing evening, or in silence, by a decaying taper, and
amidst the solitude of a half-lighted apartment, it may
redeem its character as a good ghost story.

Miss Seward always affirmed that she had derived her
information from an authentic source, although she
suppressed the names of the two persons chiefly
concerned. I will not avail myself of any particulars I may
have since received concerning the localities of the detail,
but suffer them to rest under the same general description

---

[1] Anna Seward (1747-1809)

in which they were first related to me; and, for the same
reason, I will not add to or diminish the narrative, by any
circumstances, whether more or less material, but simply
rehearse, as I heard it, a story of supernatural terror.

About the end of the American War,[2] when the officers
of Lord Cornwallis's army,[3] which surrendered at
Yorktown, and others, who had been made prisoners
during the impolitic and ill-fated controversy, were
returning to their own country, to relate their adventures,
and repose themselves after their fatigues; there was
amongst them a general officer, to whom Miss S. gave the
name of Browne, but merely, as I understood, to save the
inconvenience of introducing a nameless agent in the
narrative. He was an officer of merit, as well as a
gentleman of high consideration for family and
attainments.

Some business had carried General Browne upon a
tour through the western counties, when, in the
conclusion of a morning stage, he found himself in the
vicinity of a small country town, which presented a scene
of uncommon beauty, and of a character peculiarly
English.

The little town, with its stately old church, whose
tower bore testimony to the devotion of ages long past, lay
amidst pasture and corn-fields of small extent, but
bounded and divided with hedge-row timber of great age
and size. There were few marks of modern improvement.
The environs of the place intimated neither the solitude of
decay, nor the bustle of novelty; the houses were old, but
in good repair; and the beautiful little river murmured
freely on its way to the left of the town, neither restrained
by a dam, nor bordered by a towing-path.

Upon a gentle eminence, nearly a mile to the
southward of the town, were seen, amongst many
venerable oaks and tangled thickets, the turrets of a
castle, as old as the wars of York and Lancaster,[4] but
which seemed to have received important alterations
during the age of Elizabeth[5] and her successors. It had not

---

[2] American Revolutionary War (1775-1783)
[3] British army led by Charles Cornwallis (1738-1805)
[4] Battle of Lancaster in 1780 and Yorktown in 1781 where British
soldiers were defeated by the Americans
[5] Period that is considered the golden age of English arts during
the reign of Queen Elizabeth (1558-1603)

been a place of great size; but whatever accommodation it formerly afforded, was, it must be supposed, still to be obtained within its walls; at least, such was the inference which General Browne drew from observing the smoke arise merrily from several of the ancient wreathed and carved chimney-stalks.

The wall of the park ran alongside of the highway for two or three hundred yards; and through the different points by which the eye found glimpses into the woodland scenery, it seemed to be well stocked. Other points of view opened in succession; now a full one, of the front of the old castle, and now a side glimpse at its particular towers; the former rich in all the bizarrerie of the Elizabethan school, while the simple and solid strength of other parts of the building seemed to show that they had been raised more for defence than ostentation.

Delighted with the partial glimpses which he obtained of the castle through the woods and glades by which this ancient feudal fortress was surrounded, our military traveller was determined to inquire whether it might not deserve a nearer view, and whether it contained family pictures or other objects of curiosity worthy of a stranger's visit; when, leaving the vicinity of the park, he rolled through a clean and well-paved street, and stopped at the door of a well-frequented inn.

Before ordering horses to proceed on his journey, General Browne made inquiries concerning the proprietor of the chateau which had so attracted his admiration, and was equally surprised and pleased at hearing in reply a nobleman named whom we shall call Lord Woodville. How fortunate! Much of Browne's early recollections, both at school and at college, had been connected with young Woodville, whom, by a few questions, he now ascertained to be the same with the owner of this fair domain.

He had been raised to the peerage by the decease of his father a few months before, and, as the General learned from the landlord, the term of mourning being ended, was now taking possession of his paternal estate, in the jovial season of merry autumn, accompanied by a select party of friends to enjoy the sports of a country famous for game.

This was delightful news to our traveller. Frank Woodville had been Richard Browne's fag[6] at Eton, and his

---

[6] Underling

chosen intimate at Christ Church; their pleasures and
their tasks had been the same; and the honest soldier's
heart warmed to find his early friend in possession of so
delightful a residence, and of an estate, as the landlord
assured him with a nod and a wink, fully adequate to
maintain and add to his dignity. Nothing was more
natural than that the traveller should suspend a journey,
which there was nothing to render hurried, to pay a visit
to an old friend under such agreeable circumstances.

The fresh horses, therefore, had only the brief task of
conveying the General's travelling carriage to Woodville
Castle. A porter admitted them at a modern Gothic Lodge,
built in that style to correspond with the Castle itself, and
at the same time rang a bell to give warning of the
approach of visitors. Apparently the sound of the bell had
suspended the separation of the company, bent on the
various amusements of the morning; for, on entering the
court of the chateau, several young men were lounging
about in their sporting dresses, looking at, and criticising,
the dogs which the keepers held in readiness to attend
their pastime.

As General Browne alighted, the young lord came to
the gate of the hall, and for an instant gazed, as at a
stranger, upon the countenance of his friend, on which
war, with its fatigues and its wounds, had made a great
alteration. But the uncertainty lasted no longer than till
the visitor had spoken, and the hearty greeting which
followed was such as can only be exchanged betwixt those
who have passed together the merry days of careless
boyhood or early youth.

"If I could have formed a wish, my dear Browne," said
Lord Woodville, "it would have been to have you here, of
all men, upon this occasion, which my friends are good
enough to hold a sort of holiday. Do not think you have
been unwatched during the years you have been absent
from us. I have traced you through your dangers, your
triumphs, your misfortunes, and was delighted to see
that, whether in victory or defeat, the name of my old
friend was always distinguished with applause."

The General made a suitable reply, and congratulated
his friend on his new dignities, and the possession of a
place and domain so beautiful.

"Nay, you have seen nothing of it as yet," said Lord
Woodville, "and I trust you do not mean to leave us till you
are better acquainted with it. It is true, I confess, that my

present party is pretty large, and the old house, like other places of the kind, does not possess so much accommodation as the extent of the outward walls appears to promise. But we can give you a comfortable old-fashioned room; and I venture to suppose that your campaigns have taught you to be glad of worse quarters."

The General shrugged his shoulders, and laughed. "I presume," he said, "the worst apartment in your chateau is considerably superior to the old tobacco-cask,[7] in which I was fain to take up my night's lodging when I was in the Bush, as the Virginians call it, with the light corps. There I lay, like Diogenes[8] himself, so delighted with my covering from the elements, that I made a vain attempt to have it rolled on to my next quarters; but my commander for the time would give way to no such luxurious provision, and I took farewell of my beloved cask with tears in my eyes."

"Well, then, since you do not fear your quarters," said Lord Woodville, "you will stay with me a week at least. Of guns, dogs, fishing-rods, flies, and means of sport by sea and land, we have enough and to spare: you cannot pitch on an amusement, but we will pitch on the means of pursuing it. But if you prefer the gun and pointers, I will go with you myself, and see whether you have mended your shooting since you have been amongst the Indians of the back settlements."

The General gladly accepted his friendly host's proposal in all its points. After a morning of manly exercise, the company met at dinner, where it was the delight of Lord Woodville to conduce to the display of the high properties of his recovered friend, so as to recommend him to his guests, most of whom were persons of distinction. He led General Browne to speak of the scenes he had witnessed; and as every word marked alike the brave officer and the sensible man, who retained possession of his cool judgment under the most imminent dangers, the company looked upon the soldier with general respect, as on one who had proved himself possessed of an uncommon portion of personal courage— that attribute, of all others, of which everybody desires to be thought possessed.

---

[7] Large wooden barrel for holding tobacco
[8] Diogenes the Cynic (412 BC – 323 BC) was a Greek philosopher who chose to be homeless and live a life of poverty

The day at Woodville Castle ended as usual in such mansions. The hospitality stopped within the limits of good order; music, in which the young lord was a proficient, succeeded to the circulation of the bottle: cards and billiards, for those who preferred such amusements, were in readiness: but the exercise of the morning required early hours, and not long after eleven o'clock the guests began to retire to their several apartments.

The young lord himself conducted his friend, General Browne, to the chamber destined for him, which answered the description he had given of it, being comfortable, but old-fashioned. The bed was of the massive form used in the end of the seventeenth century, and the curtains of faded silk, heavily trimmed with tarnished gold. But then the sheets, pillows, and blankets looked delightful to the campaigner, when he thought of his mansion, the cask. There was an air of gloom in the tapestry hangings, which, with their worn-out graces, curtained the walls of the little chamber, and gently undulated as the autumnal breeze found its way through the ancient lattice-window, which pattered and whistled as the air gained entrance. The toilet too, with its mirror, turbaned, after the manner of the beginning of the century, with a coiffure[9] of murrey-coloured[10] silk, and its hundred strange-shaped boxes, providing for arrangements which had been obsolete for more than fifty years, had an antique, and in so far a melancholy, aspect. But nothing could blaze more brightly and cheerfully than the two large wax candles; or if aught could rival them, it was the flaming bickering fagots in the chimney, that sent at once their gleam and their warmth through the snug apartment; which, notwithstanding the general antiquity of its appearance, was not wanting in the least convenience that modern habits rendered either necessary or desirable.

"This is an old-fashioned sleeping apartment, General," said the young lord; "but I hope you will find nothing that makes you envy your old tobacco-cask."

"I am not particular respecting my lodgings," replied the General; "yet, were I to make any choice, I would prefer this chamber by many degrees, to the gayer and more modern rooms of your family mansion. Believe me, that when I unite its modern air of comfort with its

---

[9] Crowned with a weave
[10] Red-purple color

venerable antiquity, and recollect that it is your lordship's property, I shall feel in better quarters here, than if I were in the best hotel London could afford."

"I trust—I have no doubt—that you will find yourself as comfortable as I wish you, my dear General," said the young nobleman; and once more bidding his guest good-night, he shook him by the hand and withdrew.

The General again looked round him, and internally congratulating himself on his return to peaceful life, the comforts of which were endeared by the recollection of the hardships and dangers he had lately sustained, undressed himself, and prepared himself for a luxurious night's rest.

Here, contrary to the custom of this species of tale, we leave the General in possession of his apartment until the next morning.

The company assembled for breakfast at an early hour, but without the appearance of General Browne, who seemed the guest that Lord Woodville was desirous of honouring above all whom his hospitality had assembled around him. He more than once expressed surprise at the General's absence, and at length sent a servant to make inquiry after him. The man brought back information that General Browne had been walking abroad since an early hour of the morning, in defiance of the weather, which was misty and ungenial.

"The custom of a soldier,"—said the young nobleman to his friends; "many of them acquire habitual vigilance, and cannot sleep after the early hour at which their duty usually commands them to be alert."

Yet the explanation which Lord Woodville thus offered to the company seemed hardly satisfactory to his own mind, and it was in a fit of silence and abstraction that he awaited the return of the General. It took place near an hour after the breakfast-bell had rung. He looked fatigued and feverish. His hair, the powdering and arrangement of which was at this time one of the most important occupations of a man's whole day, and marked his fashion as much as, in the present time, the tying of a cravat,[11] or the want of one, was dishevelled, uncurled, void of powder, and dank with dew. His clothes were huddled on with a careless negligence, remarkable in a military man, whose real or supposed duties are usually held to include

---

[11] Band of fabric worn around the neck

some attention to the toilet; and his looks were haggard and ghastly in a peculiar degree.

"So you have stolen a march upon us this morning, my dear General," said Lord Woodville; "or you have not found your bed so much to your mind as I had hoped and you seemed to expect. How did you rest last night?"

"Oh, excellently well! remarkably well! never better in my life"—said General Browne rapidly, and yet with an air of embarrassment which was obvious to his friend. He then hastily swallowed a cup of tea, and, neglecting or refusing whatever eke was offered, seemed to fall into a fit of abstraction.

"You will take the gun to-day, General;" said his friend and host, but had to repeat the question twice ere he received the abrupt answer, "No, my lord; I am sorry I cannot have the honour of spending another day with your lordship; my post horses are ordered, and will be here directly."

All who were present showed surprise, and Lord Woodville immediately replied, "Post horses,[12] my good friend! what can you possibly want with them, when you promised to stay with me quietly for at least a week?"

"I believe," said the General, obviously much embarrassed, "that I might, in the pleasure of my first meeting with your lordship, have said something about stopping here a few days; but I have since found it altogether impossible."

"That is very extraordinary," answered the young nobleman. "You seemed quite disengaged yesterday, and you cannot have had a summons to-day; for our post has not come up from the town, and therefore you cannot have received any letters."

General Browne, without giving any farther explanation, muttered something of indispensable business, and insisted on the absolute necessity of his departure in a manner which silenced all opposition on the part of his host, who saw that his resolution was taken, and forbore farther importunity.

"At least, however," he said, "permit me, my dear Browne, since go you will or must, to show you the view from the terrace, which the mist, that is now rising, will soon display."

---

[12] Horses stationed at an inn for use by travelers

He threw open a sash window, and stepped down upon the terrace as he spoke. The General followed him mechanically, but seemed little to attend to what his host was saying, as, looking across an extended and rich prospect, he pointed out the different objects worthy of observation. Thus they moved on till Lord Woodville had attained his purpose of drawing his guest entirely apart from the rest of the company, when, turning round upon him with an air of great solemnity, he addressed him thus:—

"Richard Browne, my old and very dear friend, we are now alone. Let me conjure you to answer me upon the word of a friend, and the honour of a soldier. How did you in reality rest during last night?"

"Most wretchedly indeed, my lord," answered the General in the same tone of solemnity;—"so miserably, that I would not run the risk of such a second night, not only for all the lands belonging to this castle, but for all the country which I see from this elevated point of view."

"This is most extraordinary," said the young lord, as if speaking to himself; "then there must be something in the reports concerning that apartment." Again turning to the General, he said, "For God's sake, my dear friend, be candid with me, and let me know the disagreeable particulars, which have befallen you under a roof, where, with consent of the owner, you should have met nothing save comfort."

The General seemed distressed by this appeal, and paused a moment before he replied. "My dear lord," he at length said, "what happened to me last night is of a nature so peculiar and so unpleasant, that I could hardly bring myself to detail it even to your lordship, were it not that, independent of my wish to gratify any request of yours, I think that sincerity on my part may lead to some explanation about a circumstance equally painful and mysterious. To others, the communication I am about to make, might place me in the light of a weak-minded, superstitious fool, who suffered his own imagination to delude and bewilder him; but you have known me in childhood and youth, and will not suspect me of having adopted in manhood the feelings and frailties from which my early years were free." Here he paused, and his friend replied:—

"Do not doubt my perfect confidence in the truth of your communication, however strange it may be," replied

Lord Woodville; "I know your firmness of disposition too well, to suspect you could be made the object of imposition, and am aware that your honour and your friendship will equally deter you from exaggerating whatever you may have witnessed."

"Well then," said the General, "I will proceed with my story as well as I can, relying upon your candour; and yet distinctly feeling that I would rather face a battery than recall to my mind the odious recollections of last night."

He paused a second time, and then perceiving that Lord Woodville remained silent and in an attitude of attention, he commenced, though not without obvious reluctance, the history of his night's adventures in the Tapestried Chamber.

"I undressed and went to bed, so soon as your lordship left me yesterday evening; but the wood in the chimney, which nearly fronted my bed, blazed brightly and cheerfully, and, aided by a hundred exciting recollections of my childhood and youth, which had been recalled by the unexpected pleasure of meeting your lordship, prevented me from falling immediately asleep. I ought, however, to say, that these reflections were all of a pleasant and agreeable kind, grounded on a sense of having for a time exchanged the labour, fatigues, and dangers of my profession, for the enjoyments of a peaceful life, and the reunion of those friendly and affectionate ties, which I had torn asunder at the rude summons of war.

"While such pleasing reflections were stealing over my mind, and gradually lulling me to slumber, I was suddenly aroused by a sound like that of the rustling of a silken gown, and the tapping of a pair of high-heeled shoes, as if a woman were walking in the apartment. Ere I could draw the curtain to see what the matter was, the figure of a little woman passed between the bed and the fire.

"The back of this form was turned to me, and I could observe, from the shoulders and neck, it was that of an old woman, whose dress was an old-fashioned gown, which, I think, ladies call a sacque; that is, a sort of robe, completely loose in the body, but gathered into broad plaits upon the neck and shoulders, which fall down to the ground, and terminate in a species of train.

"I thought the intrusion singular enough, but never harboured for a moment the idea that what I saw was anything more than the mortal form of some old woman about the establishment, who had a fancy to dress like her grandmother, and who, having perhaps (as your lordship mentioned that you were rather straitened for room) been dislodged from her chamber for my accommodation, had forgotten the circumstance, and returned by twelve to her old haunt.

"Under this persuasion I moved myself in bed and coughed a little, to make the intruder sensible of my being in possession of the premises.—She turned slowly round, but, gracious heaven! my lord, what a countenance did she display to me! There was no longer any question what she was, or any thought of her being a living being.

"Upon a face which wore the fixed features of a corpse, were imprinted the traces of the vilest and most hideous passions which had animated her while she lived. The body of some atrocious criminal seemed to have been given up from the grave, and the soul restored from the penal fire, in order to form, for a space, a union with the ancient accomplice of its guilt.

"I started up in bed, and sat upright, supporting myself on my palms, as I gazed on this horrible spectre. The hag made, as it seemed, a single and swift stride to the bed where I lay, and squatted herself down upon it, in precisely the same attitude which I had assumed in the extremity of horror, advancing her diabolical countenance within half-a-yard of mine, with a grin which seemed to intimate the malice and the derision of an incarnate fiend."

Here General Browne stopped, and wiped from his brow the cold perspiration with which the recollection of his horrible vision had covered it.

"My lord," he said, "I am no coward. I have been in all the mortal dangers incidental to my profession, and I may truly boast, that no man ever knew Richard Browne dishonour the sword he wears; but in these horrible circumstances, under the eyes, and as it seemed, almost in the grasp of an incarnation of an evil spirit, all firmness forsook me, all manhood melted from me like wax in the furnace, and I felt my hair individually bristle. The current of my life-blood ceased to flow, and I sank back in a swoon, as very a victim to panic terror as ever was a village girl, or a child of ten years old. How long I lay in this condition I cannot pretend to guess.

"But I was roused by the castle clock striking one, so loud that it seemed as if it were in the very room. It was some time before I dared open my eyes, lest they should again encounter the horrible spectacle. When, however, I summoned courage to look up, she was no longer visible.

"My first idea was to pull my bell, wake the servants, and remove to a garret or a hay-loft, to be ensured against a second visitation. Nay, I will confess the truth, that my resolution was altered, not by the shame of exposing myself, but by the fear that, as the bellcord hung by the chimney, I might, in making my way to it, be again crossed by the fiendish hug, who, I figured to myself, might be still lurking about some corner of the apartment.

"I will not pretend to describe what hot and cold fever-fits tormented me for the rest of the night, through broken sleep, weary vigils, and that dubious state which forms the neutral ground between them. A hundred terrible objects appeared to haunt me; but there was the great difference betwixt the vision which I have described, and those which followed, that I knew the last to be deceptions of my own fancy and over-excited nerves.

"Day at last appeared, and I rose from my bed ill in health and humiliated in mind. I was ashamed of myself as a man and a soldier, and still more so, at feeling my own extreme desire to escape from the haunted apartment, which, however, conquered all other considerations; so that, huddling on my clothes with the most careless haste, I made my escape from your lordship's mansion, to seek in the open air some relief to my nervous system, shaken as it was by this horrible reencounter with a visitant, for such I must believe her, from the other world. Your lordship has now heard the cause of my discomposure, and of my sudden desire to leave your hospitable castle. In other places I trust we may often meet; but God protect me from ever spending a second night under that roof!"

Strange as the General's tale was, he spoke with such a deep air of conviction, that it cut short all the usual commentaries which are made on such stories. Lord Woodville never once asked him if he was sure he did not dream of the apparition, or suggested any of the possibilities by which it is fashionable to explain supernatural appearances, as wild vagaries of the fancy, or deceptions of the optic nerves.

On the contrary, he seemed deeply impressed with the truth and reality of what he had heard; and, after a considerable pause, regretted, with much appearance of sincerity, that his early friend should in his house have suffered so severely.

"I am the more sorry for your pain, my dear Browne," he continued, "that it is the unhappy, though most unexpected result of an experiment of my own! You must know, that for my father and grandfather's time, at least, the apartment which was assigned to you last night, had been shut on account of reports that it was disturbed by supernatural sights and noises. When I came, a few weeks since, into possession of the estate, I thought the accommodation, which the castle afforded for my friends, was not extensive enough to permit the inhabitants of the invisible world to retain possession of a comfortable sleeping apartment.

"I therefore caused the Tapestried Chamber, as we call it, to be opened; and without destroying its air of antiquity, I had such new articles of furniture placed in it as became the modern times. Yet, as the opinion that the room was haunted very strongly prevailed among the domestics, and was also known in the neighbourhood and to many of my friends, I feared some prejudice might be entertained by the first occupant of the Tapestried Chamber, which might tend to revive the evil report which it had laboured under, and so disappoint my purpose of rendering it a useful part of the house. I must confess, my dear Browne, that your arrival yesterday, agreeable to me for a thousand reasons besides, seemed the most favourable opportunity of removing the unpleasant rumours which attached to the room, since your courage was indubitable, and your mind free of any pre-occupation on the subject. I could not, therefore, have chosen a more fitting subject for my experiment.

"Upon my life," said General Browne, somewhat hastily, "I am infinitely obliged to your lordship—very particularly indebted indeed. I am likely to remember for some time the consequences of the experiment, as your lordship is pleased to call it."

"Nay, now you are unjust, my dear friend," said Lord Woodville. "You have only to reflect for a single moment, in order to be convinced that I could not augur the possibility of the pain to which you have been so unhappily exposed. I was yesterday morning a complete sceptic on the subject of supernatural appearances. Nay, I am sure that had I told you what was said about that room, those very reports would have induced you, by your own choice, to select it for your accommodation. It was my misfortune, perhaps my error, but really cannot be termed my fault, that you have been afflicted so strangely."

"Strangely indeed!" said the General, resuming his good temper; "and I acknowledge that I have no right to be offended with your lordship for treating me like what I used to think myself—a man of some firmness and courage.—But I see my post horses are arrived, and I must not detain your lordship from your amusement."

"Nay, my old friend," said Lord Woodville, "since you cannot stay with us another day, which, indeed, I can no longer urge, give me at least half-an-hour more. You used to love pictures, and I have a gallery of portraits, some of them by Vandyke,[13] representing ancestry to whom this property and castle formerly belonged. I think that several of them will strike you as possessing merit."

General Browne accepted the invitation, though somewhat unwillingly. It was evident he was not to breathe freely or at ease till he left Woodville Castle far behind him. He could not refuse his friend's invitation, however; and the less so, that he was a little ashamed of the peevishness which he had displayed towards his well-meaning entertainer.

The General, therefore, followed Lord Woodville through several rooms, into a long gallery hung with pictures, which the latter pointed out to his guest, telling the names, and giving some account of the personages whose portraits presented themselves in progression. General Browne was but little interested in the details which these accounts conveyed to him. They were, indeed, of the kind which are usually found in an old family gallery.

Here was a cavalier[14] who had ruined the estate in the royal cause; there a fine lady who had reinstated it by contracting a match with a wealthy Roundhead.[15] There hung a gallant who had been in danger for corresponding

---

[13] Sir Anthony van Dyck (1599-1641), Flemish painter of portraits
[14] Royal backers of King Charles I and Charles II from 1642-1680; Anthony van Dyck painted a portrait of James Stuart (1612-1655) and his brother Lord Bernard Stuart (1623-1645) in 1638
[15] Alternate name for a cavalier

with the exiled Court at Saint Germains;[16] here one who
had taken arms for William at the Revolution;[17] and there
a third that had thrown his weight alternately into the
scale of Whig and Tory.[18]

While Lord Woodville was cramming these words into
his guest's ear, "against the stomach of his sense," they
gained the middle of the gallery, when he beheld General
Browne suddenly start, and assume an attitude of the
utmost surprise, not unmixed with fear, as his eyes were
caught and suddenly rivetted by a portrait of an old lady
in a sacque, the fashionable dress of the end of the
seventeenth century.

"There she is!" he exclaimed; "there she is, in form and
features, though inferior in demoniac expression to the
accursed hag who visited me last night!"

"If that be the case," said the young nobleman, "there
can remain no longer any doubt of the horrible reality of
your apparition. That is the picture of a wretched
ancestress of mine, of whose crimes a black and fearful
catalogue is recorded in a family history in my charter-
chest. The recital of them would be too horrible; it is
enough to say, that in yon fatal apartment incest and
unnatural murder were committed. I will restore it to the
solitude to which the better judgment of those who
preceded me had consigned it; and never shall any one, so
long as I can prevent it, be exposed to a repetition of the
supernatural horrors which could shake such courage as
yours."

Thus the friends, who had met with such glee, parted
in a very different mood; Lord Woodville to command the
Tapestried Chamber to be unmantled, and the door built
up; and General Browne to seek in some less beautiful
country, and with some less dignified friend, forgetfulness
of the painful night which he had passed in Woodville
Castle.

---

[16] Chateau-Neuf de Saint Germain-en-Laye was the massive
castle and grounds of the French royals until 1680
[17] English Revolution of 1688 led by William of Orange (1650-
1702)
[18] After the English Revolution of 1688 both the political parties
of Whigs and Tories governed together

WASHINGTON IRVING
(1783-1859)

Introduction
to
The Legend of Sleepy Hollow

What can be said about "The Legend of Sleepy Hollow" that has not already been said? It was published in Irving's *The Sketch Book of Geoffrey Crayon* in 1820. Sir Walter Scott used his influence to popularize it in London. Irving lived a number of years in Europe and spent time with Scott in London, which prompted William Thackeray to remark that Irving was "the first ambassador whom the New World of Letters sent to the Old." Nearly 200 years after its publication, the common perception is that the headless horseman theme was an entirely original figment of Washington Irving's imagination.

It was actually derived from Irish and German legends. In the former, the headless horseman is a quick rider who races others, but is not malevolent. This legend is alluded to by Washington Irving in the story when Brom Bones offers "to race with him for a bowl of punch, and should have won it too, for Daredevil beat the goblin horse all hollow, but just as they came to the church bridge, the Hessian bolted, and vanished in a flash of fire." In the German legend an elderly man is forced to ride on the back of the headless horseman's steed and is later thrown off a bridge into a brook. Similarly, in the story Irving tells of old Brouwer who met the horseman one night and was made to ride on his steed. "[T]hey galloped over bush and brake, over hill and swamp, until they reached the bridge; when the horseman suddenly turned into a skeleton, threw old Brouwer into the brook, and sprang away over the treetops with a clap of thunder."

Irving was the first to transpose these legends into a written story, which included his excellent characters and his unique twist. In sum, Irving brought the legend to life in only the way that he could, with ample comedy sprinkled about.

This does not sit well with some modern supernatural writers. H. P. Lovecraft is an example. To be sure, there was no room for comedic effect in the horror tales of Lovecraft. To him, humor spoiled horror. The kicker is that Lovecraft's main flaw in his short tales of horror is his lack of character generation, to which Washington Irving excelled through comedic effect. If Lovecraft is to be believed, "The Legend of Sleepy Hollow" has no place in this collection. After revisiting this tale I believe Lovecraft is dead wrong. It is planted firmly among the other sequoia trees of literature found here.

This is the most comedic of the scary ghost stories that I have collected, yet the end is terrifyingly effective because of its great characters. We want to know about "the fate of poor Icabod"; he with his pointy elbows that stick out like grasshoppers' while riding Gunpowder, his old plough horse. We care whether he makes it back to the blooming lass that is Katrina Van Tassel with his saddle slipping and the headless horseman bearing down. That is when Irving has us and we are at his supernatural mercy.

Only in rare instances does the comedic effect work in a scary ghost story and "The Legend of Sleepy Hollow" is a shining jack-o'-lantern example of when it does. Before you is the first supernatural tale with great characters penned in the English language. Before you is a legend that has been made real in the hands of Irving.

The Legend of Sleepy Hollow (1820)

> A pleasing land of drowsy head it was,
> Of dreams that wave before the half-shut eye;
> And of gay castles in the clouds that pass,
> For ever flushing round a summer sky.
> *Castle of Indolence.*[1]

IN THE BOSOM OF one of those spacious coves which indent the eastern shore of the Hudson, at that broad expansion of the river denominated by the ancient Dutch navigators the Tappan Zee,[2] and where they always prudently shortened sail, and implored the protection of St. Nicholas[3] when they crossed, there lies a small market town or rural port, which by some is called Greensburgh, but which is more generally and properly known by the name of Tarry Town.[4]

This name was given it, we are told, in former days, by the good housewives of the adjacent country, from the inveterate propensity of their husbands to linger about the village tavern on market days. Be that as it may, I do not vouch for the fact, but merely advert to it, for the sake of being precise and authentic. Not far from this village, perhaps about three miles, there is a little valley or rather lap of land among high hills, which is one of the quietest places in the whole world. A small brook glides through it, with just murmur enough to lull one to repose; and the occasional whistle of a quail, or tapping of a woodpecker, is almost the only sound that ever breaks in upon the uniform tranquillity.

---

[1] Poem written by James Thomson (1700-1748) and published in 1748

[2] An expanse ten miles long and four across

[3] Also known as Nicholas the Wonderworker (276–343), this four century Greek Bishop was known for his charity, hence the association with Santa Clause, but in this context ancient sailors were known to pray to him during storms.

[4] Village of 5.7 square miles in the Town of Greenburgh, New York

I recollect that, when a stripling, my first exploit in squirrel-shooting was in a grove of tall walnut trees that shades one side of the valley. I had wandered into it at noon-time, when all nature is peculiarly quiet, and was startled by the roar of my own gun, as it broke the Sabbath[5] stillness around, and was prolonged and reverberated by the angry echoes. If ever I should wish for a retreat whither I might steal from the world and its distractions, and dream quietly away the remnant of a troubled life, I know of none more promising than this little valley.

From the listless repose of the place, and the peculiar character of its inhabitants, who are descendants from the original Dutch settlers, this sequestered glen has long been known by the name of SLEEPY HOLLOW, and its rustic lads are called the Sleepy Hollow Boys throughout all the neighbouring country. A drowsy, dreamy influence seems to hang over the land, and to pervade the very atmosphere. Some say that the place was bewitched by a high German doctor, during the early days of the settlement; others, that an old Indian chief, the prophet or wizard of his tribe, held his powwows[6] there before the country was discovered by Master Hendrick Hudson.[7]

Certain it is, the place still continues under the sway of some witching power, that holds a spell over the minds of the good people, causing them to walk in a continual reverie. They are given to all kinds of marvellous beliefs; are subject to trances and visions, and frequently see strange sights, and hear music and voices in the air. The whole neighbourhood abounds with local tales, haunted spots, and twilight superstitions; stars shoot and meteors glare oftener across-the valley than in any other part of the country, and the night-mare, with her whole nine fold,[8] seems to make it the favourite scene of her gambols.[9]

---

[5] Saturday in Jewish and Christian religions
[6] American Indian incantation ceremony
[7] Hendrick Hudson (1560-1611), Englishman who explored the area of modern New York and for whom the Hudson River, Hudson's Bay and Hudson's Straits are named after
[8] Derivation from William Shakespeare's (1564-1616) *King Lear*, Act III. Sc. 4, "He met the nightmare and her nine fold,"
[9] Playful jumping

The dominant spirit, however, that haunts this enchanted region, and seems to be commander-in-chief of all the powers of the air, is the apparition of a figure on horseback without a head. It is said by some to be the ghost of a Hessian trooper,[10] whose head had been carried away by a cannon-ball, in some nameless battle during the Revolutionary War,[11] and who is ever and anon seen by the country folk, hurrying along in the gloom of night, as if on the wings of the wind. His haunts are not confined to the valley, but extend at times to the adjacent roads, and especially to the vicinity of a church that is at no great distance.

Indeed, certain of the most authentic historians of those parts, who have been careful in collecting and collating the floating facts concerning this spectre, allege, that the body of the trooper having been buried in the churchyard, the ghost rides forth to the scene of battle in nightly quest of his head, and that the rushing speed with which he sometimes passes along the hollow, like a midnight blast, is owing to his being belated, and in a hurry to get back to the churchyard before daybreak.

Such is the general purport of this legendary superstition, which has furnished materials for many a wild story in that region of shadows; and the spectre is known at all the country firesides, by the name of The Headless Horseman of Sleepy Hollow.

It is remarkable, that the visionary propensity I have mentioned is not confined to the native inhabitants of the valley, but is unconsciously imbibed by every one who resides there for a time. However wide awake they may have been before they entered that sleepy region, they are sure, in a little time, to inhale the witching influence of the air, and begin to grow imaginative—to dream dreams, and see apparitions.

I mention this peaceful spot with all possible laud; for it is in such little retired Dutch valleys, found here and there embosomed in the great State of New-York, that population, manners, and customs, remain fixed, while the great torrent of migration and improvement, which is

---

[10] German soldiers from the area of Hesse or Hessia employed to fight with the British against the Americans during the Revolutionary War

[11] Battle for independence of American from Brittan from 1775-1883

making such incessant changes in other parts of this restless country, sweeps by them unobserved. They are like those little nooks of still water, which border a rapid stream, where we may see the straw and bubble riding quietly at anchor, or slowly revolving in their mimic harbour, undisturbed by the rush of the passing current. Though many years have elapsed since I trod the drowsy shades of Sleepy Hollow, yet I question whether I should not still find the same trees and the same families vegetating in its sheltered bosom.

In this by-place of nature there abode, in a remote period of American history, that is to say, some thirty years since, a worthy wight[12] of the name of Ichabod Crane, who sojourned, or, as he expressed it, "tarried," in Sleepy Hollow, for the purpose of instructing the children of the vicinity. He was a native of Connecticut, a State which supplies the Union[13] with pioneers for the mind as well as for the forest, and sends forth yearly its legions of frontier woodmen and country schoolmasters.

The cognomen of Crane was not inapplicable to his person. He was tall, but exceedingly lank, with narrow shoulders, long arms and legs, hands that dangled a mile out of his sleeves, feet that might have served for shovels, and his whole frame most loosely hung together. His head was small, and flat at top, with huge ears, large green glassy eyes, and a long snipe nose,[14] so that it looked like a weathercock[15] perched upon his spindle neck, to tell which way the wind blew. To see him striding along the profile of a hill on a windy day, with his clothes bagging and fluttering about him, one might have mistaken him for the genius of famine descending upon the earth, or some scarecrow eloped from a cornfield.

His school-house was a low building of one large room, rudely constructed of logs; the windows partly glazed, and partly patched with leaves of old copybooks.[16] It was most ingeniously secured at vacant hours, by a withe[17] twisted in the handle of the door, and stakes set against the

---

[12] Lad or person or creature
[13] America
[14] Reference to the long bill of the snipe bird
[15] Reference to a weathervane that were commonly in the shape of a rooster and mounted on a narrow iron rod
[16] Old books used by students for tracing letters
[17] Bendable twigs or sticks used for a tying band

window-shutters; so that though a thief might get in with perfect ease, he would find some embarrassment in getting out;—an idea most probably borrowed by the architect, Yost Van Houten, from the mystery of an eelpot.[18]

The schoolhouse stood in a rather lonely but pleasant situation, just at the foot of a woody hill, with a brook running close by, and a formidable birch-tree growing at one end of it. From hence the low murmur of his pupil's voices, conning over their lessons, might be heard of a drowsy summer's day, like the hum of a beehive; interrupted now and then by the authoritative voice of the master, in the tone of menace or command; or, peradventure, by the appalling sound of the birch, as he urged some tardy loiterer along the flowery path of knowledge. Truth to say, he was a conscientious man, that ever bore in mind the golden maxim, "spare the rod and spoil the child."[19]—Ichabod Crane's scholars certainly were not spoiled.

I would riot have it imagined, however, that he was one of those cruel potentates of the school, who joy in the smart of their subjects; on the contrary, he administered justice with discrimination rather than severity; taking the burthen off the backs of the weak, and laying it on those of the strong. Your mere puny stripling, that winced at the least flourish of the rod, was passed by with indulgence; but the claims of justice were satisfied by inflicting a double portion on some little, tough, wrong-headed, broad skirted Dutch urchin, who sulked and swelled and grew dogged and sullen beneath the birch. All this he called "doing his duty by their parents;" and he never inflicted a chastisement without following it by the assurance, so consolatory to the smarting urchin, that "he would remember it and thank him for it the longest day he had to live."

When school hours were over, he was even the companion and playmate of the larger boys; and on holyday afternoons would convoy some of the smaller ones home, who happened to have pretty sisters, or good housewifes for mothers, noted for the comforts of the

---

[18] A box trap for eels with a funnel for easy entrance and makes it difficult to escape through the small end of the funnel

[19] Biblical derivation from Proverbs 13:24 "He that spareth his rod hateth his son."

cupboard. Indeed, it behooved him to keep on good terms with his pupils. The revenue arising from his school was small, and would have been scarcely sufficient to furnish him with daily bread, for he was a huge feeder, and though lank, had the dilating powers of an anaconda; but to help out his maintenance, he was, according to country custom in those parts, boarded and lodged at the houses of the farmers, whose children he instructed. With these he lived successively a week at a time, thus going the rounds of the neighbourhood, with all his worldly effects tied up in a cotton handkerchief.

That all this might not be too onerous on the purses of his rustic patrons, who are apt to consider the costs of schooling a grievous burthen, and schoolmasters as mere drones, he had various ways of rendering himself both useful and agreeable. He assisted the farmers occasionally in the lighter labours of their farms; helped to make hay; mended the fences; took the horses to water; drove the cows from pasture; and cut wood for the winter fire.

He laid aside, too, all the dominant dignity and absolute sway, with which he lorded it in his little empire, the school, and became wonderfully gentle and ingratiating. He found favour in the eyes of the mothers, by petting the children, particularly the youngest; and like the lion bold, which whilome[20] so magnanimously the lamb did hold,[21] he would sit with a child on one knee, and rock a cradle with his foot for whole hours together. In addition to his other vocations, he was the singing-master of the neighbourhood, and picked up many bright shillings[22] by instructing the young folks in psalmody.[23]

It was a matter of no little vanity to him on Sundays, to take his station in front of the church gallery, with a band of chosen singers; where, in his own mind, he completely carried away the palm from the parson.[24]

---

[20] As of old

[21] Quote taken from the letter L example of The New England Primer, the first reading primer for America published in the late eighteenth century: "The Lion bold, the lamb doeth hold," which means if the lion is on the prowl for prey, the lamb holds still

[22] Reference to British coins still being used in America

[23] A method of singing passages from Psalms, a book of the *Bible*

[24] Ichabod believes his group of singers have out sung the parson/preacher, which is analogous to out singing the church choir and the palm is representative of victory in war

Certain it is, his voice resounded far above all the rest of the congregation, and there are peculiar quavers[25] still to be heard in that church, and which may even be heard half a mile off, quite to the opposite side of the mill-pond, on a still Sunday morning, which are said to be legitimately descended from the nose of Ichabod Crane. Thus, by divers little make-shifts, in that ingenious way which is commonly denominated "by hook and by crook," the worthy pedagogue[26] got on tolerably enough, and was thought, by all who understood nothing of the labour of head-work, to have a wonderful easy life of it.

The schoolmaster is generally a man of some importance in the female circle of a rural neighbourhood; being considered a kind of idle gentleman-like personage, of vastly superior taste and accomplishments to the rough country swains,[27] and, indeed, inferior in learning only to the parson. His appearance, therefore, is apt to occasion some little stir at the tea-table of a farm-house, and the addition of a supernumerary[28] dish of cakes or sweetmeats, or, peradventure, the parade of a silver tea-pot. Our man of letters, therefore, was peculiarly happy in the smiles of all the country damsels. How he would figure among them in the churchyard, between services on Sundays; gathering grapes for them from the wild vines that overrun the surrounding trees; reciting for their amusement all the epitaphs on the tombstones; or sauntering, with a whole bevy of them, along the banks of the adjacent mill-pond; while the more bashful country bumpkins hung sheepishly back, envying his superior elegance and address.

From his half itinerant life, also, he was a kind of travelling gazette, carrying the whole budget of local gossip from house to house; so that his appearance was always greeted with satisfaction. He was, moreover, esteemed by the women as a man of great erudition,[29] for he had read several books quite through, and was a perfect master of

---

[25] Non-harmonious vibrations of the singing voice
[26] Schoolteacher
[27] Country children
[28] Exceeding large
[29] Scholarly education

Cotton Mather's *History of New-England Witchcraft*,[30] in which, by the way, he most firmly and potently believed.

He was, in fact, an odd mixture of small shrewdness and simple credulity. His appetite for the marvellous, and his powers of digesting it, were equally extraordinary; and both had been increased by his residence in this spell-bound region. No tale was too gross or monstrous for his capacious swallow. It was often his delight, after his school was dismissed in the afternoon, to stretch himself on the rich bed of clover, bordering the little brook that whimpered by his school-house, and there con[31] over old Mather's direful tales, until the gathering dusk of evening made the printed page a mere mist before his eyes.

Then, as he wended his way, by swamp and stream and awful woodland, to the farm-house where he happened to be quartered, every sound of nature, at that witching hour,[32] fluttered his excited imagination: the moan of the whip-poor-will[33] from the hill side; the boding cry of the tree-toad, that harbinger of storm; the dreary hooting of the screech-owl; or the sudden rustling in the thicket, of birds frightened from their roost.

The fire-flies, too, which sparkled most vividly in the darkest places, now and then startled him, as one of uncommon brightness would stream across his path; and if, by chance, a huge blockhead of a beetle came winging his blundering flight against him, the poor varlet[34] was ready to give up the ghost,[35] with the idea that he was struck with a witch's token.[36] His only resource on such occasions, either to drown thought, or drive away evil

---

[30] Puritan minister, Cotton Mather (1663-1728), whose books are thought to have incited the witch trials

[31] Short for convene

[32] Thomas Moore's (1779-1852) famous poem *Lalla Rookh. An Oriental Romance.* published in 1817 uses the phrase "Alone, at this same witching hour," which may be where Washington Irving saw it; yet the first instance is in Richard Cumberland's (1732-1811) British poem *Ode to the Sun* published in 1789, "And the witching hour of night, Whilst thy pale sister lends her shadowy light, Summon the naked wood-nymphs to my sight."

[33] Bird that only sings at night

[34] Excitable

[35] Die, reference here to giving up the Holy Ghost in death

[36] Being struck with a witch's token meant a spell was cast on that person

spirits, was to sing Psalm tunes;—and the good people of Sleepy Hollow, as they sat by their doors of an evening, were often filled with awe, at hearing his nasal melody, "in linked sweetness long drawn out,"[37] floating from the distant hill, or along the dusky road.

Another of his sources of fearful pleasure was, to pass long winter evenings with the old Dutch wives, as they sat spinning by the fire, with a row of apples roasting and sputtering along the hearth, and listen to their marvellous tales of ghosts, and goblins, and haunted fields and haunted brooks, and haunted bridges and haunted houses, and particularly of the headless horseman, or galloping Hessian of the Hollow, as they sometimes called him. He would delight them equally by his anecdotes of witchcraft, and of the direful omens and portentous sights and sounds in the air, which prevailed in the earlier times of Connecticut; and would frighten them woefully with speculations upon comets and shooting stars, and with the alarming fact that the world did absolutely turn round, and that they were half the time topsy-turvy!

But if there was a pleasure in all this, while snugly cuddling in the chimney corner of a chamber that was all of a ruddy glow from the crackling wood fire and where, of course, no spectre dared to show its face, it was dearly purchased by the terrors of his subsequent walk homewards. What fearful shapes and shadows beset his path, amidst the dim and ghastly glare of a snowy night!— With what wistful look did he eye every trembling ray of light streaming across the waste fields from some distant window!—How often was he appalled by some shrub covered with snow, which like a sheeted spectre beset his very path!—How often did he shrink with curdling awe at the sound of his own steps on the frosty crust beneath his feet; and dread to look over his shoulder, lest he should behold some uncouth being tramping close behind him!— and how often was he thrown into complete dismay by some rushing blast, howling among the trees, in the idea that it was the galloping Hessian on one of his nightly scourings!

All these, however, were mere terrors of the night, phantoms of the mind, that walk in darkness: and though he had seen many spectres in his time, and been more

---

[37] John Milton's (1608-1674) pastoral poem *L'allegro*, published in 1631, includes the line, "Of linked sweetness long drawn out."

than once beset by Satan in divers shapes, in his lonely perambulations,[38] yet day-light put an end to all these evils; and he would have passed a pleasant life of it, in despite of the Devil and all his works, if his path had not been crossed by a being that causes more perplexity to mortal man, than ghosts, goblins, and the whole race of witches put together; and that was—a woman.

Among the musical disciples who assembled, one evening in each week, to receive his instructions in psalmody, was Katrina Van Tassel, the daughter and only child of a substantial Dutch farmer. She was a blooming lass of fresh eighteen; plump as a partridge; ripe and melting and rosy-cheeked as one of her father's peaches, and universally famed, not merely for her beauty, but her vast expectations. She was withal a little of a coquette,[39] as might be perceived even in her dress, which was a mixture of ancient and modern fashions, as most suited to set off her charms. She wore the ornaments of pure yellow gold, which her great-great-grandmother had brought over from Saardam;[40] the tempting stomacher[41] of the olden time, and withal a provokingly short petticoat, to display the prettiest foot and ankle in the country round.

Ichabod Crane had a soft and foolish heart toward the sex; and it is not to be wondered at, that so tempting a morsel soon found favour in his eyes, more especially after he had visited her in her paternal mansion. Old Baltus Van Tassel was a perfect picture of a thriving, contented, liberal-hearted farmer. He seldom, it is true, sent either his eyes or his thoughts beyond the boundaries of his own farm; but within these, every thing was snug, happy, and well conditioned. He was satisfied with his wealth, but not proud of it; and piqued himself upon the hearty abundance, rather than the style in which he lived. His strong-hold was situated on the banks of the Hudson, in one of those green, sheltered, fertile nooks, in which the Dutch farmers are so fond of nestling.

A great elm-tree spread its broad branches over it, at the foot of which bubbled up a spring of the softest and sweetest water, in a little well, formed of a barrel; and then stole sparkling away through the grass, to a neighbouring

---

[38] Aimless walks
[39] Flirt
[40] A city in the western Netherlands
[41] Front of a woman's dress

brook, that babbled along among alders and dwarf willows. Hard by the farm-house was a vast barn, that might have served for a church; every window and crevice of which seemed bursting forth with the treasures of the farm; the flail was busily resounding within it from morning to night; swallows and martins skimmed twittering about the eaves; and rows of pigeons, some with one eye turned up, as if watching the weather, some with their heads under their wings, or buried in their bosoms, and others, swelling, and cooing, and bowing about their dames, were enjoying the sunshine on the roof.

Sleek, unwieldy porkers were grunting in the repose and abundance of their pens, from whence sallied forth, now and then, troops of sucking pigs, as if to snuff the air. A stately squadron of snowy geese were riding in an adjoining pond, convoying whole fleets of ducks; regiments of turkeys were gobbling through the farm-yard, and guinea-fowls fretting about it like ill-tempered housewives, with their peevish, discontented cry. Before the barn door strutted the gallant cock, that pattern of a husband, a warrior, and a fine gentleman; clapping his burnished wings and crowing in the pride and gladness of his heart— sometimes tearing up the earth with his feet, and then generously calling his ever-hungry family of wives and children to enjoy the rich morsel which he had discovered.

The pedagogue's mouth watered, as he looked upon this sumptuous promise of luxurious winter fare. In his devouring mind's eye, he pictured to himself every roasting pig running about, with a pudding in its belly, and an apple in its mouth; the pigeons were snugly put to bed in a comfortable pie, and tucked in with a coverlet of crust; the geese were swimming in their own gravy; and the ducks pairing cosily in dishes, like snug married couples, with a decent competency of onion sauce. In the porkers he saw carved out the future sleek side of bacon, and juicy relishing ham; not a turkey, but he beheld daintily trussed up, with its gizzard under its wing, and, peradventure, a necklace of savoury sausages; and even bright chanticleer[42] himself, lay sprawling on his back, in a side dish, with uplifted claws, as if craving that quarter which his chivalrous spirit disdained to ask while living.

As the enraptured Ichabod fancied all this, and as he rolled his great green eyes over the fat meadow lands, the

---

[42] Rooster

rich fields of wheat, of rye, of buckwheat, and Indian corn, and the orchards burthened with ruddy fruit, which surrounded the warm tenement of Van Tassel, his heart yearned after the damsel who was to inherit these domains, and his imagination expanded with the idea, how they might be readily turned into cash, and the money invested in immense tracts of wild land, and shingle palaces in the wilderness. Nay, his busy fancy already realized his hopes, and presented to him the blooming Katrina, with a whole family of children, mounted on the top of a wagon loaded with household trumpery, with pots and kettles dangling beneath; and he beheld himself bestriding a pacing mare, with a colt at her heels, setting out for Kentucky, Tennessee—or the Lord knows where!

When he entered the house, the conquest of his heart was complete. It was one of those spacious farm-houses, with high-ridged, but lowly-sloping roofs built in the style handed down from the first Dutch settlers. The low projecting eaves forming a piazza along the front, capable of being closed up in bad weather. Under this were hung flails,[43] harness, various utensils of husbandry,[44] and nets for fishing in the neighbouring river. Benches were built along the sides for summer use; and a great spinning-wheel at one end, and a churn at the other, showed the various uses to which this important porch might be devoted. From this piazza the wonderful Ichabod entered the hall, which formed the centre of the mansion, and the place of usual residence.

Here, rows of resplendent pewter, ranged on a long dresser, dazzled his eyes. In one corner stood a huge bag of wool, ready to be spun; in another, a quantity of linsey-woolsey[45] just from the loom;[46] ears of Indian corn,[47] and strings of dried apples and peaches, hung in gay festoons along the walls, mingled with the gaud of red peppers; and a door left ajar, gave him a peep into the best parlour, where the claw-footed chairs, and dark mahogany tables, shone like mirrors; andirons, with their accompanying shovel and tongs, glistened from their covert of asparagus

---

[43] A threshing tool used by farmers
[44] Profession of growing and harvesting crops
[45] Rough cloth weaved out of linen and wool
[46] Manual apparatus for weaving cloth
[47] Multi-colored corn used by American Indians

tops; mock-oranges and conch shells decorated the mantelpiece; strings of various coloured birds' eggs were suspended above it; a great ostrich egg was hung from the centre of the room, and a corner cupboard, knowingly left open, displayed immense treasures of old silver and well-mended china.

From the moment Ichabod laid his eyes upon these regions of delight, the peace of his mind was at an end, and his only study was how to gain the affections of the peerless daughter of Van Tassel. In this enterprise, however, he, had more real difficulties than generally fell to the lot of a knight-errant of yore, who seldom had any thing but giants, enchanters, fiery dragons, and such like easily conquered adversaries, to contend with; and had to make his way merely through gates of iron and brass, and walls of adamant to the castle-keep, where the lady of his heart was confined; all which he achieved as easily as a man would carve his way to the centre of a Christmas pie,[48] and then the lady gave him her hand as a matter of course.

Ichabod, on the contrary, had to win his way to the heart of a country coquette, beset with a labyrinth of whims and caprices, which were for ever presenting new difficulties and impediments, and he had to encounter a host of fearful adversaries of real flesh and blood, the numerous rustic admirers, who beset every portal to her heart; keeping a watchful and angry eye upon each other, but ready to fly out in the common cause against any new competitor.

Among these, the most formidable was a burley, roaring, roistering blade, of the name of Abraham, or, according to the Dutch abbreviation, Brom Van Brunt,[49] the hero of the country round, which rung with his feats of strength and hardihood. He was broad-shouldered and double-jointed, with short curly black hair, and a bluff, but not unpleasant countenance, having a mingled air of fun and arrogance. From his Herculean frame and great powers of limb he had received the nickname of BROM BONES, by which he was universally known. He was famed

---

[48] Perhaps a mincemeat pie

[49] It is claimed that the character is based off a real person by the name of Abraham (or Abram) Van Tassel; *see* "Irving's Ichabod Crane Again," Edgar Mayhew Bacon, *New York Times*, March 12, 1898

for great knowledge and skill in horsemanship, being as dexterous on horseback as a Tartar.[50]

He was foremost at all races and cock-fights, and with the ascendancy which bodily strength always acquires in rustic life, was the umpire in all disputes, setting his hat on one side, and giving his decisions with an air and tone that admitted of no gainsay or appeal. He was always ready for either a fight or a frolic; had more mischief than ill-will in his composition; and with all his overbearing roughness, there was a strong dash of waggish good-humour at bottom. He had three or four boon[51] companions of his own stamp,[52] who regarded him as their model, and at the head of whom he scoured the country, attending every scene of feud or merriment for miles round. In cold weather, he was distinguished by a fur cap, surmounted with a flaunting fox's tail; and when the folks at a country gathering descried this well-known crest at a distance, whisking about among a squad of hard riders, they always stood by for a squall.

Sometimes his crew would be heard dashing along past the farmhouses at midnight, with whoop and halloo, like a troop of Don Cossacks,[53] and the old dames, startled out of their sleep, would listen for a moment till the hurry-scurry had clattered by, and then exclaim, "Ay, there goes Brom Bones and his gang!" The neighbours looked upon him with a mixture of awe, admiration, and good-will; and when any madcap prank, or rustic brawl occurred in the vicinity, always shook their heads, and warranted Brom Bones was at the bottom of it.

This rantipole[54] hero had for some time singled out the blooming Katrina for the object of his uncouth gallantries, and though his amorous toyings were something like the gentle caresses and endearments of a bear, yet it was whispered that she did not altogether discourage his hopes. Certain it is, his advances were signals for rival candidates to retire, who felt no inclination to cross a lion in his amours; insomuch, that when his horse was seen tied to Van Tassel's paling, on a Sunday night, a sure sign

---

50 Men from Tartary, a huge tract of land in northern and central Asia, were known for their horse-riding skills
51 Jovial
52 Similar in looks and personality
53 Skilled horsemen of the Don River in Russia
54 Loud, wild and romping

that his master was courting, or, as it is termed, "sparking," within, all other suitors passed by in despair, and carried the war into other quarters.

Such was the formidable rival with whom Ichabod Crane had to contend, and considering all things, a stouter man than he would have shrunk from the competition, and a wiser man would have despaired. He had, however, a happy mixture of pliability and perseverance in his nature; he was in form and spirit like a supple-jack[55]—yielding, but tough; though he bent, he never broke; and though he bowed beneath the slightest pressure, yet, the moment it was away—jerk!—he was as erect, and carried his head as high as ever.

To have taken the field openly against his rival, would have been madness; for he was not a man to be thwarted in his amours, any more than that stormy lover, Achilles.[56] Ichabod, therefore, made his advances in a quiet and gently-insinuating manner. Under cover of his character of singing-master, he made frequent visits at the farm-house; not that he had any thing to apprehend from the meddlesome interference of parents, which is so often a stumbling block in the path of lovers. Bait Van Tassel was an easy indulgent soul; he loved his daughter better even than his pipe, and like a reasonable man, and an excellent father, let her have her way in every thing.

His notable little wife, too, had enough to do to attend to her housekeeping and manage the poultry; for, as she sagely observed, ducks and geese are foolish things, and must be looked after, but girls can take care of themselves. Thus, while the busy dame bustled about the house, or plied her spinning wheel at one end of the piazza, honest Bait would sit smoking his evening pipe at the other, watching the achievements of a little wooden warrior, who, armed with a sword in each hand, was most valiantly fighting the wind on the pinnacle of the barn. In the mean time, Ichabod would carry on his suit with the daughter by the side of the spring under the great elm, or sauntering along in the twilight, that hour so favourable to the lover's eloquence.

I profess not to know how women's hearts are wooed and won. To me they have always been matters of riddle and admiration. Some seem to have but one vulnerable

---

55 Pliable vine that grows in the southern United States
56 Quick and brave Greek warrior in Homer's *Iliad*, Book I

point, or door of access; while others have a thousand
avenues, and may be captured in a thousand different
ways. It is a great triumph of skill to gain the former, but a
still greater proof of generalship to maintain possession of
the latter, for a man must battle for his fortress at every
door and window. He that wins a thousand common
hearts, is therefore entitled to some renown; but he who
keeps undisputed sway over the heart of a coquette, is
indeed a hero. Certain it is, this was not the case with the
redoubtable[57] Brom Bones; and from the moment Ichabod
Crane made his advances, the interests of the former
evidently declined: his horse was no longer seen tied at the
palings on Sunday nights, and a deadly feud gradually
arose between him and the preceptor of Sleepy Hollow.

Brom, who had a degree of rough chivalry in his
nature, would fain have carried matters to open warfare,
and settled their pretensions to the lady, according to the
mode of those most concise and simple reasoners, the
knights errant of yore—by single combat; but Ichabod was
too conscious of the superior might of his adversary to
enter the lists against him; he had overheard the boast of
Bones, that he would "double the schoolmaster up, and
put him on a shelf;" and he was too wary to give him an
opportunity. There was something extremely provoking in
this obstinately pacific system;[58] it left Brom no alternative
but to draw upon the funds of rustic waggery in his
disposition, and to play off boorish practical jokes upon
his rival.

Ichabod became the object of whimsical persecution to
Bones, and his gang of rough riders. They harried his
hitherto peaceful domains; smoked out his singing-school,
by stopping up the chimney; broke into the schoolhouse at
night, in spite of its formidable fastenings of withe and
window-stakes, and turned every thing topsy-turvy; so
that the poor schoolmaster began to think all the witches
in the country held their meetings there. But what was
still more annoying, Brom took all opportunities of turning
him into ridicule in presence of his mistress, and had a
scoundrel dog whom he taught to whine in the most
ludicrous manner, and introduced as a rival of Ichabod's,
to instruct her in psalmody.

---

[57] Formidable
[58] Peaceful

In this way, matters went on for some time, without producing any material effect on the relative situations of the contending powers. On a fine autumnal afternoon, Ichabod, in pensive mood, sat enthroned on the lofty stool from whence he usually watched all the concerns of his little literary realm. In his hand he swayed a ferule,[59] that sceptre of despotic power; the birch of justice reposed on three nails, behind the throne, a constant terror to evil doers; while on the desk before him might be seen sundry contraband articles and prohibited weapons, detected upon the persons of idle urchins; such as half-munched apples, popguns, whirligigs,[60] fly-cages, and whole legions of rampant little paper game-cocks.

Apparently there had been some appalling act of justice recently inflicted, for his scholars were all busily intent upon their books, or slyly whispering behind them with one eye kept upon the master; and a kind of buzzing stillness reigned throughout the school-room. It was suddenly interrupted by the appearance of a negro in tow-cloth jacket and trowsers, a round crowned fragment of a hat, like the cap of Mercury,[61] and mounted on the back of a ragged, wild, half-broken colt, which he managed with a rope by way of halter. He came clattering up to the school-door with an invitation to Ichabod to attend a merry-making, or "quilting frolic,"[62] to be held that evening at Mynheer Van Tassel's; and having delivered his message with that air of importance, and effort at fine language, which a negro is apt to display on petty embassies of the kind, he dashed over the brook, and was seen scampering away up the hollow, full of the importance and hurry of his mission.

All was now bustle and hubbub in the late quiet school-room. The scholars were hurried through their lessons, without stopping at trifles; those who were nimble, skipped over half with impunity, and those who were tardy, had a smart application now and then in the rear, to quicken their speed, or help them over a tall word. Books were flung aside, without being put away on the shelves; inkstands were overturned, benches thrown

---

[59] Ruler
[60] A spinning toy like a top
[61] Pointed cap worn by Mercury, the messenger of the gods in Roman mythology
[62] Reference to party after long quilting sessions

down, and the whole school was turned loose an hour before the usual time; bursting forth like a legion of young imps, yelping and racketing about the green, in joy at their early emancipation.

The gallant Ichabod now spent at least an extra half-hour at his toilet, brushing and furbishing up his best, and indeed only suit of rusty black, and arranging his looks by a bit of broken looking-glass, that hung up in the school-house. That he might make his appearance before his mistress in the true style of a cavalier, he borrowed a horse from the farmer with whom he was domiciliated, a choleric[63] old Dutchman, of the name of Hans Van Ripper, and thus gallantly mounted, issued forth like a knight errant in quest of adventures.

But it is meet I should, in the true spirit of romantic story, give some account of the looks and equipments of my hero and his steed. The animal he bestrode was a broken down plough-horse, that had outlived almost every thing but his viciousness. He was gaunt and shagged, with a ewe[64] neck and a head like a hammer; his rusty mane and tail were tangled and knotted with burrs; one eye had lost its pupil, and was glaring and spectral, but the other had the gleam of a genuine devil in it. Still he must have had fire and mettle in his day, if we may judge from his name, which was Gunpowder. He had, in fact, been a favourite steed of his master's, the choleric Van Ripper, who was a furious rider, and had infused, very probably, some of his own spirit into the animal; for, old and broken-down as he looked, there was more of the lurking devil in him than in any young filly[65] in the country.

Ichabod was a suitable figure for such a steed. He rode with short stirrups, which brought his knees nearly up to the pommel[66] of the saddle; his sharp elbows stuck out like grasshoppers'; he carried his whip perpendicularly in his hand, like a sceptre, and as the horse jogged on, the motion of his arms was not unlike the flapping of a pair of wings. A small wool hat rested on the top of his nose, for so his scanty strip of forehead might be called, and the skirts of his black coat fluttered out almost to the horse's

---

[63] Of sour disposition
[64] Female sheep
[65] Mare less than three years old
[66] Stub that sticks above the saddle

tail. Such was the appearance of Ichabod and his steed, as they shambled out of the gate of Hans Van Ripper, and it was altogether such an apparition as is seldom to be met with in broad daylight.

It was, as I have said, a fine autumnal day; the sky was clear and serene, and nature wore that rich and golden livery which we always associate with the idea of abundance. The forests had put on their sober brown and yellow, while some trees of the tenderer kind had been nipped by the frosts into brilliant dyes of orange, purple, and scarlet. Streaming files of wild ducks began to make their appearance high in the air; the bark of the squirrel might be heard from the groves of beech and hickory-nuts, and the pensive whistle of the quail at intervals from the neighbouring stubble field.

The small birds were taking their farewell banquets. In the fullness of their revelry, they fluttered chirping and frolicking, from bush to bush, and tree to tree, capricious from the very profusion and variety around them. There was the honest cockrobin, the favourite game of stripling sportsmen, with its loud querulous note, and the twittering blackbirds flying in sable clouds; and the golden-winged woodpecker, with his crimson crest, his broad black gorget, and splendid plumage; and the cedar-bird, with its red-tipt wings and yellow-tipt tail, and its little monteiro cap of feathers; and the blue jay, that noisy coxcomb, in his gay light blue coat and white underclothes, screaming and chattering, nodding, and bobbing, and bowing, and pretending to be on good terms with every songster of the grove.

As Ichabod jogged slowly on his way, his eye, ever open to every symptom of culinary abundance, ranged with delight over the treasures of jolly autumn. On all sides he beheld vast store of apples, some hanging in oppressive opulence on the trees; some gathered into baskets and barrels for the market; others heaped up in rich piles for the cider-press. Farther on he beheld great fields of Indian corn, with its golden ears peeping from their leafy coverts, and holding out the promise of cakes and hasty-pudding; and the yellow pumpkins lying beneath them, turning up their fair round bellies to the sun, and giving ample prospects of the most luxurious of pies; and anon he passed the fragrant buckwheat fields, breathing the odour of the bee-hive, and as he beheld them, soft anticipations stole over his mind of dainty slapjacks,[67] well buttered, and garnished with honey or treacle,[68] by the delicate little dimpled hand of Katrina Van Tassel.

Thus feeding his mind with many sweet thoughts and "sugared suppositions," he journeyed along the sides of a range of hills which look out upon some of the goodliest scenes of the mighty Hudson. The sun gradually wheeled his broad disk down into the west. The wide bosom of the Tappan Zee lay motionless and glassy, excepting that here and there a gentle undulation waved and prolonged the blue shadow of the distant mountain. A few amber clouds floated in the sky, without a breath of air to move them. The horizon was of a fine golden tint, changing gradually into a pure apple green, and from that into the deep blue of the mid-heaven.

A slanting ray lingered on the woody crests of the precipices that overhung some parts of the river, giving greater depth to the dark gray and purple of their rocky sides. A sloop was loitering in the distance, dropping slowly down with the tide, her sail hanging uselessly against the mast; and as the reflection of the sky gleamed along the still water, it seemed as if the vessel was suspended in the air.

It was toward evening that Ichabod arrived at the castle of the Heer Van Tassel, which he found thronged with the pride and flower of the adjacent country. Old farmers, a spare leathern-faced race, in homespun coats and breeches, blue stockings, huge shoes, and magnificent pewter buckles. Their brisk, withered little dames, in close crimped caps, long-waisted gowns, homespun petticoats, with scissors and pincushions, and gay calico[69] pockets hanging on the outside. Buxom lasses, almost as antiquated as their mothers, excepting where a straw hat, a fine riband,[70] or perhaps a white frock,[71] gave symptoms of city innovations. The sons, in short square-skirted coats, with rows of stupendous brass buttons, and their hair generally queued in the fashion of the times, especially if they could procure an eelskin for

---

[67] Pancakes
[68] Sugar cane syrup
[69] White, red and black
[70] Ribbon
[71] Loose-fitting dress

the purpose, it being esteemed throughout the country, as a potent nourisher and strengthener of the hair.

Brom Bones, however, was the hero of the scene, having come to the gathering on his favourite steed Daredevil, a creature, like himself, full of mettle and mischief, and which no one but himself could manage. He was, in fact, noted for preferring vicious animals, given to all kinds of tricks which kept the rider in constant risk of his neck, for he held a tractable well broken horse as unworthy of a lad of spirit.

Fain would I pause to dwell upon the world of charms that burst upon the enraptured gaze of my hero, as he entered the state parlour of Van Tassel's mansion. Not those of the bevy of buxom lasses, with their luxurious display of red and white; but the ample charms of a genuine Dutch country teatable, in the sumptuous time of autumn. Such heaped-up platters of cakes of various and almost indescribable kinds, known only to experienced Dutch housewives! There was the doughty dough-nut, the tender oly-koek,[72] and the crisp and crumbling cruller; sweet cakes and short cakes, ginger cakes and honey cakes, and the whole family of cakes.

And then there were apple pies, and peach pies, and pumpkin pies; besides slices of ham and smoked beef; and moreover delectable dishes of preserved plums, and peaches, and pears, and quinces;[73] not to mention broiled shad[74] and roasted chickens; together with bowls of milk and cream, all mingled higgledy-piggledy, pretty much as I have enumerated them, with the motherly tea-pot sending up its clouds of vapour from the midst—Heaven bless the mark! I want breath and time to discuss this banquet as it deserves, and am too eager to get on with my story. Happily, Ichabod Crane was not in so great a hurry as his historian, but did ample justice to every dainty.

He was a kind and thankful creature, whose heart dilated in proportion as his skin was filled with good cheer, and whose spirits rose with eating, as some men's do with drink. He could not help, too, rolling his large eyes round him as he ate, and chuckling with the possibility that he might one day be lord of all this scene of almost unimaginable luxury and splendour. Then, he thought,

---

[72] Cake fried in lard
[73] Hard and sour fruit in the shape of a pear
[74] Fish

how soon he'd turn his back upon the old school-house; snap his fingers in the face of Hans Van Ripper, and every other niggardly[75] patron, and kick any itinerant pedagogue out of doors that should dare to call him comrade!

Old Baltus Van Tassel moved about among his guests with a face dilated with content and good-humour, round and jolly as the harvest moon. His hospitable attentions were brief, but expressive, being confined to a shake of the hand, a slap on the shoulder, a loud laugh, and a pressing invitation to "fall to, and help themselves."

And now the sound of the music from the common room, or hall, summoned to the dance. The musician was an old gray-headed negro, who had been the itinerant orchestra of the neighbourhood for more than half a century. His instrument was as old and battered as himself. The greater part of the time he scraped away on two or three strings, accompanying every movement of the bow with a motion of the head; bowing almost to the ground, and stamping with his foot whenever a fresh couple were to start.

Ichabod prided himself upon his dancing as much as upon his vocal powers. Not a limb, not a fibre about him was idle; and to have seen his loosely hung frame in full motion, and clattering about the room, you would have thought St. Vitus[76] himself, that blessed patron of the dance, was figuring before you in person. He was the admiration of all the negroes; who, having gathered, of all ages and sizes, from the farm and the neighbourhood, stood forming a pyramid of shining black faces at every door and window; gazing with delight at the scene; rolling their white eye-balls, and showing grinning rows of ivory from ear to ear. How could the flogger of urchins be otherwise than animated and joyous? the lady of his heart was his partner in the dance, and smiling graciously in reply to all his amorous oglings; while Brom Bones, sorely smitten with love and jealousy, sat brooding by himself in one corner.

When the dance was at an end, Ichabod was attracted to a knot of the sager folks, who, with Old Van Tassel, sat

---

[75] Cheapskate, stingy

[76] Imprisoned by his father for adopting the Christian religion, he was purported to be seen dancing with seven angels, considered the saint of dancers

smoking at one end of the piazza, gossiping over former times, and drawling out long stories about the war.

This neighbourhood, at the time of which I am speaking, was one of those highly favoured places which abound with chronicle and great men. The British and American line had run near it during the war; it had, therefore, been the scene of marauding, and infested with refugees, cow-boys, and all kind of border chivalry. Just sufficient time had elapsed to enable each story-teller to dress up his tale with a little becoming fiction, and, in the indistinctness of his recollection, to make himself the hero of every exploit.

There was the story of Doffue Martling, a large blue-bearded Dutchman, who had nearly taken a British frigate with an old iron nine-pounder from a mud breastwork, only that his gun burst at the sixth discharge. And there was an old gentleman who shall be nameless, being too rich a mynheer[77] to be lightly mentioned, who, in the battle of Whiteplains,[78] being an excellent master of defence, parried a musket-ball with a small-sword, insomuch that he absolutely felt it whiz round the blade, and glance off at the hilt; in proof of which he was ready at any time to show the sword, with the hilt a little bent. There were several more that had been equally great in the field, not one of whom but was persuaded that he had a considerable hand in bringing the war to a happy termination.

But all these were nothing to the tales of ghosts and apparitions that succeeded. The neighbourhood is rich in legendary treasures of the kind. Local tales and superstitions thrive best in these sheltered, long-settled retreats; but are trampled under foot, by the shifting throng that forms the population of most of our country places. Besides, there is no encouragement for ghosts in most of our villages, for they have scarcely had time to finish their first nap, and turn themselves in their graves, before their surviving friends have travelled away from the neighbourhood: so that when they turn out at night to walk their rounds, they have no acquaintance left to call upon. This is perhaps the reason why we so seldom hear

---

[77] Dutch gentleman
[78] Battle between America and Brittan in White Plains, New York on October 28, 1776

of ghosts except in our long-established Dutch communities.

The immediate cause, however, of the prevalence of supernatural stories in these parts, was doubtless owing to the vicinity of Sleepy Hollow. There was a contagion in the very air that blew from that haunted region; it breathed forth an atmosphere of dreams and fancies infecting all the land. Several of the Sleepy Hollow people were present at Van Tassel's, and, as usual, were doling out their wild and wonderful legends. Many dismal tales were told about funeral trains, and mourning cries and wailings heard and seen about the great tree where the unfortunate Major Andre[79] was taken, and which stood in the neighbourhood. Some mention was made also of the woman in white, that haunted the dark glen at Raven Rock, and was often heard to shriek on winter nights before a storm, having perished there in the snow. The chief part of the stories, however, turned upon the favourite spectre of Sleepy Hollow, the headless horseman, who had been heard several times of late, patroling the country; and it is said, tethered his horse nightly among the graves in the churchyard.

The sequestered situation of this church seems always to have made it a favourite haunt of troubled spirits. It stands on a knoll, surrounded by locust trees and lofty elms, from among which its decent, whitewashed walls shine modestly forth, like Christian purity, beaming through the shades of retirement. A gentle slope descends from it to a silver sheet of water, bordered by high trees, between which, peeps may be caught at the blue hills of the Hudson.

To look upon its grass-grown yard, where the sunbeams seem to sleep so quietly, one would think that there at least the dead might rest in peace. On one side of the church extends a wide woody dell, along which raves a large brook among broken rocks and trunks of fallen trees. Over a deep black part of the stream, not far from the church, was formerly thrown a wooden bridge; the road that led to it, and the bridge itself, were thickly shaded by overhanging trees, which cast a gloom about it, even in the day-time; but occasioned a fearful darkness at night. Such was one of the favourite haunts of the

---

[79] Major John Andre (1750-1780) was a British solider hanged as during the American Revolutionary War

headless horseman, and the place where he was most frequently encountered.

The tale was told of old Brouwer, a most heretical disbeliever in ghosts, how he met the horseman returning from his foray into Sleepy Hollow, and was obliged to get up behind him; how they galloped over bush and brake, over hill and swamp, until they reached the bridge; when the horseman suddenly turned into a skeleton, threw old Brouwer into the brook, and sprang away over the tree-tops with a clap of thunder.[80]

This story was immediately matched by a thrice marvellous adventure, of Brom Bones, who made light of the galloping Hessian as an arrant jockey. He affirmed, that on returning one night from the neighbouring village of Sing-Sing, he had been overtaken by this midnight trooper; that he had offered to race with him for a bowl of punch, and should have won it too, for Daredevil beat the goblin horse all hollow, but just as they came to the church bridge, the Hessian bolted, and vanished in a flash of fire.[81]

All these tales, told in that drowsy under tone with which men talk in the dark, the countenances of the listeners only now and then receiving a casual gleam from the glare of a pipe, sunk deep in the mind of Ichabod. He repaid them in kind with large extracts from his invaluable author, Cotton Mather, and added many marvellous events that had taken place in his native State of Connecticut, and fearful sights which he had seen in his nightly walks about Sleepy Hollow.

The revel now gradually broke up. The old farmers gathered together their families in their wagons, and were heard for some time rattling along the hollow roads, and over the distant hills. Some of the damsels mounted on pillions[82] behind their favourite swains,[83] and their light-hearted laughter, mingling with the clatter of hoofs,

---

[80] A recounting of the prior German legend where an elderly man is forced to ride on the back of the headless horseman's steed and is later thrown off a bridge into a brook

[81] A recounting of the prior Irish legend where a rider must race the headless horseman

[82] Long pad that a woman sits on when she rides behind another on a horse

[83] Young lover

echoed along the silent woodlands, sounding fainter and fainter, until they gradually died away—and the late scene of noise and frolic was all silent and deserted. Ichabod only lingered behind, according to the custom of country lovers, to have a *tete-a-tete*[84] with the heiress, fully convinced that he was now on the high road to success. What passed at this interview I will not pretend to say, for in fact I do not know.

Something, however, I fear me, must have gone wrong, for he certainly sallied forth, after no very great interval, with an air quite desolate and chapfallen[85]—Oh, these women! these women! Could that girl have been playing off any of her coquettish tricks?—Was her encouragement of the poor pedagogue all a mere sham to secure her conquest of his rival?—Heaven only knows, not I!—Let it suffice to say, Ichabod stole forth with the air of one who had been sacking a henroost, rather than a fair lady's heart. Without looking to the right or left to notice the scene of rural wealth, on which he had so often gloated, he went straight to the stable, and with several hearty cuffs and kicks, roused his steed most uncourteously from the comfortable quarters in which he was soundly sleeping, dreaming of mountains of corn and oats, and whole valleys of timothy[86] and clover.

It was the very witching time of night[87] that Ichabod, heavy-hearted and crest-fallen,[88] pursued his travel homewards, along the sides of the lofty hills which rise above Tarry Town, and which he had traversed so cheerily in the afternoon. The hour was as dismal as himself. Far below him the Tappan Zee spread its dusky and indistinct waste of waters, with here and there the tall mast of a sloop, riding quietly at anchor under the land.

In the dead hush of midnight, he could even hear the barking of the watchdog from the opposite shore of the Hudson; but it was so vague and faint as only to give an idea of his distance from this faithful companion of man. Now and then, too, the long-drawn crowing of a cock,

---

[84] One-on-one meeting
[85] Disheartened
[86] Thick, long grass on which cattle graze
[87] See William Shakespeare's *Hamlet*, Act III. Sc. ii, "'tis now the very witching time of night, When churchyards yawn, and Hell itself breathes out contagion to this world;"
[88] Overwhelming sadness

accidentally awakened, would sound far, far off, from some farm-house away among the hills—but it was like a dreaming sound in his ear. No signs of life occurred near him, but occasionally the melancholy chirp of a cricket, or perhaps the guttural twang of a bull-frog from a neighbouring marsh, as if sleeping uncomfortably, and turning suddenly in his bed.

All the stories of ghosts and goblins that he had heard in the afternoon, now came crowding upon his recollection. The night grew darker and darker; the stars seemed to sink deeper in the sky, and driving clouds occasionally hid them from his sight. He had never felt so lonely and dismal. He was, moreover, approaching the very place where many of the scenes of the ghost stories had been laid. In the centre of the road stood an enormous tulip-tree, which towered like a giant above all the other trees of the neighbourhood, and formed a kind of landmark. Its limbs were gnarled and fantastic, large enough to form trunks for ordinary trees, twisting down almost to the earth, and rising again into the air.

It was connected with the tragical story of the unfortunate Andre, who had been taken prisoner hard by; and was universally known by the name of Major Andre's tree.[89] The common people regarded it with a mixture of respect and superstition, partly out of sympathy for the fate of its ill-starred namesake, and partly from the tales of strange sights, and doleful lamentations, told concerning it.

As Ichabod approached this fearful tree, he began to whistle; he thought his whistle was answered: it was but a blast sweeping sharply through the dry branches. As he approached a little nearer, he thought he saw something white, hanging in the midst of the tree: he paused, and ceased whistling; but on looking more narrowly, perceived that it was a place where the tree had been scathed by lightning, and the white wood laid bare. Suddenly he heard a groan—his teeth chattered, and his knees smote against the saddle: it was but the rubbing of one huge bough upon another, as they were swayed about by the breeze. He passed the tree in safety, but new perils lay before him.

About two hundred yards from the tree, a small brook crossed the road, and ran into a marshy and thickly-

---

[89] Reference to the tree where Major John Andre was hanged

wooded glen, known by the name of Wiley's Swamp.[90] A
few rough logs, laid side by side, served for a bridge over
this stream. On that side of the road where the brook
entered the wood, a group of oaks and chestnuts, matted
thick with wild grape-vines, threw a cavernous gloom over
it. To pass this bridge, was the severest trial. It was at this
identical spot that the unfortunate Andre was captured,
and under the covert of those chestnuts and vines were
the sturdy yeomen[91] concealed who surprised him. This
has ever since been considered a haunted stream, and
fearful are the feelings of the school-boy who has to pass it
alone after dark.

As he approached the stream, his heart began to
thump; he summoned up, however, all his resolution, gave
his horse half a score of kicks in the ribs, and attempted
to dash briskly across the bridge; but instead of starting
forward, the perverse old animal made a lateral
movement, and ran broadside against the fence. Ichabod,
whose fears increased with the delay, jerked the reins on
the other side, and kicked lustily with the contrary foot; it
was all in vain; his steed started, it is true, but it was only
to plunge to the opposite side of the road into a thicket of
brambles and alder-bushes.

The schoolmaster now bestowed both whip and heel
upon the starveling ribs of old Gunpowder, who dashed
forwards, snuffling and snorting, but came to a stand just
by the bridge, with a suddenness that had nearly sent his
rider sprawling over his head. Just at this moment plashy
tramp by the side of the bridge caught the sensitive ear of
Ichabod. In the dark shadow of the grove, on the margin of
the brook, he beheld something huge, misshapen, black
and towering. It stirred not, but seemed gathered up in
the gloom, like some gigantic monster ready to spring
upon the traveller.

The hair of the affrighted pedagogue rose upon his
head with terror. What was to be done? To turn and fly
was now too late; and besides, what chance was there of
escaping ghost or goblin, if such it was, which could ride
upon the wings of the wind? Summoning up, therefore, a
show of courage, he demanded in stammering accents—
"Who are you?" He received no reply. He repeated his
demand in a still more agitated voice. Still there was no

---

[90] Actual swamp in Tarrytown, New York
[91] Military officer of lesser rank

answer. Once more he cudgelled the sides of the inflexible Gunpowder, and shutting his eyes, broke forth with involuntary fervour into a psalm tune. Just then the shadowy object of alarm put itself in motion, and with a scramble and a bound, stood at once in the middle of the road.

Though the night was dark and dismal, yet the form of the unknown might now in some degree be ascertained. He appeared to be a horseman of large dimensions, and mounted on a black horse of powerful frame. He made no offer of molestation or sociability, but kept aloof on one side of the road, jogging along on the blind side of old Gunpowder, who had now got over his fright and waywardness.

Ichabod, who had no relish for this strange midnight companion, and bethought himself of the adventure of Brom Bones with the galloping Hessian, now quickened his steed, in hopes of leaving him behind. The stranger, however, quickened his horse to an equal pace. Ichabod pulled up, and fell into a walk, thinking to lag behind—the other did the same. His heart began to sink within him; he endeavoured to resume his psalm tune, but his parched tongue clove to the roof of his mouth, and he could not utter a stave.[92]

There was something in the moody and dogged silence of this pertinacious companion, that was mysterious and appalling. It was soon fearfully accounted for. On mounting a rising ground, which brought the figure of his fellow-traveller in relief against the sky, gigantic in height, and muffled in a cloak, Ichabod was horror-struck, on perceiving that he was headless! but his horror was still more increased, on observing that the head, which should have rested on his shoulders, was carried before him on the pommel of his saddle! His terror rose to desperation; he rained a shower of kicks and blows upon Gunpowder, hoping, by a sudden movement, to give his companion the slip—but the spectre started full jump with him. Away, then, they dashed, through thick and thin; stones flying and sparks flashing at every bound. Ichabod's flimsy garments fluttered in the air, as he stretched his long lank body away over his horse's head, in the eagerness of his flight.

---

[92] Tune

They had now reached the road which turns off to Sleepy Hollow; but Gunpowder, who seemed possessed with a demon, instead of keeping up it, made an opposite turn, and plunged headlong down hill to the left. This road leads through a sandy hollow, shaded by trees for about a quarter of a mile, where it crosses the bridge famous in goblin story and just beyond swells the green knoll on which stands the whitewashed church.

As yet the panic of the steed had given his unskillful rider an apparent advantage in the chase; but just as he had got half-way through the hollow, the girths of the saddle gave way, and he felt it slipping from under him. He seized it by the pommel, and endeavoured to hold it firm, but in vain; and had just time to save himself by clasping old Gunpowder round the neck, when the saddle fell to the earth, and he heard it trampled under foot by his pursuer. For a moment the terror of Hans Van Ripper's wrath passed across his mind—for it was his Sunday saddle; but this was no time for petty fears: the goblin was hard on his haunches; and, (unskillful rider that he was!) he had much ado to maintain his seat; sometimes slipping on one side, sometimes on another, and sometimes jolted on the high ridge of his horse's backbone, with a violence that he verily feared would cleave him asunder.

An opening in the trees now cheered him with the hopes that the church bridge was at hand. The wavering reflection of a silver star in the bosom of the brook told him that he was not mistaken. He saw the walls of the church dimly glaring under the trees beyond. He recollected the place where Brom Bones's ghostly competitor had disappeared. "If I can but reach that bridge," thought Ichabod, "I am safe."[93]

Just then he heard the black steed panting and blowing close behind him; he even fancied that he felt his hot breath. Another convulsive kick in the ribs, and old Gunpowder sprung upon the bridge; he thundered over the resounding planks; he gained the opposite side, and now Ichabod cast a look behind to see if his pursuer should vanish, according to rule, in a flash of fire and brimstone. Just then he saw the goblin rising in his stirrups, and in the very act of hurling his head at him. Ichabod endeavoured to dodge the horrible missile, but too late. It encountered his cranium with a tremendous

---

[93] Common belief that spirits cannot cross running water

crash—he was tumbled headlong into the dust, and Gunpowder, the black steed, and the goblin rider, passed by like a whirlwind.

The next morning the old horse was found without his saddle, and with the bridle under his feet, soberly cropping the grass at his master's gate. Ichabod did not make his appearance at breakfast—dinner-hour came, but no Ichabod. The boys assembled at the school-house, and strolled idly about the banks of the brook; but no schoolmaster. Hans Van Ripper now began to feel some uneasiness about the fate of poor Ichabod, and his saddle.

An inquiry was set on foot, and after diligent investigation they came upon his traces. In one part of the road leading to the church, was found the saddle trampled in the dirt; the tracks of horses' hoofs deeply dented in the road, and evidently at furious speed, were traced to the bridge, beyond which, on the bank of a broad part of the brook, where the water ran deep and black, was found the hat of the unfortunate Ichabod, and close beside it a shattered pumpkin.

The brook was searched, but the body of the schoolmaster was not to be discovered. Hans Van Ripper, as executor of his estate, examined the bundle which contained all his worldly effects. They consisted of two shirts and a half; two stocks for the neck; a pair or two of worsted stockings; an old pair of corduroy small-clothes; a rusty razor; a book of psalm tunes full of dog's ears; and a broken pitchpipe. As to the books and furniture of the schoolhouse, they belonged to the community, excepting Cotton Mather's *History of Witchcraft*, a New-England Almanac, and a book of dreams and fortune-telling; in which last was a sheet of foolscap[94] much scribbled and blotted, by several fruitless attempts to make a copy of verses in honour of the heiress of Van Tassel.

These magic books and the poetic scrawl were forthwith consigned to the names by Hans Van Ripper; who, from that time forward, determined to send his children no more to school; observing, that he never knew any good come of this same reading and writing. Whatever money the schoolmaster possessed, and he had received his quarter's pay but a day or two before, he must have had about his person at the time of his disappearance.

---

94 Large writing paper that is 13 by 16 inches

The mysterious event caused much speculation at the church on the following Sunday. Knots of gazers and gossips were collected in the churchyard, at the bridge, and at the spot where the hat and pumpkin had been found. The stories of Brouwer, of Bones, and a whole budget of others, were called to mind; and when they had diligently considered them all, and compared them with the symptoms of the present case, they shook their heads, and came to the conclusion, that Ichabod had been carried off by the galloping Hessian. As he was a bachelor, and in nobody's debt, nobody troubled his head any more about him; the school was removed to a different quarter of the Hollow, and another pedagogue reigned in his stead.

It is true, an old farmer, who had been down to New-York on a visit several years after, and from whom this account of the ghostly adventure was received, brought home the intelligence that Ichabod Crane was still alive; that he had left the neighbourhood partly through fear of the goblin and Hans Van Ripper, and partly in mortification at having been suddenly dismissed by the heiress; that he had changed his quarters to a distant part of the country; had kept school and studied law at the same time; had been admitted to the bar; turned politician; electioneered; written for the newspapers; and finally, had been made a Justice of the Ten Pound Court.[95]

Brom Bones, too, who, shortly after his rival's disappearance, conducted the blooming Katrina in triumph to the altar, was observed to look exceedingly knowing whenever the story of Ichabod was related, and always burst into a hearty laugh at the mention of the pumpkin; which led some to suspect that he knew more about the matter than he chose to tell.

The old country wives, however, who are the best judges of these matters, maintain to this day, that Ichabod was spirited away by supernatural means; and it is a favourite story often told about the neighbourhood round the winter evening fire. The bridge became more than ever an object of superstitious awe; and that may be the reason why the road has been altered of late years, so as to approach the church by the border of the mill-pond. The schoolhouse being deserted, soon fell to decay, and was reported to be haunted by the ghost of the unfortunate

---

[95] Equivalent to modern day small claims court that deal with civil matter where no more than ten pounds was in dispute

pedagogue; and the plough-boy, loitering homeward of a still summer evening, has often fancied his voice at a distance, chanting a melancholy Psalm tune among the tranquil solitudes of Sleepy Hollow.

EDGAR ALLAN POE
(1809-1849)

Introduction
to
The Mask of the Red Death

During the first half of the nineteenth century one man towered above all others in penning short horror stories. He wrote an amazing one third of the dozen selected for *The Best Horror Short Stories 1800-1849,* that were culled from over 300 I read for this period. He arguably created the science fiction genre (*see* "[The Balloon Hoax]," "Mellonta Tauta," "The Unparalleled Adventure of One Hans Pfaall," etc.), wrote the first cryptography short story ("The Gold-Bug"), and invented the closed room murder story ("The Murders in the Rue Morgue"). And none of this takes into consideration the poems from America's first great poet.

That man was Edgar Allan Poe. In the May 1842 issue of *Graham's Magazine* he published his best ghost story "The Mask of the Red Death." Applicable to any modern age, the story tells of a disease ravaging the land—a disease with no cure. Here Poe calls it the Red Death in a play on the term Black Death that previously invaded Europe. This is the first instance I have found during the period in review of a spectre spreading disease or pestilence in a short story. Consider the many literary items and artifacts Poe placed in the text.

The seven differently colored rooms in the palace represent the seven stages of life, with the last being the black room, or death. Poe may have drawn on the famous lines from Act II. Sc. vii of William Shakespeare's play *As You Like It.*

"All the world's a stage, and all the men and women merely players: They have their exits and their entrances; and one man in his time plays many parts, his acts being seven ages. As, first the infant, mewling and pewking in his nurse's arms. And then the whining schoolboy, with his satchel and shining morning face, creeping like snail unwillingly to school. And then the lover, sighing like furnace, with a woeful ballad made to his mistress' eyebrow. Then the soldier, full of strange oaths, and bearded like the pard, jealous in honor, sudden and quick in quarrel, seeking the bubble reputation even in the cannon's mouth. And then the justice in fair round belly with good capon lined, with eyes severe and beard of formal cut, full of wise saws and modern instances; and so he plays his part. The sixth age slips into the lean and slipper'd pantaloon, with spectacles on nose and pouch on side; his youthful hose, well saved, a world too wide for his shrunk shrank; and his manly voice, turning again toward childish treble, pipes and whistles in his sound. Last scene of all, that ends this strange eventful history, is second childishness and mere oblivion, sans teeth, sans eyes, sans taste, sans everything."

Life truly is a stage.

Prince Prospero (also the name of a character in Shakespeare's *The Tempest*) chases the figure who has returned from the grave. Note the first room is on the east end of the abbey and the final death room is on the west, mirroring the birth and death of the sun each day and its parallel to life.

Poe is also saying that no matter how rich one is and no matter what lengths one goes to avoid death, it is inevitable; just as he knew it was inevitable for his wife Virginia to die of tuberculosis that she contracted just a few months before this story was published. The disease may have prompted his idea for it. Here the contagion is spread by the dead who have power over the living. It is the first ghost story where the specter is bloody and shows the ravages of the disease that ushered in his death. It is a story that could only be told by Edgar Allan Poe.

The Mask of the Red Death
(1842)

THE "RED DEATH" HAD long devastated the country. No pestilence had been ever so fatal, or so hideous. Blood was its Avatar[1] and its seal — the redness and the horror of blood. There were sharp pains, and sudden dizziness, and then profuse bleedings at the pores, with dissolution. The scarlet stains upon the body and especially upon the face of the victim, were the pest-ban which shut him out from the aid and from the sympathy of his fellow-men. And the whole seizure, progress and termination of the disease were the incidents of half an hour.

But the Prince Prospero[2] was happy and dauntless, and sagacious. When his dominions were half depopulated, he summoned to his presence a thousand hale and light-hearted friends from among the knights and dames of his court, and with these retired to the deep seclusion of one of his castellated abbeys.[3] This was an extensive and magnificent structure, the creation of the prince's own eccentric yet august[4] taste. A strong and lofty wall girdled it in.

This wall had gates of iron. The courtiers, having entered, brought furnaces and massy hammers and welded the bolts. They resolved to leave means neither of ingress or egress to the sudden impulses of despair from without or of frenzy from within. The abbey was amply provisioned. With such precautions the courtiers might bid defiance to contagion. The external world could take care of itself.

In the meantime it was folly to grieve, or to think. The prince had provided all the appliances of pleasure. There were buffoons, there were improvisatori, there were ballêt-dancers, there were musicians, there were cards, there was Beauty, there was wine. All these and security were within. Without was the "Red Death."

---

[1] Manifestation
[2] Character in William Shakespeare's (1564-1616) *The Tempest*
[3] Residence, typically part of a monetary or covenant
[4] Majestic or high-class

It was towards the close of the fifth or sixth month of his seclusion, and while the pestilence raged most furiously abroad, that the Prince Prospero entertained his thousand friends at a masked ball of the most unusual magnificence. It was a voluptuous scene that masquerade.

But first let me tell of the rooms in which it was held. There were seven[5] — an imperial suite. In many palaces, however, such suites form a long and straight vista, while the folding doors slide back nearly to the walls on either hand, so that the view of the whole extent is scarcely impeded. Here the case was very different; as might have been expected from the duke's love of the *bizarre*.

The apartments were so irregularly disposed that the vision embraced but little more than one at a time. There was a sharp turn at every twenty or thirty yards, and at each turn a novel effect. To the right and left, in the middle of each wall, a tall and narrow Gothic window looked out upon a closed corridor which pursued the windings of the suite.

These windows were of stained glass whose color varied in accordance with the prevailing hue of the decorations of the chamber into which it opened. That at the eastern extremity was hung, for example, in blue — and vividly blue were its windows. The second chamber was purple in its ornaments and tapestries, and here the panes were purple. The third was green throughout, and so were the casements. The fourth was furnished and lighted with orange — the fifth with white — the sixth with violet. The seventh apartment was closely shrouded in black velvet tapestries that hung all over the ceiling and down the walls, falling in heavy folds upon a carpet of the same material and hue.

But, in this chamber only, the color of the windows failed to correspond with the decorations. The panes here were scarlet — a deep blood color. Now in no one of the seven apartments was there any lamp or candelabrum, amid the profusion of golden ornaments that lay scattered to and fro or depended from the roof.

There was no light of any kind emanating from lamp or candle within the suite of chambers. But in the corridors that followed the suite, there stood, opposite to each window, a heavy tripod, bearing a brazier of fire that projected its rays through the tinted glass and so glaringly

---

[5] Seven stages of life

illumined the room. And thus were produced a multitude of gaudy and fantastic appearances. But in the western or black chamber the effect of the fire-light that streamed upon the dark hangings through the blood-tinted panes, was ghastly in the extreme, and produced so wild a look upon the countenances of those who entered, that there were few of the company bold enough to set foot within its precincts at all.

It was in this apartment, also, that there stood against the western wall, a gigantic clock of ebony. Its pendulum swung to and fro with a dull, heavy, monotonous clang; and when its minute-hand made the circuit of the face, and the hour was to be stricken, there came forth from the brazen lungs of the clock a sound which was clear and loud and deep and exceedingly musical, but of so peculiar a note and emphasis that, at each lapse of an hour, the musicians in the orchestra were constrained to pause, momently, in their performance, to harken to the sound; and thus the waltzers perforce ceased their evolutions; and there was a brief disconcert of the whole gay company; and, while the chimes of the clock yet rang, it was observed that the giddiest grew pale, and that the more aged and sedate passed their hands over their brows as if in confused reverie or meditation.

But when the echoes had fully ceased, a light laughter at once pervaded the assembly; the musicians looked at each other and smiled as if at their own nervousness and folly, and made whispering vows, each to the other, that the next chiming of the clock should produce in them no similar emotion; and then, after the lapse of sixty minutes, (which embrace three thousand and six hundred seconds of the Time that flies,) there came yet another chiming of the clock, and then were the same disconcert and tremulousness and meditation as before.

But, in spite of these things, it was a gay and magnificent revel. The tastes of the duke were peculiar. He had a fine eye for colors and effects. He disregarded the *decora* of mere fashion. His plans were bold and fiery, and his conceptions glowed with barbaric lustre. There are some who would have thought him mad. His followers felt that he was not. It was necessary to hear and see and touch him to be *sure* that he was not.

He had directed, in great part, the moveable embellishments of the seven chambers, upon occasion of this great *fête*, and it was his own guiding taste which had

given character to the costumes of the masqueraders. Be
sure they were grotesque. There were much glare and
glitter and piquancy and phantasm — much of what has
been since seen in "Hernani."[6] There were arabesque
figures with unsuited limbs and appointments. There were
delirious fancies such as the madman fashions. There was
much of the beautiful, much of the wanton, much of the
bizarre, something of the terrible, and not a little of that
which might have excited disgust.

To and fro in the seven chambers there stalked, in
fact, a multitude of dreams. And these, the dreams —
writhed in and about, taking hue from the rooms, and
causing the wild music of the orchestra to seem as the
echo of their steps. And, anon, there strikes the ebony
clock which stands in the hall of the velvet. And then,
momently, all is still, and all is silent save the voice of the
clock.

The dreams are stiff-frozen as they stand. But the
echoes of the chime die away — they have endured but an
instant — and a light, half-subdued laughter floats after
them as they depart. And now again the music swells, and
the dreams live, and writhe to and fro more merrily than
ever, taking hue from the many-tinted windows through
which stream the rays from the tripods.

But to the chamber which lies most westwardly of the
seven there are now none of the maskers who venture;
for the night is waning away; and there flows a ruddier
light through the blood-colored panes; and the blackness
of the sable drapery appalls; and to him whose foot falls
upon the sable carpet, there comes from the near clock of
ebony a muffled peal more solemnly emphatic than any
which reaches *their* ears who indulge in the more remote
gaieties of the other apartments.

But these other apartments were densely crowded, and
in them beat feverishly the heart of life. And the revel went
whirlingly on, until at length was sounded the twelfth
hour upon the clock. And then the music ceased, as I have
told; and the evolutions of the waltzers were quieted; and
there was an uneasy cessation of all things as before. But
now there were twelve strokes to be sounded by the bell of
the clock; and thus it happened, perhaps, that more of

---

[6] Dramatic 1830 play by Victor Hugo (1802-1885) fully titled
Hernani; or, Castilian Honor

thought crept, with more of time, into the meditations of the thoughtful among those who revelled.

And thus, again, it happened, perhaps, that before the last echoes of the last chime had utterly sunk into silence, there were many individuals in the crowd who had found leisure to become aware of the presence of a masked figure which had arrested the attention of no single individual before. And the rumor of this new presence having spread itself whisperingly around, there arose at length from the whole company a buzz, or murmur, expressive at first of disapprobation and surprise — then, finally, of terror, of horror, and of disgust.

In an assembly of phantasms such as I have painted, it may well be supposed that no ordinary appearance could have excited such sensation. In truth the masquerade license of the night was nearly unlimited; but the figure in question had out-Heroded Herod,[7] and gone beyond the bounds of even the prince's indefinite decorum. There are chords in the hearts of the most reckless which cannot be touched without emotion. Even with the utterly lost, to whom life and death are equally jests, there *are* matters of which no jest can be properly made.

The whole company, indeed, seemed now deeply to feel that in the costume and bearing of the stranger neither wit nor propriety existed. The figure was tall and gaunt, and shrouded from head to foot in the habiliments of the grave. The mask which concealed the visage was made so nearly to resemble the countenance of a stiffened corpse that the closest scrutiny must have had difficulty in detecting the cheat. And yet all this might have been endured, if not approved, by the mad revellers around. But the mummer had gone so far as to assume the type of the Red Death. His vesture was dabbled in *blood* — and his broad brow, with all the features of the face, was besprinkled with the scarlet horror.

When the eyes of the Prince Prospero fell upon this spectral image (which with a slow and solemn movement, as if more fully to sustain its *rôle*, stalked to and fro among the waltzers) he was seen to be convulsed, in the first moment, with a strong shudder either of terror or distaste; but, in the next, his brow reddened with rage.

---

[7] Phrase from William Shakespeare's (1564-1616) *Hamlet* Act III. Sc. 2, in reference to exceeding evil or wrongdoing

"Who dares?" he demanded hoarsely of the group that stood around him, "who dares thus to make mockery of our woes? Uncase the varlet that we may know whom we have to hang to-morrow at sunrise from the battlements.[8] Will no one stir at my bidding? — stop him and strip him, I say, of those reddened vestures of sacrilege!"

It was in the eastern or blue chamber in which stood the Prince Prospero as he uttered these words. They rang throughout the seven rooms loudly and clearly — for the prince was a bold and robust man, and the music had become hushed at the waving of his hand.

It was in the blue room where stood the prince, with a group of pale courtiers by his side. At first, as he spoke, there was a slight rushing movement of this group in the direction of the intruder, who at the moment was also near at hand, and now, with deliberate and stately step, made closer approach to the speaker.

But from a certain nameless awe with which the mad assumptions of the mummer had inspired the whole party, there were found none who put forth hand to seize him; so that, unimpeded, he passed within a yard of the prince's person; and, while the vast assembly, as if with one impulse, shrank from the centres of the rooms to the walls, he made his way uninterruptedly, but with the same solemn and measured step which had distinguished him from the first, through the blue chamber to the purple — through the purple to the green — through the green to the orange, — through this again to the white — and even thence to the violet, ere a decided movement had been made to arrest him.

It was then, however, that the Prince Prospero, maddening with rage and the shame of his own momentary cowardice, rushed hurriedly through the six chambers — while none followed him on account of a deadly terror that had seized upon all. He bore aloft a drawn dagger, and had approached, in rapid impetuosity, to within three or four feet of the retreating figure, when the latter, having attained the extremity of the velvet apartment, turned suddenly round and confronted his pursuer. There was a sharp cry — and the dagger dropped gleaming upon the sable carpet, upon which instantly afterwards, fell prostrate in death the Prince Prospero.

---

[8] Walls used for defense and offensive strikes

Then, summoning the wild courage of despair, a throng of the revellers at once threw themselves into the black apartment, and, seizing the mummer, whose tall figure stood erect and motionless within the shadow of the ebony clock, gasped in unutterable horror at finding the grave-cerements and corpse-like mask which they handled with so violent a rudeness, untenanted by any tangible form.

And now was acknowledged the presence of the Red Death. He had come like a thief in the night. And one by one dropped the revellers in the blood-bedewed halls of their revel, and died each in the despairing posture of his fall. And the life of the ebony clock went out with that of the last of the gay. And the flames of the tripods expired. And Darkness and Decay and the Red Death held illimitable dominion over all.

JOSEPH SHERIDAN LE FANU
(1814-1873)

Introduction
to
A Chapter in the History of a Tyrone Family

Edgar Allan Poe is the king of the early horror story and Joseph Sheridan le Fanu is the king of the early ghost story given the sheer number he penned, their high level of writing, and originality.

And it is Fanu's originality that calls into question the novelty of a key section of Charlotte Brontë's most famous novel—*Jane Eyre*. The similarities will become apparent as you read it. They are so strong—so uncanny—that I am convinced Brontë lifted them from Fanu. In the afterword to this story I will compare and analyze them so the story is not given away here.

The resemblance to real life events does not stop with Charlotte Brontë. Unknown to Fanu at the time he was penning "A Chapter in the History of a Tyrone Family," the eerie story would soon draw striking parallels to his own life. In 1844 he married Susanna Bennett. About a decade later she began suffering from a neurological disease, causing the struggling writer (who desperately needed popularity) to limit her interaction with the public. In 1858 an extreme attack of hysteria ushered in Bennett's death, which happened the following day.

"A Chapter in the History of a Tyrone Family" was first published in 1839 as a "tenth extract from the legacy of the late Francis Purcell FP, of Drumcoolagh." The fictional

Francis Purcell is presented to readers in the preface of "The Ghost and the Bone-Setter" (Fanu's first published ghost story) as a real priest with an antiquary and literary hobby. "A Chapter in the History of a Tyrone Family" was expanded by Fanu in 1869 and published as a novel titled *The Wyvern Mystery*.

Sometimes the most frightening ghost stories are when the reader does not see the ghost but instead experiences their aftermath. M. R. James makes this evident in many of this stories and that is certainly the case here. Thanks to a 1923 introduction to *Madam Crowl's Ghost and Other Tales of Mystery* by M. R. James, Fanu's stories were foisted back into the public eye and are read to this day. A number of his ghost stories, and his superb vampire tale "Carmilla," have stood the test of time and he greatly influenced M. R. James's (perceive but don't show) style of supernatural writing.

If Fanu was the father of the Victorian ghost story, then M. R. James was certainly one of his sons. Perhaps M. R. James is the first born and deserving heir to Fanu's inheritance in this line of ghost story construction where the ghost is only partially shown to the reader, or never at all.

A Chapter in the History
of a Tyrone Family
(1839)

[IN THE FOLLOWING NARRATIVE, I have endeavoured to give as nearly as possible the *"ipsisiima verba"*[1] of the valued friend from whom I received it, conscious that any aberration from *her* mode of telling the tale of her own life, would at once impair its accuracy and its effect.

Would, that, with her words, I could also bring before you her animated gesture, her expressive countenance, the solemn and thrilling air and accent with which she related the dark passages in her strange story; and, above all, that I could communicate the impressive consciousness that the narrator had seen with her own eyes, and personally acted in the scenes which she described; these accompaniments, taken with the additional circumstance, that she who told the tale was one far too deeply and sadly impressed with religious principle, to misrepresent or fabricate what she repeated as fact, gave to the tale a depth of interest which the events recorded could hardly, themselves, have produced.

I became acquainted with the lady from whose lips I heard this narrative, nearly twenty years since, and the story struck my fancy so much, that I committed it to paper while it was still fresh in my mind, and should its perusal afford you entertainment for a listless half hour, my labour shall not have been bestowed in vain. I find that I have taken the story down as she told it, in the first person, and, perhaps, this is as it should be. She began as follows.]

My maiden name was Richardson[2] the designation of a family of some distinction in the county of Tyrone. I was

---

[1] The exact words

[2] [Fanu footnote] I have carefully altered the names as they appear in the original MSS., for the reader will see that some of the circumstances recorded are not of a kind to reflect honour upon those involved in them; and, as many are still living, in every way honoured and honourable, who stand in close relation

the younger of two daughters, and we were the only
children. There was a difference in our ages of nearly six
years, so that I did not, in my childhood, enjoy that close
companionship which sisterhood, in other circumstances,
necessarily involves; and while I was still a child, my sister
was married. The person upon whom she bestowed her
hand, was a Mr. Carew, a gentleman of property and
consideration in the north of England. I remember well the
eventful day of the wedding; the thronging carriages, the
noisy menials, the loud laughter, the merry faces, and the
gay dresses. Such sights were then new to me, and
harmonized ill with the sorrowful feelings with which I
regarded the event which was to separate me, as it turned
out, for ever, from a sister whose tenderness alone had
hitherto more than supplied all that I wanted in my
mother's affection.

The day soon arrived which was to remove the happy
couple from Ashtown-house. The carriage stood at the
hall-door, and my poor sister kissed me again, and again,
telling me that I should see her soon. The carriage drove
away, and I gazed after it until my eyes filled with tears,
and, returning slowly to my chamber, I wept more bitterly,
and so, to speak more desolately, than ever I had done
before.

My father had never seemed to love, or to take an
interest in me. He had desired a son, and I think he never
thoroughly forgave me my unfortunate sex. My having
come into the world at all as his child, he regarded as a
kind of fraudulent intrusion, and, as his antipathy to me
had its origin in an imperfection of mine, too radical for
removal, I never even hoped to stand high in his good
graces. My mother was, I dare say, as fond of me as she
was of any one; but she was a woman of a masculine and
a worldly cast of mind. She had no tenderness or
sympathy for the weaknesses, or even for the affections of
woman's nature, and her demeanour towards me was
peremptory, and often even harsh. It is not to be
supposed, then, that I found in the society of my parents
much to supply the loss of my sister.

About a year after her marriage, we received letters
from Mr. drew, containing accounts of my sister's health,
which, though not actually alarming, were calculated to

---

to the principal actors in this drama, the reader will see the
necessity of the course which we have adopted.

make us seriously uneasy. The symptoms most dwelt upon, were, loss of appetite and cough. The letters concluded by intimating that he would avail himself of my father and mother's repeated invitation to spend some time at Ashtown, particularly as the physician who had been consulted as to my sister's health had strongly advised a removal to her native air.

There were added repeated assurances that nothing serious was apprehended, as it was supposed that a deranged state of the liver was the only source of the symptoms which seemed to intimate consumption.[3] In accordance with this announcement, my sister and Mr. Carew arrived in Dublin, where one of my father's carriages awaited them, in readiness to start upon whatever day or hour they might choose for their departure. It was arranged that Mr. Carew was, as soon as the day upon which they were to leave Dublin was definitely fixed, to write to my father, who intended that the two last stages should be performed by his own horses, upon whose speed and safety far more reliance might be placed than upon those of the ordinary *post horses,*[4] which were, at that time, almost without exception, of the very worst order. The journey, one of about ninety miles, was to be divided; the larger portion to be reserved for the second day.

On Sunday, a letter reached us, stating that the party would leave Dublin on Monday, and, in due course, reach Ashtown upon Tuesday evening. Tuesday came: the evening closed in, and yet no carriage appeared; darkness came on, and still no sign of our expected visitors. Hour after hour passed away, and it was now past twelve; the night was remarkably calm, scarce a breath stirring, so that any sound, such as that produced by the rapid movement of a vehicle, would have been audible at a considerable distance.

For some such sound I was feverishly listening. It was, however, my father's rule to close the house at nightfall, and the window-shutters being fastened, I was unable to reconnoitre the avenue as I would have wished. It was nearly one o'clock, and we began almost to despair of seeing them upon that night, when I thought I distinguished the sound of wheels, but so remote and

---

3 Tuberculosis
4 Horses kept at an inn for rental by travellers

faint as to make me at first very uncertain. The noise
approached; it become louder and clearer; it stopped for a
moment. I now heard the shrill screaking of the rusty iron,
as the avenue gate revolved on its hinges; again came the
sound of wheels in rapid motion.

"It is they," said I, starting up, "the carriage is in the
avenue."

We all stood for a few moments, breathlessly listening.
On thundered the vehicle with the speed of a whirlwind;
crack went the whip, and clatter went the wheels, as it
rattled over the uneven pavement of the court; a general
and furious barking from all the dogs about the house,
hailed its arrival.

We hurried to the hall in time to hear the steps let
down with the sharp clanging noise peculiar to the
operation, and the hum of voices exerted in the bustle of
arrival. The hall-door was now thrown open, and we all
stepped forth to greet our visitors. The court was perfectly
empty; the moon was shining broadly and brightly upon
all around; nothing was to be seen but the tall trees with
their long spectral shadows, now wet with the dews of
midnight.

We stood gazing from right to left, as if suddenly
awakened from a dream; the dogs walked suspiciously,
growling and snuffing about the court, and by totally and
suddenly ceasing their former loud barking, as also by
carrying their tails between their legs, expressing the
predominance of fear. We looked one upon the other in
perplexity and dismay, and I think I never beheld more
pale faces assembled. By my father's direction, we looked
about to find anything which might indicate or account for
the noise which we had heard; but no such thing was to
be seen—even the mire which lay upon the avenue was
undisturbed. We returned to the house, more panic struck
than I can describe. On the next day, we learned by a
messenger, who had ridden hard the greater part of the
night, that my sister was dead. On Sunday evening, she
had retired to bed rather unwell, and, on Monday, her
indisposition declared itself unequivocally to be malignant
fever.

She became hourly worse, and, on Tuesday night, a
little after midnight, she expired.[5] I mention this

------

5 [Fanu footnote] The residuary legatee of the late Frances
Purcell, who has the honour of selecting such of his lamented old

circumstance, because it was one upon which a thousand wild and fantastical reports were founded, though one would have thought that the truth scarcely required to be improved upon; and again, because it produced a strong and lasting effect upon my spirits, and indeed, I am inclined to think, upon my character. I was, for several years after this occurrence, long after the violence of my grief subsided, so wretchedly low-spirited and nervous, that I could scarcely be said to live, and during this time, habits of indecision, arising out of a listless acquiescence

---

friend's manuscripts as may appear fit for publication, in order that the lore which they contain may reach the world before scepticism and utility have robbed our species of the precious gift of credulity, and scornfully kicked before them, or trampled into annihilation, those harmless fragments of picturesque superstition, which it is our object to preserve, has been subjected to the charge of dealing too largely in the marvellous; and it has been half insinuated that such is his love for *diablerie,* that he is content to wander a mile out of his way, in order to meet a fiend or a goblin, and thus to sacrifice all regard for truth and accuracy to the idle hope of affrighting the imagination, and thus pandering to the bad taste of his reader.

He begs leave, then, to take this opportunity of asserting his perfect innocence of all the crimes laid to his charge, and to assure his reader that he never *pandered to his bad taste,* nor went one inch out of his way to introduce witch, fairy, devil, ghost, or any other of the grim fraternity of the redoubted Raw-head and bloody-bones. His province, touching these tales, has been attended with no difficulty and little responsibility; indeed, he is accountable for nothing more than an alteration in the names of persons mentioned therein, when such a step seemed necessary, and for an occasional note, whenever he conceived it possible, innocently, to edge in a word. These tales have been *written down,* as the heading of each announces, by the Rev. Francis Purcell, P. P. of Drumcoolagh; and in all the instances, which are many, in which the present writer has had an opportunity of comparing the manuscript of his departed friend with the actual traditions which are current . amongst the families whose fortunes they pretend to illustrate, he has uniformly found that whatever of supernatural occurred in the story, so far from having been exaggerated by him, had been rather softened down, and, wherever it could be attempted, accounted for.

in the will of others, a fear of encountering even the slightest opposition, and a disposition to shrink from what are commonly called amusements, grew upon me so strongly, that I have scarcely even yet, altogether overcome them.

We saw nothing more of Mr. Carew. He returned to England as soon as the melancholy rites attendant upon the event which I have just mentioned were performed; and not being altogether inconsolable, he married again within two years; after which, owing to the remoteness of our relative situations, and other circumstances, we gradually lost sight of him.

I was now an only child; and, as my elder sister had died without issue, it was evident that, in the ordinary course of things, my father's property, which was altogether in his power, would go to me, and the consequence was, that before I was fourteen, Ashtown-house was besieged by a host of suitors; however, whether it was that *I* was too young, or that none of the aspirants to my hand stood sufficiently high in rank or wealth, I was suffered by both parents to do exactly as I pleased; and well was it for me, as I afterwards found that fortune, or, rather Providence, had so ordained it, that I had not suffered my affections to become in any degree engaged, for my mother would never have suffered any *silly fancy* of mine, as she was in the habit of styling an attachment, to stand in the way of her ambitious views; views which she was determined to carry into effect, in defiance of every obstacle, and in order to accomplish which, she would not have hesitated to sacrifice anything so unreasonable and contemptible as a girlish passion.

When I reached the age of sixteen, my mother's plans began to develope themselves, and, at her suggestion, we moved to Dublin to sojourn for the winter, in order that no time might be lost in disposing of me to the best advantage. I had been too long accustomed to consider myself as of no importance whatever, to believe for a moment that I was in reality the cause of all the bustle and preparation which surrounded me, and being thus relieved from the pain which a consciousness of my real situation would have inflicted, I journeyed towards the capital with a feeling of total indifference.

My father's wealth and connection had established him in the best society, and, consequently, upon our arrival in the metropolis, we commanded whatever enjoyment or advantages its gaieties afforded. The tumult and novelty of the scenes in which I was involved did not fail considerably to amuse me, and my mind gradually recovered its tone, which was naturally cheerful. It was almost immediately known and reported that I was an heiress, and of course my attractions were pretty generally acknowledged. Among the many gentlemen whom it was my fortune to please, one, ere long, established himself in my mother's good graces, to the exclusion of all less important aspirants. However, I had not understood, or even remarked his attentions, nor, in the slightest degree, suspected his or ray mother's plans respecting me, when I was made aware of them rather abruptly by my mother herself. We had attended a splendid ball, given by Lord M_____, at his residence in Stephen's-green,[6] and I was, with the assistance of my waiting-maid, employed in rapidly divesting myself of the rich ornaments which, in profuseness and value, could scarcely have found their equals in any private family in Ireland.

I had thrown myself into a lounging chair beside the fire, listless and exhausted, after the fatigues of the evening, when I was aroused from the reverie into which I had fallen, by the sound of footsteps approaching my chamber, and my mother entered.

"Fanny, my dear," said she, in her softest tone. "I wish to say a word or two with you before I go to rest. You are not fatigued, love, I hope?"

"No, no, madam, I thank you," said I, rising at the same time from my seat with the formal respect so little practised now.

"Sit down, my dear," said she, placing herself upon a chair beside me;" I must chat with you for a quarter of an hour or so. Saunders, (to the maid) you may leave the room; do not close the room door, but shut that of the lobby."

This precaution against curious ears having been taken as directed, my mother proceeded.

"You have observed, I should suppose, my dearest Fanny; indeed, you *must* have observed, Lord Glenfallen's marked attentions to you?"

"I assure you, madam," I began.

"Well, well, that is all right," interrupted my mother; "of course you must be modest upon the matter; but listen

---

[6] City park in Dublin, Ireland

to me for a few moments, my love, and I will prove to your satisfaction that your modesty is quite unnecessary in this case. You have done better than we could have hoped, at least, so very soon. Lord Glenfallen is in love with you. I give you joy o your conquest," and saying this, my mother kissed my forehead.

"In love with me!" I exclaimed, in unfeigned astonishment.

"Yes, in love with you," repeated my mother; "devotedly, distractedly in love with you. Why, my dear, what is there wonderful in it; look in the glass, and look at these," she continued, pointing with a smile to the jewels which I had just removed from my person, and which now lay a glittering heap upon the table.

"May there not," said I, hesitating between confusion and real alarm; "is it not possible that some mistake may be at the bottom of all this?"

"Mistake! dearest; none," said my mother. "None; none in the world; judge for yourself; read this, my love," and she placed in my hand a letter, addressed to herself, the seal of which was broken. I read it through with no small surprise. After some very fine complimentary flourishes upon my beauty and perfections, as, also, upon the antiquity and high reputation of our family, it went on to make a formal proposal of marriage, to be communicated or not to me at present, as my mother should deem expedient; and the letter wound up by a request that the writer might be permitted, upon our return to Ashtown-house, which was soon to take place, as the spring was now tolerably advanced, to visit us for a few days, in case his suit was approved.

"Well, well, my dear," said my mother, impatiently; "do you know who Lord Glenfallen is?"

"I do, madam," said I rather timidly, for I dreaded an altercation with my mother.

"Well, dear, and what frightens you?" continued she; "are you afraid of a title? What has he done to alarm you? he is neither old nor ugly."

I was silent, though I might have said, "he is neither young nor handsome."

"My dear Fanny," continued my mother, "in sober seriousness you have been most fortunate in engaging the affections of a nobleman such as Lord Glenfallen, young and wealthy, with first-rate, yes, acknowledged *first-rate* abilities, and of a family whose influence is not exceeded by that of any in Ireland—of course you see the offer in the same light that I do—indeed I think you *must.*"

This was uttered in no very dubious tone. I was so much astonished by the suddenness of the whole communication that I literally did not know what to say.

"You are not in love?" said my mother, turning sharply, and fixing her dark eyes upon me, with severe scrutiny.

"No, madam," said I, promptly; horrified, as what young lady would not have been, at such a query.

"I'm glad to hear it," said my mother, drily. "Once, nearly twenty years ago, a friend of mine consulted me how he should deal with a daughter who had made what they call a love match, beggared herself, and disgraced her family; and I said, without hesitation, take no care for her, but cast her off; such punishment I awarded for an offence committed against the reputation of a family not my own; and what I advised respecting the child of another, with full as small compunction I would *do* with mine. I cannot conceive anything more unreasonable or intolerable than that the fortune and the character of a family should be marred by the idle caprices of a girl."

She spoke this with great severity, and paused as if she expected some observation from me. I, however, said nothing.

"But I need not explain to you, my dear Fanny," she continued, "my views upon this subject; you have always known them well, and I have never yet had reason to believe you likely, voluntarily, to offend me, or to abuse or neglect any of those advantages—which reason and duty tell you should be improved—come hither, my dear, kiss me, and do not look so frightened. Well, now, about this letter, you need not answer it yet; of course you must be allowed time to make up your mind; in the mean time I will write to his lordship to give him my permission to visit us at Ashtown—good night, my love."

And thus ended one of the most the disagreeable, not to say astounding, conversations I had ever had; it would not be easy to describe exactly what where my feelings towards Lord Glenfallen; whatever might have been my mother's suspicions, my heart was perfectly disengaged; and hitherto, although I had not been made in the slightest degree acquainted with his real views, I had liked him very much, as an agreeable, well informed man, whom I was always glad to meet in society; he had served in the navy in early life, and the polish which his manners received in his after intercourse with courts and cities had but served to obliterate that frankness of *manner* which belongs proverbially to the sailor.

Whether this apparent candour went deeper than the outward bearing I was yet to learn; however there was no doubt that as far as I had seen of Lord Glenfallen, he was, though perhaps not so young as might have been desired in a lover, a singularly pleasing man, and whatever feeling unfavourable to him had found its way into my mind, arose altogether from the dread, not an unreasonable one, that constraint might be practised upon my inclinations. I reflected, however, that Lord Glenfallen was a wealthy man, and one highly thought of; and although I could never expect to love him in the romantic sense of the term, yet I had no doubt but that, all things considered, I might be more happy with him than I could hope to be at home.

When next I met him it was with no small embarrassment, his tact and good breeding, however, soon reassured me, and effectually prevented my awkwardness being remarked upon; and I had the satisfaction of leaving Dublin for the country with the full conviction that nobody, not even those most intimate with me, even suspected the fact of Lord Glenfallen's having made me a formal proposal. This was to me a very serious subject of self gratulation, for, besides my instinctive dread of becoming the topic of the speculations of gossip, I felt that if the situation which I occupied in relation to him were made publicly known, I should stand committed in a mariner which would scarcely leave me the power of retraction.

The period at which Lord Glenfallen had arranged to visit Ashtown house was now fast approaching, and it became my mother's wish to form me thoroughly to her will, and to obtain my consent to the proposed marriage before his arrival, so that all things might proceed smoothly without apparent opposition or objection upon my part; whatever objections, therefore, *I* had entertained were to be subdued; whatever disposition to resistance I had exhibited or had been supposed to feel, were to be completely eradicated before he made his appearance, and my mother addressed herself to the task with a decision and energy against which even the barriers, which hot imagination had created, could hardly have stood.

If she had, however, expected any determined opposition from me, she was agreeably disappointed; my heart was perfectly free, and all my feelings of liking and preference were in favour of Lord Glenfallen, and I well knew that in case I refused to dispose of myself as I was desired, my mother had alike the power and the will to render my existence as utterly miserable as any, even the most ill assorted marriage could possibly have done.

You wilt remember, my good friend, that I was very young and very completely under the controul of my parents, both of whom, my mother particularly, were unscrupulously determined in matters of this kind, and willing, when voluntary obedience on the part of those within their power was withheld, to compel a forced acquiescence by an unsparing use of all the engines of the most stern and rigorous domestic discipline. All these combined, not unnaturally, induced me to resolve upon yielding at once, and without useless opposition, to what appeared almost to be my fate. The appointed time was come, and my now accepted suitor arrived; he was in high spirits, and, if possible, more entertaining than ever. I was not, however, quite in the mood to enjoy his sprightliness; but whatever I wanted in gaiety was amply made up in the triumphant and gracious good humour of my mother, whose smiles of benevolence and exultation were showered around as bountifully as the summer sunshine.

I will not weary you with unnecessary prolixity. Let it suffice to say, that I was married to Lord Glenfallen with all the attendant pomp and circumstance of wealth, rank, and grandeur. According to the usage of the times, now humanely reformed, the ceremony was made until long past midnight, the season of wild, uproarious, and promiscuous feasting and revelry. Of all this I have a painfully vivid recollection, and particularly of the little annoyances inflicted upon me by the dull and coarse jokes of the wits and wags who abound in all such places, and upon all such occasions. I was not sorry, when, after a few days, Lord Glenfallen's carriage appeared at the door to convey us both from Ashtown; for any change would have been a relief from the irksomeness of ceremonial and formality which the visits received in honour of my newly acquired titles hourly entailed upon me. It was arranged that we were to proceed to Cahergillagh, one of the Glenfallen estates, lying, however, in a southern county, so that a tedious journey (then owing to the impracticability of the roads,) of three days intervened.

I set forth with my noble companion, followed by the regrets of some, and by the envy of many, though God knows I little deserved the latter; the three days of travel were now almost spent, when passing the brow of a wild heathy hill, the domain of Cahergillagh opened suddenly upon our view. It formed a striking and a beautiful scene. A lake of considerable extent stretching away towards the west, and reflecting from its broad, smooth waters, the rich glow of the setting sun, was overhung by steep hills, covered by a rich mantle of velvet sward, broken here and there by the grey front of some old rock, and exhibiting on their shelving sides, their slopes and hollows, every variety of light and shade; a thick wood of dwarf oak, birch, and hazel skirted these hills, and clothed the shores of the lake, running out in rich luxuriance upon every promontory, and spreading upward considerably upon the side of the hills.

"There lies the enchanted castle," said Lord Glenfallen, pointing towards a considerable level space intervening between two of the picturesque hills, which rose dimly around the lake. This little plain was chiefly occupied by the same low, wild wood which covered the other parts of the domain; but towards the centre a mass of taller and statelier forest trees stood darkly grouped together, and among them stood an ancient square tower, with many buildings of an humbler character, forming together the manor house, or, us it was more usually called, the court of Cahergillagh.

As we approached the level upon which the mansion stood, the winding road gave us many glimpses of the time-worn castle and its surrounding buildings; and seen as it was through the long vistas of the tine old trees, and with the rich glow of evening upon it, I have seldom beheld an object more picturesquely striking. I was glad to perceive, too, that here and there the blue curling smoke ascended from stacks of chimneys now hidden by the rich, dark ivy, which, in a great measure, covered the building; other indications of comfort made themselves manifest as we approached; and indeed, though the place was evidently one of considerable antiquity, it had nothing whatever of the gloom of decay about it.

"You must not, my love," said Lord Glenfallen, "imagine this place worse than it is. I have no taste for antiquity, at least I should not choose a house to reside in because it is old. Indeed I do not recollect that I was even so romantic as to overcome my aversion to rats and rheumatism, those faithful attendants upon your noble relics of feudalism; and I much prefer a snug, modern, unmysterious bedroom, with well-aired sheets, to the waving tapestry, mildewed cushions, and all the other interesting appliances of romance; however, though I cannot promise you all the discomfort generally pertaining to an old castle, you will find legends and ghostly lore enough to claim your respect; and if old Martha be still to the fore, as I trust she is, you will soon have a supernatural and appropriate anecdote for every closet and corner of the mansion; but here we are—so, without more ado, welcome to Cahergillagh."

We now entered the hall of the castle, and while the domestics were employed in conveying our trunks and other luggage which we had brought with us for immediate use to the apartments which Lord Glenfallen had selected for himself and me, I went with him into a spacious sitting room, wainscoted with finely polished black oak, and hung round with the portraits of various of the worthies of the Glenfallen family.

This room looked out upon an extensive level covered with the softest green sward, and irregularly bounded by the wild wood I have before mentioned, through the leafy arcade formed by whose boughs and trunks the level beams of the setting sun were pouring; in the distance, a group of dairy maids were plying their task, which they accompanied throughout with snatches of Irish songs which, mellowed by the distance, floated not unpleasingly to the ear; and beside them sat or lay, with all the grave importance of conscious protection, six or seven large dogs of various kinds; farther in the distance, and through the cloisters of the arching wood, two or three ragged urchins were employed in driving such stray kine[7] as had wandered farther than the rest to join their fellows.

As I looked upon this scene which I have described, a feeling of tranquillity and happiness came upon me, which I have never experienced in so strong a degree; and so strange to me was the sensation that my eyes filled with tears. Lord Glenfallen mistook the cause of my emotion, and taking me kindly and tenderly by the hand he said,

---

[7] Cattle

"Do not suppose, my love, that it is my intention to *settle* here, whenever you desire to leave this, you have only to let me know your wish and it shall be complied with, so I must entreat of you not to surfer any circumstances which I can controul to give you one moment's uneasiness; but here is old Martha, you must be introduced to her, one of the heir-looms of our family."

A hale, good-humoured, erect, old woman was Martha, and an agreeable contrast to the grim, decrepit hag, which my fancy had conjured up, as the depository of all the horrible tales in which I doubted not this old place was most fruitful. She welcomed me and her master with a profusion of gratulations, alternately kissing our hands and apologising for the liberty, until at length Lord Glenfallen put an end to this somewhat fatiguing ceremonial, by requesting her to conduct me to my chamber if it were prepared for my reception. I followed Martha up an old-fashioned, oak stair-case into a long, dim passage at the end of which lay the door which communicated with the apartments which had been selected for our use; here the old woman stopped, and respectfully requested me to proceed.

I accordingly opened the door and was about to enter, when something like a mass of black tapestry as it appeared disturbed by my sudden approach, fell from above the door, so as completely to screen the aperture; the startling unexpectedness of the occurrence, and the rustling noise which the drapery made in its descent, caused me involuntarily to step two or three paces backwards, I turned, smiling and half ashamed to the old servant, and said, "You see what a coward I am."

The woman looked puzzled, and without saying any more, I was about to draw aside the curtain and enter the room, when upon turning to do so, I was surprised to find that nothing whatever interposed to obstruct the passage. I went into the room, followed by the servant woman, and was amazed to find that it, like the one below, was wainscoted, and that nothing like drapery was to be found near the door.

"Where is it," said I; "what has become of it?"

"What does your ladyship wish to know?" said the old woman.

"Where is the black curtain that fell across the door, when I attempted first to come to my chamber," answered I.

"The cross of Christ about us," said the old woman, turning suddenly pale.

"What is the matter, my good friend," said I; "you seem frightened."

"Oh, no, no, your ladyship," said the old woman, endeavouring to conceal her agitation; but in vain, for tottering towards a chair, she sunk into it, looking so deadly pale and horrorstruck that I thought every moment she would faint.

"Merciful God, keep us from harm and danger," muttered she at length.

"What can have terrified you so," said I, beginning to fear that she had seen, something more than had met my eye, "you appear ill, my poor woman."

"Nothing, nothing, my lady," said she, rising; "I beg your ladyship's pardon for making so bold; may the great God defend us from misfortune."

"Martha," said I, "something *has* frightened you very much, and I insist on knowing what it is; your keeping me in the dark upon the subject will make me much more uneasy than any thing you could tell me; I desire you, therefore, to let me know what agitates you; I command you to tell me."

"Your ladyship said you saw a black curtain falling across the door when you were coming into the room," said the old woman.

"I did," said I; "but though the whole thing appears somewhat strange I cannot see any thing in the matter to agitate you so excessively."

"It's for no good you saw that, my lady," said the Crone; "something terrible is coming; its a sign, my lady— a sign that never fails."

"Explain, explain what you mean, my good woman," said I, in spite of myself, catching more than I could account for of her superstitious terror.

"Whenever something—something *bad* is going to happen to the Glenfallen family, some one that belongs to them sees a black handkerchief or curtain just waved or falling before their faces; I saw it myself," continued she, lowering her voice, "when I was only a little girl, and I'll never forget it; I often heard of it before, though I never saw it till then, nor since, praised be God; but I was going into Lady Jane's room to waken her in the morning; and sure enough when I got first to the bed and began to draw the curtain, something dark was waved across the division, but only for a moment; and when I saw rightly into the bed, there was she lying cold and dead, God be merciful to me; so my lady there is small blame to me to be daunted when any one of the family sees it, for it's many's the story I heard of it, though I saw it but once."

I was not of a superstitious turn of mind; yet I could not resist a feeling of awe very nearly allied to the fear which my companion had so unreservedly expressed; and when you consider my situation, the loneliness, antiquity, and gloom of the place, you will allow that the weakness was not without excuse. In spite of old Martha's boding predictions, however, time flowed on in an unruffled course; one little incident, however, though trifling in itself, I must relate as it serves to make what follows more intelligible.

Upon the day after my arrival, Lord Glenfallen of course desired to make me acquainted with the house and domain; and accordingly we set forth upon our ramble; when returning, he became for some time silent and moody, a state so unusual with him as considerably to excite my surprise, I endeavoured by observations and questions to arouse him—but in vain; at length as we approached the house, he said, as if speaking to himself, "'twere madness—madness—madness," repeating the word bitterly—"sure and speedy ruin." There was here a long pause; and at length turning sharply towards me in a tone very unlike that in which he had hitherto addressed me, he said, "do you think it possible that a woman can keep a secret?"

"I am sure," said I, "that women are very much belied upon the score of talkativeness, and that I may answer your question with the same directness with which you put it; I reply that I *do* think a woman can keep a secret."

"But I do not," said he, drily.

We walked on in silence for a time; I was much astonished at his unwonted abruptness; I had almost said rudeness. After a considerable pause he seemed to recollect himself, and with an effort resuming his sprightly manner, he said, "well, well, the next thing to keeping a secret well is, not to desire to possess one—talkativeness and curiosity generally go together; now I shall make test of you in the first place, respecting the latter of these qualities. I shall be your *Bluebeard*[8]—tush, why do I trifle thus; listen to me, my dear Fanny, I speak now in solemn earnest; what I desire is, intimately, inseparably, connected with your happiness and honour as well as my own; and your compliance with my request will not be difficult; it will impose upon you a very trifling restraint during your sojourn here, which certain events which have occurred since our arrival, have determined me shall not be a long one.

"You must promise me, upon your sacred honour, that you will visit *only* that part of the castle which can be reached from the front entrance, leaving the back entrance and the part of the building commanded immediately by it, to the menials, as also the small garden whose high wall you see yonder; and never at any time seek to pry or peep into them, nor to open the door which communicates from the front part of the house through the corridor with the back. I do not urge this in jest or in caprice, but from a solemn conviction that danger and misery will be the certain consequences of your not observing what I prescribe. I cannot explain myself further at present—promise me, then, these things as you hope for peace here and for mercy hereafter."

I did make the promise as desired, and he appeared relieved; his manner recovered all its gaiety and elasticity, but the recollection of the strange scene which I have just described dwelt painfully upon my mind.

More than a month passed away without any occurrence worth recording; but I was not destined to leave Cahergillagh without further adventure; one day intending to enjoy the pleasant sunshine in a ramble through the woods, I ran up to my room to procure my bonnet and shawl; upon entering the chamber, I was surprised and somewhat startled to find it occupied; beside the fireplace and nearly opposite the door, seated in a large, old-fashioned elbow-chair, was placed the figure of a lady; she appeared to be nearer fifty than forty, and was dressed suitably to her age, in a handsome suit of flowered silk; she had a profusion of trinkets and jewellery about her person, and many rings upon her fingers; but

---

[8] "Bluebeard," published in 1697 by Charles Perrault (1628-1703), tells of a rich man whose wives disappear; when he invites a new romance into his castle she is forbidden to enter one room; when she does she finds the remains of his other wives

although very rich, her dress was not gaudy or in ill taste; but what was remarkable in the lady was, that although her features were handsome, and upon the whole pleasing; the pupil of each eye was dimmed with the whiteness of cataract, and she was evidently stone blind. I was for some seconds so surprised at this unaccountable apparition, that I could not find words to address her.

"Madam," said I, "there most be some mistake here—this is my bedchamber."

"Marry come up," said the lady, sharply; "*your* chamber! Where is Lord Glenfallen?"

"He is below, madam," replied I; "and I am convinced he will be not a little surprised to find you here."

"I do not think he will," said she; "with your good leave, talk of what you know something about; tell him I want him; why does the minx dilly dally so?"

In spite of the awe which this grim lady inspired, there was something in her air of confident superiority which, when I considered our relative situations was not a little irritating.

"Do you know, madam to whom you speak," said I?

"I neither know nor care," said she; "but I presume that you are some one about the house, so, again, I desire you, if you wish to continue here, to bring your master hither forthwith."

"I must tell you madam," said I "that I am Lady Glenfallen."

"What's that," said the stranger, rapidly.

"I say, madam," I repeated, approaching her, that I might be more distinctly heard, "that I am Lady Glenfallen."

"It's a lie, you trull," cried she, in an accent which made me start, and, at the same time, springing forward, she seized me in her grasp and shook me violently, repeating, "it's a lie, it's a lie," with a rapidity and vehemence which swelled every vein of her face; the violence of her action, and the fury which convulsed her face, effectually terrified me, and disengaging myself from her grasp, I screamed as loud as I could for help; the blind woman continued to pour out a torrent of abuse upon me, foaming at the mouth with rage, and impotently shaking her clenched fists towards me.

I heard Lord Glenfallen's step upon the stairs, and I instantly ran out; as I past him I perceived that he was deadly pale, and just caught the words, "I hope that demon has not hurt you?"

I made some answer, I forget what, and he entered the chamber, the door of which he locked upon the inside; what passed within I know not; but I heard the voices of the two speakers raised in loud and angry altercation. I thought I heard the shrill accents of the woman repeat the words, "let her look to herself;" but I could not be quite sure. This short sentence, however, was, to my alarmed imagination, pregnant with fearful meaning; the storm at length subsided, though not until after a conference of more than two long hours.

Lord Glenfallen then returned, pale and agitated, "that unfortunate woman," said he, "is out of her mind; I dare say she treated you to some of her ravings, but you need not dread any further interruption from her, I have brought her so far to reason. She did not hurt you I trust."

"No, no," said I; "but she terrified me beyond measure."

"Well," said he, "she is likely to behave better for the future, and I dare swear that neither you nor she would desire after what has passed to meet again."

This occurrence, so startling and unpleasant, so involved in mystery, and giving rise to so many painful surmises, afforded me no very agreeable food for rumination. All attempts on my part to arrive at the truth were baffled; Lord Glenfallen evaded all my enquiries, and at length peremptorily forbid any further allusion to the matter. I was thus obliged to rest satisfied with what I had actually seen, and to trust to time to resolve the perplexities in which the whole transaction had involved me. Lord Glenfallen's temper and spirits gradually underwent a complete and most painful change; he became silent and abstracted, his manner to me was abrupt and often harsh, some grievous anxiety seemed ever present to his mind; and under its influence his spirits sunk and his temper became toured.

I soon perceived that his gaiety was rather that which the stir and excitement of society produces, than the result of a healthy habit of mind; and every day confirmed me in the opinion, that the considerate good nature which I had so much admired in him was little more than a mere manner; and to my infinite grief and surprise, the gay, kind, open-hearted nobleman who had for months followed and flattered me, was rapidly assuming the form of a gloomy, morose, and singularly selfish man; this was a bitter discovery, and I strove to conceal it from my myself as long as I could, but the truth was not to be denied, and I was forced to believe that Lord Glenfallen no longer loved me, and that he was at little pains to conceal the alteration in his sentiments.

One morning after breakfast, Lord Glenfallen had been for some time walking silently up and down the room, buried in his moody reflections, when pausing suddenly, and turning towards me, he exclaimed, "I have it, I have it; we must go abroad and stay there, too, and if that does not answer, why—why we must try some more effectual expedient. Lady Glenfallen, I have become involved in heavy embarrassments, a wife you know must share the fortunes of her husband, for better for worse, but I will waive my right if you prefer remaining here—here at Cahergillagh; for I would not have you seen elsewhere without the state to which your rank entitles you; besides it would break your poor mother's heart," he added, with sneering gravity, "so make up your mind—Cahergillagh or France. I will start if possible in a week, so determine between this and then."

He left the room, and in a few moments I saw him ride past the window, followed by a mounted servant; he had directed a domestic to inform me that he should not be back until the next day. I was in very great doubt as to what course of conduct I should pursue, as to accompanying him in the continental tour so suddenly determined upon, I felt that it would be a hazard too great to encounter; for at Cahergillagh I had always the consciousness to sustain me, that if his temper at any time led him into violent or unwarrantable treatment of me, I had a remedy within reach, in the protection and support of my own family, from all useful and effective communication with whom, if once in France, I should be entirely debarred.

As to remaining at Cahergillagh in solitude, and for aught I knew, exposed to hidden dangers, it appeared to me scarcely less objectionable than the former proposition; and yet I feared that with one or other I must comply, unless I was prepared to come to an actual breach with Lord Glenfallen; full of these unpleasing doubts and perplexities, I retired to rest. I was wakened, after having slept uneasily for some hours, by some person shaking me rudely by the shoulder; a small lamp burned in my room, and by its light, to my horror and amazement, I discovered that my visitant was the self-same blind, old lady who had so terrified me a few weeks before.

I started up in the bed, with a view to ring the bell, and alarm the domestics, but she instantly anticipated me by saying, "do not be frightened, silly girl; if I had wished to harm you I could have done it while you were sleeping, I need not have wakened you; listen to me, now, attentively and fearlessly; for what I have to say, interests you to the full as much as it docs me; tell me, here, in the presence of God, did Lord Glenfallen marry you, *actually marry you?*—speak the truth, woman."

"As surely as I live and speak," I replied, "did Lord Glenfallen marry me in presence of more than a hundred witnesses."

"Well," continued she, "he should have told you *then,* before you married him, that he had a wife living, which wife I am; I feel you tremble—tush! do not be frightened. I do not mean to harm you—mark me now—you are *not* his wife. When I make my story known you will be so, neither in the eye of God nor of man; you must leave this house upon to-morrow; let the world know that your husband has another wife living; go, you, into retirement, and leave him to justice, which will surely overtake him. If you remain in this house alter to-morrow you will reap the bitter fruits of your sin," so saying, she quitted the room, leaving me very little disposed to sleep.

Here was food for my very worst and most terrible suspicions; still there was not enough to remove all doubt. I had no proof of the truth of this woman's statement. Taken by itself there was nothing to induce me to attach weight to it; but when I viewed it in connection with the extraordinary mystery of some of Lord Glenfallen's proceedings, his strange anxiety to exclude me from certain portions of the mansion, doubtless, lest I should encounter this person—the strong influence, nay, command, which she possessed over him, a circumstance clearly established by the very fact of her residing in the very place, where of all others, he should least have desired to find her—her thus acting, and continuing to act in direct contradiction to his wishes; when I say I viewed her disclosure in connection with all these circumstances, I could not help feeling that there was at least a fearful verisimilitude in the allegations which she had made.

Still I was not satisfied, nor nearly so; young minds
have a reluctance almost insurmountable to believing
upon any thing short of unquestionable proof, the
existence of premeditated guilt in any one whom they have
ever trusted; and in support of this feeling I was assured
that if the assertion of Lord Glenfallen, which nothing in
this woman's manner had led me to disbelieve, were true,
namely, that her mind was unsound, the whole fabric of
my doubts and fears must fall to the ground. I determined
to state to Lord Glenfallen freely and accurately the
substance of the communication which I had just heard,
and in his words and looks to seek for its proof or
refutation; full of these thoughts I remained wakeful and
excited all night, every moment fancying that I heard the
step, or saw the figure of my recent visitor towards whom I
felt a species of horror and dread which I can hardly
describe.

There was something in her face, though her features
had evidently been handsome, and were not, at first sight,
unpleasing, which, upon a nearer inspection, seemed to
indicate the habitual prevalence and indulgence of evil
passions, and a power of expressing mere animal anger,
with an intenseness that I have seldom seen equalled, and
to which an almost unearthly effect was given by the
convulsive quivering of the sightless eyes.

You may easily suppose that it was no very pleasing
reflection to me to consider, that whenever caprice might
induce her to return, I was within the reach of this violent,
and, for aught I knew, insane woman, who had, upon that
very night, spoken to me in a tone of menace, of which her
mere words, divested of the manner and look with which
she uttered them, can convey but a faint idea. Will you
believe me when I tell you that I was actually afraid to
leave my bed in order to secure the door, lest I should
again encounter the dreadful object lurking in some
corner or peeping from behind the window curtains, so
very a child was I in my fears.

The morning came, and with it Lord Glenfallen. I knew
not, and indeed I cared not, where he might have been; my
thoughts were wholly engrossed by the terrible fears and
suspicions which my last night's conference had
suggested to me; he was, as usual, gloomy and abstracted,
and I feared in no very fitting mood to hear what I had to
say with patience, whether the charges were true or false.
I was, however, determined not to suffer the opportunity

to pass, or Lord Glenfallen to leave the room, until, at all hazards, I had unburdened my mind.

"My Lord," said I, after a long silence, summoning up all my firmness, "my lord, I wish to say a few words to you upon a matter of very great importance, of very deep concernment to you and to me." I fixed my eyes upon him to discern, if possible, whether the announcement caused him any uneasiness, but no symptom of any such feeling was perceptible.

"Well, my dear," said he, "this is, no doubt, a very grave preface, and portends, I have no doubt, something extraordinary—pray let us have it without more ado."

He took a chair, and seated himself nearly opposite to me.

"My lord," said I, "I have seen the person who alarmed me so much a short time since, the blind lady, again, upon last night;" his face upon which my eyes were fixed, turned pale, he hesitated for a moment, and then said—

"And did you, pray madam, so totally forget or spurn my express command, as to enter that portion of the house from which your promise, I might say, your oath, excluded you—answer me that?" he added, fiercely.

"My lord," said I, "I have neither forgotten your *commands,* since such they were, nor disobeyed them. I was, last night, wakened from my sleep, as I lay in my own chamber, and accosted by the person whom I have mentioned—how she found access to the room I cannot pretend to say."

"Ha! this must be looked to," said he, half reflectively; "and pray," added he, quickly, while in turn he fixed his eyes upon me, "what did this person say, since some comment upon her communication forms, no doubt, the sequel to your preface."

"Your lordship is not mistaken," said I, "her statement was so extraordinary that I could not think of withholding it from you; she told me, my lord, that you had a wife living at the time you married me, and that she was that wife."

Lord Glenfallen became ashy pale, almost livid; he made two or three efforts to clear his voice to speak, but in vain, and turning suddenly from me, he walked to the window; the horror and dismay, which, in the olden time, overwhelmed the woman of Endor,[9] when her spells unexpectedly conjured the dead into her presence, were but types of what I felt, when thus presented with what appeared to be almost unequivocal evidence of the guilt, whose existence I had before so strongly doubted. There was a silence of some moments, during which it were hard to conjecture whether I or my companion suffered most.

Lord Glenfallen soon recovered his self command; he returned to the table, again sat down and said—"What you have told me has so astonished me, has unfolded such a tissue of motiveless guilt, and in a quarter from which I had so little reason to look for ingratitude or treachery, that your announcement almost deprived me of speech; the person in question, however, has one excuse, her mind is, as I told you before, unsettled.

"You should have remembered that, and hesitated to receive as unexceptionable evidence against the honour of your husband, the ravings of a lunatic. I now tell you that this is the last time I shall speak to you upon this subject, and, in the presence of the God who is to judge me, and as I hope for mercy in the day of judgment, I swear that the charge thus brought against me, is utterly false, unfounded, and ridiculous; I defy the world in any point to taint my honour; and, as I have never taken the opinion of madmen touching your character or morals, I think it but fair to require that you will evince a like tenderness for me; and now, once for all, never again dare to repeat to me your insulting suspicions, or the clumsy and infamous calumnies of fools. I shall instantly let the worthy lady who contrived this somewhat original device, understand fully my opinion upon the matter—good morning;" and with these words he left me again in doubt, and involved in all horrors of the most agonizing suspense.

I had reason to think that Lord Glenfallen wreaked his vengeance upon the author of the strange story which I had heard, with a violence which was not satisfied with mere words, for old Martha, with whom I was a great favourite, while attending me in my room, told me that she feared her master had ill used the poor, blind, Dutch woman, for that she had heard her scream as if the very

9 The Bible (I Samuel 28:7-20) describes the curious passage of the woman at Endor, a medium, who is contacted by Saul to conjure the dead and when Samuel appears to them both they are very afraid

life were leaving her, but added a request that I should not speak of what she had told me to any one, particularly to the master.

"How do you know that she is a Dutch woman?" inquired I, anxious to learn anything whatever that might throw a light upon the history of this person, who seemed to have resolved to mix herself up in my fortunes.

"Why, my lady," answered Martha, "the master often calls her the Dutch hag, and other names you would not like to hear, and I am sure she is neither English nor Irish; for, whenever they talk together, they speak some queer foreign lingo, and fast enough, I'll be bound; but I ought not to talk about her at all; it might be as much as my place is worth to mention her—only you saw her first yourself, so there can be no great harm in speaking of her now."

"How long has this lady been here?" continued I.

"She came early on the morning after your ladyship's arrival," answered she; "but do not ask me any more, for the master would think nothing of turning me out of doors for daring to speak of her at all, much less to *you*, my lady."

I did not like to press the poor woman further; for her reluctance to speak on this topic was evident and strong. You will readily believe that upon the very slight grounds which my information afforded, contradicted as it was by the solemn oath of my husband, and derived from what was, at best, a very questionable source, I could not take any very decisive measure whatever; and as to the menace of the strange woman who had thus unaccountably twice intruded herself into my chamber, although, at the moment, it occasioned me some uneasiness, it was not, even in my eyes, sufficiently formidable to induce my departure from Cahergillagh.

A few nights after the scene which I have just mentioned. Lord Glenfallen having, as usual, early retired to his , study, I was left alone in the parlour to amuse myself as best I might. It was not strange that my thoughts should often recur to the agitating scenes in which I had recently taken a part; the subject of my reflections, the solitude, the silence, and the lateness of the hour, as also the depression of spirits to which I had of late been a constant prey, tended to produce that nervous excitement which places us wholly at the mercy of the imagination. In order to calm my spirits, I was endeavouring to direct my thoughts into some more pleasing channel, when I heard, or thought I heard, uttered, within a few yards of me, in an odd half-sneering tone, the words, "There is blood upon your ladyship's throat."

So vivid was the impression, that I started to my feet, and involuntarily placed my hand upon my neck. I looked around the room for the speaker, but in vain. I went then to the room door, which I opened, and peered into the passage, nearly faint with horror, lest some leering, shapeless thing should greet me upon the threshold. When I had gazed long enough to assure myself that no strange object was within sight, "I have been too much of a rake, lately; I am racking out my nerves," said I, speaking aloud, with a view to reassure myself.

I rang the bell, and, attended by old Martha, I retired to settle for the night. While the servant was, as was her custom, arranging the lamp which I have already stated always burned during the night in my chamber, I was employed in undressing, and, in doing so, I had recourse to a large looking-glass which occupied a considerable portion of the nail in which it was fixed, rising from the ground to a height of about six feet; this mirror filled the space of a large panel in the wainscoting opposite the foot of the bed. I had hardly been before it for the lapse of a minute, when something like a black pall was slowly waved between me and it.

"Oh, God! there it is," I exclaimed wildly. "I have seen it again, Martha—the black cloth."

"God be merciful to us, then!" answered she, tremulously crossing herself. "Some misfortune is over us."

"No, no, Martha," said I, almost instantly recovering my collectedness; for, although of a nervous temperament, I had never been superstitious. "I do not believe in omens. You know, I saw, or fancied I saw, this thing before, and nothing followed."

"The Dutch lady came the next morning," replied she.

"Methinks, such an occurrence scarcely deserved a supernatural announcement," I replied.

"She is a strange woman, my lady," said Martha, "and she is not *gone* yet—mark my words."

"We'll, well, Martha," said I, "I have not wit enough to change your opinions, nor inclination to alter mine; so I will talk no more of the matter. Good night," and so I was left to my reflections.

After lying for about an hour awake, I at length fell into a kind of doze; but my imagination was still busy, for I was startled from this unrefreshing sleep by fancying that I heard a voice close to my face exclaim as before, "There is blood upon your ladyship's throat." The words were instantly followed by a loud burst of laughter.

Quaking with horror, I awakened, and heard my husband enter the room. Even this was a relief. Scared as I was, however, by the tricks which my imagination had played me, I preferred remaining silent, and pretending to sleep, to attempting to engage my husband in conversation, for I well knew that his mood was such, that his words would not, in all probability, convey anything that had not better be unsaid and unheard.

Lord Glenfallen went into his dressing-room, which lay upon the right-hand side of the bed. The door lying open, I could see him by himself, at full length upon a sofa, and, in about half an hour, I became aware, by his deep and regularly drawn respiration, that he was fast asleep. When slumber refuses to visit one, there is something peculiarly irritating, not to the temper, but to the nerves, in the consciousness that some one is in your immediate presence, actually enjoying the boon which you are seeking in vain; at least, I have always found it so, and never more than upon the present occasion.

A thousand annoying imaginations harassed and excited me, every object which I looked upon, though ever so familiar, seemed to have acquired a strange phantomlike character, the varying shadows thrown by the flickering of the lamplight, seemed shaping themselves into grotesque and unearthly forms, and whenever my eyes wandered to the sleeping figure of my husband, his features appeared to undergo the strangest and most demoniacal contortions.

Hour after hour was told by the old clock, and each succeeding one found me, if possible, less inclined to sleep than its predecessor. It was now considerably past three; my eyes, in their involuntary wanderings, happened to alight upon the large mirror which was, as I have said, fixed in the wall opposite the foot of the bed.

A view of it was commanded from where I lay, through the curtains, as I gazed fixedly upon it, I thought I perceived the broad sheet of glass shifting its position in relation to the bed; I riveted my eyes upon it with intense scrutiny; it was no deception, the mirror, as if acting of its own impulse, moved slowly aside, and disclosed a dark aperture in the wall, nearly as large as an ordinary door; a figure evidently stood in this; but the light was too dim to define it accurately. It stepped cautiously into the chamber, and with so little noise, that had I not actually seen it, I do not think I should have been aware of its presence. It was arrayed in a kind of woollen nightdress, and a white handkerchief or cloth was bound tightly about the head; I had no difficulty spite of the strangeness of the attire in recognising the blind woman whom I so much dreaded.

She stooped down, bringing her head nearly to the ground, and in that attitude she remained motionless for some moments, no doubt in order to ascertain if any suspicious sound were stirring. She was apparently satisfied by her observations, for she immediately recommenced her silent progress towards a ponderous mahogany dressing table of my husband's; when she had reached it, she paused again, and appeared to listen attentively for some minutes; she then noiselessly opened one of the drawers from which, having groped for some time, she took something which I soon perceived to be a case of razors; she opened it and tried the edge of each of the two instruments upon the skin of her hand; she quickly selected one, which she fixed firmly in her grasp; she now stooped down as before, and having listened for a time, she, with the hand that was disengaged, groped her way into the dressing room where Lord Glenfallen lay fast asleep.

I was fixed as if in the tremendous spell of a night mare. I could not stir even a ringer; I could not lift my voice; I could not even breathe, and though I expected every moment to see the sleeping man murdered, I could not even close my eyes to shut out the horrible spectacle, which I had not the power to avert. I saw the woman approach the sleeping figure, she laid the unoccupied hand lightly along his clothes, and having thus ascertained his identity, she, after a brief interval, turned back and again entered my chamber; here she bent down again to listen.

I had now not a doubt but that the razor was intended for my throat; yet the terrific fascination which had locked all my powers so long, still continued to bind me fast. I felt that my life depended upon the slightest ordinary exertion, and yet I could not stir one joint from the position in which I lay, nor even make noise enough to waken Lord Glenfallen.

The murderous woman now, with long, silent steps, approached the bed; my very heart seemed turning to ice; her left hand, that which was disengaged, was upon the pillow; she gradually slid it forward towards my head, and in an instant, with the speed of lightning, it was clutched in my hair, while, with the other hand, she dashed the razor at my throat.

A slight inaccuracy saved me from instant death; the blow fell short, the point of the razor grazing my throat; in a moment I know not how, I found myself at the other side of the bed uttering shriek after shriek; the wretch was, however, determined if possible to murder me, scrambling along by the curtains; she rushed round the bed towards me; I seized the handle of the door to make my escape; it was, however, fastened; at all events I could not open it, from the mere instinct of recoiling terror, I shrunk back into a corner—she was now within a yard of me—her hand was upon my face—I closed my eyes fast, expecting never to open them again, when a blow, inflicted from behind by a strong arm, stretched the monster senseless at my feet; at the same moment the door opened, and several domestics, alarmed by my cries, entered the apartment.

I do not recollect what followed, for I fainted. One swoon succeeded another so long and death-like, that my life was considered very doubtful. At about ten o'clock, however, I sunk into a deep and refreshing sleep, from which I was awakened at about two, that I might swear my deposition before a magistrate, who attended for that purpose.

I, accordingly, did so, as did also Lord Glenfallen; and the woman was fully committed to stand her trial at the ensuing assizes.[10] I shall never forget the scene which the examination of the blind woman and of the other parties afforded. She was brought into the room in the custody of two servants; she wore a kind of flannel wrapper which had not been changed since the night before; it was torn and soiled, and here and there smeared with blood, which had flowed in large quantities from a wound in her head;

---

[10] An intermittent court in Ireland and Wales that heard various civil and criminal cases

the white handkerchief had fallen off in the scuffle; and her drizzled hair fell in masses about her wild and deadly pale countenance.

She appeared perfectly composed, however, and the only regret she expressed throughout, was at not having succeeded in her attempt, the object of which she did not pretend to conceal. On being asked her name, she called herself the Countess Glenfallen, and refused to give any other title.

"The woman's name is Flora VanKemp," said Lord Glenfallen.

"It *was,* it *was,* you perjured traitor and cheat," screamed the woman; and then there followed a volley of words in some foreign language. "Is there a magistrate here," she resumed; "I am Lord Glenfallen's wife—I'll prove it—write down my words. I am willing to be hanged or burned, so *he* meets his deserts. I did try to kill that doll of his; but it was he who put it into my head to do it—two wives were too many—I was to murder her, or she was to hang me—listen to all I have to say."

Here Lord Glenfallen interrupted. "I think sir," said he, addressing the magistrate, "that we had better proceed to business, this unhappy woman's furious recriminations but waste our time; if she refuses to answer your questions, you had better, I presume, take my depositions."

"And are you going to swear away my life, you black perjured murderer!" shrieked the woman. "Sir, sir, sir, you must hear me," she continued, addressing the magistrate, "I can convict him—he bid me murder that girl, and then when I failed, he came behind me, and struck me down, and now he wants to swear away my life—take down all I say."

"If it is your intention," said the magistrate, "to confess the crime with which you stand charged, you may, upon producing sufficient evidence, criminate whom you please."

"Evidence!—I have no evidence but myself," said the woman. "I will swear it all—write down my testimony— write it down, I say—we shall hang side by side, my brave Lord—all your own handy-work, my gentle husband." This was followed by a low, insolent, and sneering laugh, which, from one in her situation, was sufficiently horrible.

"I will not at present hear anything," replied he, "but distinct answers to the questions which I shall put to you upon this matter."

"Then you shall hear nothing," replied she sullenly, and no inducement or intimidation could bring her to speak again.

Lord Glenfallen's deposition and mine were then given, as also those of the servants who had entered the room at the moment of my rescue; the magistrate then intimated that she was committed, and must proceed directly to gaol, whither she was brought in a carriage of Lord Glenfallen's, for his lordship was naturally by no means indifferent to the effect which her vehement accusations against himself might produce, if uttered before every chance nearer whom she might meet with between Cahergillagh and the place of confinement whither she was dispatched.

During the time which intervened between the committal and the trial of the prisoner, Lord Glenfallen seemed to suffer agonies of mind which baffle all description, he hardly ever slept, and when he did, his slumbers seemed but the instruments of new tortures, and his waking hours were, if possible, exceeded in intensity of terrors by the dreams which disturbed his sleep. Lord Glenfallen rested, if to lie in the mere attitude of repose were to do so, in his dressing-room, and thus I had an opportunity of witnessing, far oftener than I wished it, the fearful workings of his mind; his agony often broke out into such fearful paroxysms that delirium and total loss of reason appeared to be impending; he frequently spoke of flying from the country, and bringing with him all the witnesses of the appalling scene upon which the prosecution was founded; then again he would fiercely lament that the blow which he had inflicted had not ended all.

The assizes arrived, however, and upon the day appointed, Lord Glenfallen and I attended in order to give our evidence. The cause was called on, and the prisoner appeared at the bar. Great curiosity and interest were felt respecting the trial, so that the court was crowded to excess. The prisoner, however, without appearing to take the trouble of listening to the indictment, pleaded guilty, and no representations on the part of the court, availed to induce her to retract her plea. After much time had been wasted in a fruitless attempt to prevail upon her to reconsider her words, the court proceeded according to the usual form, to pass sentence.

This having been done, the prisoner was about to be removed, when she said in a low, distinct voice—"A word— a word, my Lord:—is Lord Glenfallen here in the court?" On being told that he was, she raised her voice to a tone of loud menace, and continued—"Hardress, Earl of Glenfallen, I accuse you here in this court of justice of two crimes,—first, that you married a second wife, while the first was living, and again, that you prompted me to the murder, for attempting which I am to die;—secure him— chain him—bring him here."

There was a laugh through the court at those words, which were naturally treated by the judge as a violent extemporary recrimination, and the woman was desired to be silent.

"You won't take him, then," she said, "you won't try him? You'll let him go free?"

It was intimated by the court that he would certainly be allowed "to go free," and she was ordered again to be removed. Before, however, the mandate was executed, she threw her arms wildly into the air, and uttered one piercing shriek so full of preternatural rage and despair, that it might fitly have ushered a soul into those realms where hope can come no more.

The sound still rang in my ears, months after the voice that had uttered it was for ever silent. The wretched woman was executed in accordance with the sentence which had been pronounced. For some time after this event, Lord Glenfallen appeared, if possible, to suffer more than he had done before, and altogether, his language, which often amounted to half confessions of the guilt imputed to him, and all the circumstances connected with the late occurrences, formed a mass of evidence so convincing that I wrote to my father, detailing the grounds of my fears, and imploring him to come to Cahergillagh. without delay, in order to remove me from my husband's control, previously to taking legal steps for a final separation.

Circumstanced as I was, my existence was little short of intolerable, for, besides the fearful suspicions which attached to my husband, I plainly perceived that if Lord Glenfallen were not relieved, and that speedily, insanity must supervene. I therefore expected my father's arrival, or at least a letter to announce it, with indescribable impatience.

About a week after the execution had taken place, Lord Glenfallen one morning met me with an unusually sprightly air—"Fanny," said he, "I have it now for the first time, in my power to explain to your satisfaction every thing which has hitherto appeared suspicious or mysterious in my conduct. After breakfast come with me to my study, and I shall, I hope, make all things clear."

This invitation afforded me more real pleasure than I had experienced for months; something had certainly occurred to tranquillize my husband's mind, in no ordinary decree, and I thought it by no means impossible that he would, in the proposed interview, prove himself the most injured and innocent of men.

Full of this hope I repaired to his study at the appointed hour; he was writing busily when I entered the room, and just raising his eyes, he requested me to be seated. I took a chair as he desired, and remained silently awaiting his leisure, while he finished, folded, directed, and sealed his letter; laying it then upon the table, with the address downward, he said—"My dearest Fanny, I know I must have appeared very strange to you and very unkind—often even cruel; before the end of this week I will show you the necessity of my conduct; how impossible it was that I should have seemed otherwise. I am conscious that many acts of mine must have inevitably given rise to painful suspicions—suspicious, which indeed, upon one occasion you very properly communicated to me.

"I have gotten two letters from a quarter which commands respect, containing information as to the course by which I may be enabled to prove the negative of all the crimes which even the most credulous suspicion could lay to my charge. I expected a third by this morning's post, containing documents which will set the matter forever at rest, but owing, no doubt, to some neglect, or, perhaps, to some difficulty in collecting the papers, some inevitable delay, it has not come to hand this morning, according to my expectation. I was finishing one to the very same quarter when you came in, and if a sound routing be worth any thing, I think I shall have a special messenger before two days have passed. I have been thinking over the matter within myself, whether I had better imperfectly clear up your doubt by submitting to your inspection the two letters which I have already

received, or wait till I can triumphantly vindicate myself by
the production of the documents which I have already
mentioned, and I have, I think, not unnaturally decided
upon the latter course; however, there is a person in the
next room, whose testimony is not without its value—
excuse me for one moment."

So saying, he arose and went to the door of a closet
which opened from the study, this he unlocked, and half
opening the door, he said, "it is only I," and then slipped
into the room, and carefully closed and locked the door
behind him. I immediately heard his voice in animated
conversation; my curiosity upon the subject of the letter
was naturally great, so smothering any little scruples
which I might have felt, I resolved to look at the address of
the letter which lay as my husband had left it, with its
face upon the table. I accordingly drew it over to me, and
turned up the direction. For two or three moments I could
scarce believe my eyes, but there could be no mistake—in
large characters were traced the words, "To the Archangel
Gabriel in heaven."

I had scarcely returned the letter to its original
position, and in some degree recovered the shock which
this unequivocal proof of insanity produced, when the
closet door was unlocked, and Lord Glenfallen re-entered
the study, carefully closing and locking the door again
upon the outside.

"Whom have you there?" inquired I, making a strong
effort to appear calm.

"Perhaps," said he musingly, "you might have some
objection to seeing her, at least for a time."

"Who is it?" repeated I.

"Why," said he, "I see no use in hiding it—the blind
Dutchwoman; I have been with her the whole morning.
She is very anxious to get out of that closet, but you know
she is odd, she is scarcely to be trusted."

A heavy gust of wind shook the door at this moment
with a sound as if something more substantial were
pushing against it.

"Ha, ha, ha!—do you hear her," said he, with an
obstreperous burst of laughter. The wind died away in a
long howl, and Lord Glenfallen, suddenly checking his
merriment, shrugged his shoulders, and muttered—, "Poor
devil, she has been hardly used."

"We had better not tease her at present with questions," said I, in as unconcerned a tone as I could assume, although I felt every moment as if I should faint.

"Humph I may be so," said he, "well come back in an hour or two, or when you please, and you will find us here."

He again unlocked the door, and entered with the same precautions which he had adopted before, locking the door upon the inside, and as I hurried from the room, I heard his voice again exerted as if in eager parley. I can hardly describe my emotions; my hopes had been raised to the highest, and now in an instant, all was gone—the dreadful consummation was accomplished—the fearful retribution had fallen upon the guilty man—the mind was destroyed—the power to repent was gone. The agony of the hours which followed what I would still call my *awful* interview with Lord Glenfallen, I cannot describe; my solitude was, however, broken in upon by Martha, who came to inform me of the arrival of a gentleman, who expected me in the parlour.

I accordingly descended, and to my great joy, found my father seated by the fire. This expedition, upon his part, was easily accounted for: my communications had touched the honor of the family. I speedily informed him of the dreadful malady which had fallen upon the wretched man. My father suggested the necessity of placing some person to watch him, to prevent his injuring himself or others. I rang the bell, and desired that one Edward Cooke, an attached servant of the family, should be sent to me.

I told him distinctly and briefly, the nature of the service required of him, and, attended by him, my father and I proceeded at once to the study; the door of the inner room was still closed, and everything in the outer chamber remained in the same order in which I had left it. We then advanced to the closet door, at which we knocked, but without receiving any answer. We next tried to open the door, but in vain—it was locked upon the inside; we knocked more loudly, but in vain. Seriously alarmed, I desired the servant to force the door, which was, after several violent efforts, accomplished, and we entered the closet. Lord Glenfallen was lying on his face upon a sofa.

"Hush," said I, "he is asleep;" we paused for a moment.

"He is too still for that," said my father; we all of us felt a strong reluctance to approach the figure.

"Edward," said I, "try whether your master sleeps."

The servant approached the sofa where Lord Glenfallen lay; he leant his ear towards the head of the recumbent figure, to ascertain whether the sound of breathing was audible; he turned towards us, and said—

"My Lady, you had better not wait here, I am sure he is dead!"

"Let me see the face," said I, terribly agitated, "you *may* be mistaken."

The man then, in obedience to my command, turned the body round, and, gracious God! what a sight met my view;—he was, indeed, perfectly dead. The whole breast of the shirt, with its lace frill, was drenched with gore, as was the couch underneath the spot where he lay. The head hung back, as it seemed almost severed from the body by a frightful gash, which yawned across the throat.

The instrument which had inflicted it, was found under his body. All, then, was over; I was never to learn the history in whose termination I had been so deeply and so tragically involved.

The severe discipline which my mind had undergone was not bestowed in vain. I directed my thoughts and my hopes to that place where there is no more sin, nor danger, nor sorrow.

Thus ends a brief tale, whose prominent incidents many will recognize as having marked the history of a distinguished family, and though it refers to a somewhat distant date, we shall be found not to have taken, upon that account, any liberties with the facts, but in our statement of all the incidents, to have rigorously and faithfully adhered to the truth.

Afterword
to
A Chapter in the History of a Tyrone Family

I'll admit straightaway that it's odd to publish an afterword to only one of the these stories, especially when I have included an introduction. Not wanting to ruin the dramatic effects of the story, and given the overwhelming similarities of the plot and portions of *Jane Eyre*, I am compelled to do it here.

"A History in the Life of a Tyrone Family" was first published (anonymously) in the October 1839 issue of *The Dublin University Magazine*. *Jane Eyre* was published (under the penname "Currer Bell") in October of 1847 in three bound volumes. At that time the industry would first publish the novel in three volumes, then two volumes in a subsequent year, and finally in one bound volume. *Jane Eyre* skipped the second step. In 1850 it was first published in one volume, never in two, and *never* giving any attribution to Joseph Sheridan le Fanu for his outstanding story that you have just read.

Following are some uncanny—perhaps too uncanny—similarities between "A History in the Life of a Tyrone Family" and a major theme of *Jane Eyre*.

First, a Young Woman (Fanny Glenfallen vs. Jane Eyre) is taken to a Gothic mansion (Cahergillagh vs. Thornfield Hall) owned by a handsome yet Strange Man (Lord Glenfallen vs. Edward Fairfax Rochester). Next, the young woman experiences haunting, unexplained events in the mansion.

An insane woman (Flora VanKemp vs. Bertha Rochester) lives in an upper room of the mansion who is the true wife of the strange man. The insane woman finds a way to escape from her upper room and haunts the young woman. The insane woman ultimately confronts the young woman and divulges that she is the *true* wife of the strange man.

Yet the similarities do not stop there. The insane woman in each story viciously goes for the throat of a man. Consider this from *Jane Eyre*, "the lunatic sprung and grappled his throat viciously, and laid her teeth to his cheek." In the "Tyrone Family" the insane woman takes a knife to the throat of Fanny Glenfallen—barely missing—and in the closing scene Lord Glenfallen is found with his throat slit by the specter of Flora VanKemp, the insane first wife.

These striking similarities between the stories make clear that Charlotte Brontë borrowed liberally and sloppily from Joseph Sheridan le Fanu when penning *Jane Eyre*. The originality of this classic novel is tarnished as a result.

Yet Fanu may not have been completely inventive in defining the building blocks of this tale as he admits in the introduction. He claims to have had a lady friend who told him the story in a very theatrical way around 1819. If that is the case, perhaps this mysterious lady is the true genius behind it and Fanu is merely the ghost writer (every pun intended).

ANONYMOUS

Introduction
to
The Deaf and Dumb Girl

This jewel of a ghost story was published on page 37 of *Atkinson's Casket* for July 1839. The sparse introduction tells only that it is "From the French." There is no mention of what area of France, the author, translator nor where it was first published in the French. In the language of the Parisians I can find no other publication that included the story within its pages, which leads me to believe it was derived from French legend and codified for the first time in English.

Regardless, this is truly one of the great ghost stories for the early half of the nineteenth century. The writing is good and so are the characters. As for the plot, there is nothing quite like it for this period. The ending will not soon be forgotten and demonstrates the unique disembodied personification of a haunting.

This is the first time "The Deaf and Dumb Girl" has been republished. It has been nearly 175 years since this ghost story has haunted us and hopefully it will continue to haunt us in the chronicles of our best literature.

The Deaf and Dumb Girl
(1839)

IN THE AUTUMN OF 18—, I was making "the grand tour,"[1] and on my way from Paris to Marseilles, I met with an extraordinary adventure, which I will relate in all its strange and harrowing details. The hill at Autun,[2] covered with its vineyards and their rich fruit, is picturesque and pleasing; but the gathering time was then past, and the scene was flat and dismal; my companions in the diligence were by no means persons of elegant manners, and to make bad worse, a drizzling rain kept falling, and the dampness of the atmosphere caused a depression in the spirits of myself and fellow-travellers.

We had not gone far beyond Autun, when the diligence stopped at the entrance of an avenue, which opened into the high Toad, and led to a splendid mansion, evidently the abode of a person of rank and distinction. A small party of elegantly dressed persons stood at the gate, and it appeared that one of them was about to proceed with us in the conveyance.

Two servants came forward, bringing travelling bags and trunks which were duly fastened upon the roof, and this done, a fine looking young man, in a military cloak and travelling cap, separated himself from the party, which consisted besides himself of an elderly gentleman and two ladies, one of whom seemed to be the mamma of the other, and after kissing the ladies' hands, he advanced and took his seat, without taking the slightest notice of the other passengers, and then putting his head and part of his body out from the window, he maintained a conversation with the ladies until all was ready for starting; and then came the parting words, the words which always fall mournfully on the heart, but most mournfully upon young hearts that love. Several voices exclaimed "A pleasant journey!" but one small timid voice added, *"Adieu, Jules!"* There was sweet music in that timid

---

[1] The grand tour of Europe in the early nineteenth was a tour by wealthy Europeans to see the major cities of the continent and to learn about its art, history, languages and foods
[2] Burgundy area of France

voice; it spoke audibly to the heart, though it scarcely reached the ear. And all who heard it, felt that by the speaker of those parting words, our fellow traveller was *beloved*.

The young man also repeated the word "adieu!" but it was in a much firmer and gayer tone, and he waved his hand and agitated his body, without seeming to care in the least for the other passengers, or to mind the personal inconvenience he put them to. At length the diligence moved on, and the chateau and the party at the gate were left far behind. M. Jules now began to settle himself in his seat, and to cast inquiring glances at his fellow-travellers, by all of whom he was similarly regarded.

He was a fine looking young man, with symmetric figure and a dark expressive countenance; but his eye had an expression of gay recklessness in it, which did not raise him in my estimation; and there was a thoughtless light-hearted joyance in his manner which vexed me. I had at first set him down as a perfect hero of romance. He was very communicative, and gave us to understand that he was a military officer, that the old gentleman, from whom he had just parted, was his uncle, one of the richest land proprietors in Burgundy, and that the younger of the two ladies was his daughter, Josephine, to whom our companion was on the point of being married; and, of course, we were favored with very glowing descriptions of her beauty and virtues.

He was journeying now to make preparations for the wedding; and intended to throw up his commission, abandon a military life, and reside with his wife six months in the country, and the rest of the year in Paris. Such were his arrangements, stated in the course of a lively and animated conversation, which was only interrupted by the sudden stoppage of the vehicle, and we found that our journey was arrested by a multitude of persons of all sexes and ages, singing, shouting, dancing, fiddling. We soon discovered that we were in the midst of a fair. "Why," exclaimed a fellow-passenger, Madame Vernet, after taking an almanac from her reticule, and inspecting it rapidly, "this is St. Ursula's day."[3]

---

[3] St. Ursula's Day is October 21st and a Catholic feast is had in some areas in honor of this saint and the purported 11,000 virgins that were killed in Cologne, Germany by the Huns

"*Ursula!*" exclaimed M. Jules with an expression of surprise, with which alarm appeared to be associated.

"Yea!" rejoined Madame Vernet, handing the almanac to him; "you see, it is St. Ursula's day."

M. Jules took the almanac in his hand, and appeared to look, at it, then repeating the word "Ursula" in a low tone, he returned the book to its owner.

"Ah!" said Madame Vernet, "I suppose Ursula is the second name of your destined bride."

"No!" replied Jules, faintly, and then became silent, thoughtful and reserved.

Evening had by this time drawn imperceptibly on, and upon the hills appeared the last faint reflection of the departed luminary of day; all nature appeared to be calm: the trees were still, the birds sung not among the leaves, the very air was mute, and silence led to reverie—reverie to sleep; the postilions[4] had ceased to swear, and none of us knew how the time had passed when the coach had stopped for supper at Chalons-sur-Saone.[5]

After a hasty meal, again we set out upon our journey, none more anxious than M. Jules. "Are we out of Chalons?" he was constantly enquiring. So frequently was this question put, that at length one of the passengers said "Why do you ask?"

"I have no particular reason for asking," he replied.

"Were you ever at Chalons before?" rejoined the passenger.

"Yes, I was quartered there with my regiment once."

"You have some friends here, then?"

"No," he rejoined quickly, and hastily; the conversation therefore dropped, and very soon afterward the whole of the passengers were in the arms of Morpheus.[6] We could not have slept long before a terrible shake awakened us all; the vehicle had stopped again. The night was extremely dark, and the wind howled mournfully through the trees that skirted the road, a small light upon which, as if from a lanthorn,[7] indicated that we were about to receive an accession to our numbers. The diligence had stopped to take up their passenger.

---

4 Driver of a horse drawn carriage
5 City in the southern region of Burgundy
6 Greek mythological god of dreams
7 Lantern

"We are quite full already," was the general exclamation, when this discovery was made.

"There is still one vacant place," growled the conductor.

There was no disputing this point; but we grumbled, nevertheless, for we had been very comfortable hitherto, and the addition of another person was by no means welcome.

"It's only a young lady," said the conductor, in a tone of voice which indicated he was in a very bad temper. "It's only a young lady, who will not take up much room."

Presently a small figure in white appeared upon the steps; "She will not trouble you," added the conductor, "for she is deaf and dumb; I have carried her before now to Lyons—the devil take her! She has always occasioned me some misfortune." The female had by this time got in, and taken her seat. "Wo-o! wo-o!" cried the conductor, addressing the postilion, "Mind the horses, they are rearing terribly." And then directing his conversation to a man in the garb of a priest, whom we could see by the light of a lanthorn, standing in the road. "Adieu, M. le Cure, you may be sure I'll take care of the young lady!"

Crack went the postilion's whip, and again we were proceeding on our journey.

We were all very desirous of knowing something about our fellow passenger, but as she was deaf and dumb, it was of no use saying a word to her; the ladies, indeed, got up a conversation upon the double misfortune of the poor girl, but that soon ended, and then they moved and fidgeted, to attract attention, but she sat very quiet, and took no notice of any body.

An unpleasant chilliness now came over us; we pulled up the windows, drew our cloaks close around us, and the ladies put shawls over their bonnets. But we still felt uncomfortable, so much so, indeed, that M. Jules let down one of the windows, declaring that the external air was warmer than the atmosphere we breathed in the diligence.

We found this to be the case, and all of us were puzzled to solve this philosophical mystery. We did not shiver now so much as we had done before, but nevertheless, all complained of a very uneasy sensation; and many jests were made upon the subject, and at length some one said that it was entirely attributable to the deaf and dumb girl.

We again endeavored to lull ourselves off to sleep, but could not, one awoke in a fright, another was constantly starting, a third had frightful dreams, and M. Jules moaned so dreadfully, that we were obliged to shake him, and then he told us he had been troubled with a dreadful nightmare.

"Ah!" exclaimed Madame Vernet, "we ate too much for supper at Chalons." And every, body concurred in the opinion thus expressed.

At length day dawned, and the first beams of morning falling upon the white dress of the deaf and dumb girl, again collected our attention toward her. We looked at her in silent amazement. Such a form we had none of us ever beheld before; we were fearful of trusting to our senses, and thought it an illusion. But the sun rising above the horizon put an end to our doubts, and the frightful appearance of our companion became evident.

Her skin was of a deadly white color, and it seemed to cover nothing but bare bones; her lips were thin, so thin indeed, that they scarcely enclosed a perfect set of projecting teeth, and two small eyes sparkled like live coals from the bottom of immense orbits with a vivacity of motion which made her turn her singular countenance from one aide to another with an appearance of insatiable curiosity. Her eyes seemed to interrogate us all in succession, and there was a smile upon her lips, but it was so inconsistent with the general character of her countenance that we averted our heads: it was as if death's head[8] were laughing on our faces.

The silence which the contemplation of this strange figure led to, was first broken by M. Jules, who said, "Were it not for the respect I entertain for the present company, I would say with the conductor, I wish the d—l would take her. Did you ever see such a face as hers? She makes us all shudder."

His observations were interrupted by the extraordinary looks of the subject of them; she gazed rapidly upon us all, and then burst into a fit of laughter but to the sight only, for we heard no sound. This silent laughter raised in us feelings of horror; but not the least sympathy for her misfortunes. We had not time to express our feelings to each other, for directly afterward a sudden jolt occurred,

---

[8] Typically the form of a skull and cross bones, in this instance perhaps only a white skull

and the falling of the diligence intimated that the axle-tree[9] had broken. The confusion which this accident threw us into was great, the females shrieked, the gentlemen expressed themselves in terms not to be mentioned by ears polite. The deaf and dumb girl quickly scrambled over the other passengers and got out first. Happily no one was hurt, and as soon as we extricated ourselves we all congratulated ourselves, except the conductor, who gave vent to loud imprecations. "I knew how it would be," he said, "that speechless woman has brought all this misfortune upon us. This is the third time she has wrought mischief."

Happily there was on inn by the road side in which we could take our breakfast, while the diligence was being put in travelling order again. It was a delightful morning, and though there was nothing in the scenery to make it attractive, we, nevertheless, preferred a ramble to staying at the inn, while breakfast was being prepared for us. At a short distance from the house there was a large cross, surrounded by young elm trees. A small hedge, formed by sweetbriar and common bramble waved gently around a grass-plat, extended round the stone at the foot of the cross. It was the most picturesque object in the neighborhood, and M. Jules resolved upon taking a sketch of it.

"We only want the speechless woman." said he, "to complete the picture."

"Possibly," said I, "it would not be difficult to induce her to sit to *you* for her portrait, for in the diligence she seemed to flirt with you. She looked at you as if she desired to catch your attention."

"The poor wretch," replied M. Jules, as he raised his black silk D'Orsay,[10] and twirled his moustache. "The speechless woman is a coquette![11] And why not! O, woman, woman, you are alike, all the world over."

"I should not suppose that you had much reason to complain. Have you been often in love?"

"Yes; but it seldom lasted for more than a week."

"And yet you are going to be married."

---

[9] Axle for the wheels on the carriage
[10] Silk top hat modeled after that worn by Count Alfred d'Orsay (1801-1852)
[11] Flirt

"Oh, that's a different thing altogether. When a man gets thirty years old, it looks respectable to have a wife. A woman takes your name, and you avail yourself of her property, and leave your titles and estates to your children. It is decidedly respectable to have a wife when you become thirty years old. But that is not what I call love. Josephine is charming, beautiful as an angel, but I have known many angels. Marriage is good, because it fixes you in the station you are to live in. But love is the most delightful thing in the world."

The *roué* would have proceeded, but old Madame Venet, who did not at all agree with him upon these subjects suddenly arose, and fetching the deaf and dumb girl who was playing with a herd of goats, a short distance off, made some signs to the poor creature to kneel and pray with her at the foot of the cross. I know not what the poor girl had at first thought Madame Vernet wished her to do; but she had quietly suffered herself to be led under the elms; but when the good old lady importuned her to kneel, she tripped away, laughing, and returned to the goats, which she at length led to browse upon the briar that formed a hedge round the cross.

"I verily believe," exclaimed Jules, "that the speechless woman is the genius of evil. Look, she is destroying the only beautiful object in this landscape!"

He would have gone and desired her to desist; but at that moment the old goat-herd and his dogs advanced, and drove away the goats from the hedge. The speechless woman looked for a moment at the old man, and then skipped after the animals, whilst Jules and I advanced and desired the goat-herd to continue to protect this pretty little spot. The old man knew nothing of landscape effects, his only motive he said for driving away the goats was, that they should not eat the bushes and grass where a female had been buried about eighteen months before. The whole party were astonished, and made inquiry for further particulars; but the old man knew nothing more, and referred them to the landlady of the inn, where the female had died.

We all returned to the house, and upon making inquiry, were informed by the hostess, that the female in question arrived at her house one rainy night, weary and sad; and her eyes were inflamed with weeping. She asked to have a private room, and being so accommodated, had resided there for nearly a month, paying her expenses every day; but small those expenses were, for the poor creature ate scarcely any thing. She used to wander about at night, and was often seen sitting upon the stones at the foot of the cross, and at other times was heard praying devoutly, and in extreme agony. At length she was one day found suspended from a branch of one of the elms by a silk handkerchief. This was all the hostess knew of he poor girl's story.

"The victim of man's perfidy,[12] no doubt," exclaimed Madame Venet, and the good old lady retired from the company to weep.

"The mayor came," continued the landlady; "and scolded us for giving shelter to a vagabond, for she had no writing about her to indicate who she was; and the priest refused to bury her, or allow her remains to be interred in consecrated ground; but I had pity," said the good hearted creature, "and I begged that the body might be buried near the cross, thinking that the ground there must be almost as good as consecrated ground; and they granted my request." The old woman wiped away a tear, and added, "I have, besides, what I may call her will; it was the only thing she ever wrote in this house, and I have put it into an old frame which she would buy of me for the purpose, after taking from it a fine portrait of the Emperor; and I have also placed it in the public room, according to her last request."

Our curiosity being strongly excited, we desired the landlady to show us this paper, and presently she brought in a glazed frame of black wood, but the glass was so dirty that cot a word could be read until the dirt was removed, M. Jules then took it in his hand; he gazed upon it and changed color, "Heavens!" he exclaimed, "how singular!"

"Do you know the hand-writing?" I inquired.

"I—I," he replied, much embarrassed, "how should I know it?" And he gave the frame into my hands.

The writing was to the following effect:

"If you recognise my hand-writing, be silent, I beseech you;—I implore you not to tell my name, for I shall be afraid of my father, even after death. I am dishonored, and I must die. It is a dreadful thing; but I cannot look my friends in the face again—I cannot endure my mother's rebuke;—I cannot endure my father's curse. I have no more money;—I have not strength to work; and he whom I

---

[12] Deception

love bade me *farewell,* with laughter! Would that I were mad. I fear death—greatly do I fear it; but still I must die. I am not yet eighteen. Let poor girls beware of men who come to them with smiling looks, and words of love;— their voices are ever soft—their promises are always great; they swear before the face of Heaven;—but O! believe them not. I erred, but I dearly loved him who destroyed my peace. All must now end. I hope for the prayers of every Christian soul who passes this way. Let them pray also for *him,* for he is the cause of all. But let them say nothing to my father."

The sobs of the female passengers, and of our good hostess, while I read these simple writings of a seared heart showed how much they were affected—even the men betrayed emotion, and, "albeit unused to the melting mood," I found it impossible to restrain the tears which *would* gush out, despite my efforts to restrain them, when I reflected upon the condition of this wretched girl, *murdered* by some heartless villain; for he who brought ruin upon her was the murderer. Poor girl! poor girl! heaven will have mercy on thee, though the man she loved had none!

Madame Venet uttered a vehement philippic[13] against male perfidy as soon as she could well speak, and became much warmer when M. Jules, who had recovered his presence of mind, endeavored to turn the whole into ridicule. "It is a very lucky thing," he said, "that our *beautiful* little fellow-traveller from Chalons is condemned to silence, for I should have had her also for an antagonist; and it must be confessed, that such a face, talking of love and romance, would have been irresistible."

This observation recalled the speechless lady to our recollection; and we new, for the first time, remarked that she was not present at the breakfast table. We were informed by the conductor that she never sat at table, but contented herself with a crust of dry bread. Upon looking through the open door, I saw her distributing this bread to the goats by which she was surrounded. Poor creature! the goats, after taking from her hand the bread she proffered them, fled away hastily, as if frightened by her looks.

It was at length announced that the damage experienced by the diligence had been repaired; and

---

[13] Fervent speech

accordingly our journey was resumed. During the whole of the way we constantly felt a damp chill, which we could not account for, and experienced much physical and mental uneasiness. M. Jules endeavored to re-assume his wonted gay and easy manner, but vain was his attempt; and we were all well pleased when the diligence stopped at Lyons.

After partaking of some refreshment, M. Jules and I agreed to embark in one of the passage boats which descends the Rhone, he for Valence, and I for Avignon. Freed from the looks of the strange girl in the diligence, my companion renewed his self-possession, and again amused me much by his gay and lively recitals and descriptions of adventures and places. The subject of his approaching marriage, was, of course, uppermost in his mind, and, really, he seemed to be a most fortunate fellow, for his cousin, whom he was about to lead to the altar, was extremely beautiful, and very rich.

The navigation of the Rhone was by no means pleasant, for the sources whence the river is supplied were obstructed, and the water was so extremely low, that our boat frequently touched the bottom; so, that on the second evening, we thought it advisable to put up at a miserable inn at Pomiar; but there we found the food was detestable, and the beds worse. You may be sure that our contemplation of the exchange we had made, did not produce any very pleasant feelings; and, in a state of vexation and discontent, we retired for an inspection of the inn-kitchen, which was, indeed, the only public room in the house. Imagine our surprise when, by the dim light of a solitary iron lamp, we discovered, in a corner, the speechless woman, with her flashing eye-balls fixed upon us."

"Horrible!" exclaimed Jules, "I cannot endure this. I will return and sleep in the boat. Had I been aware that she had chosen this conveyance, I should not have come by it."

I endeavored to prevail upon him to abandon his intention, but in vain, and he quitted the house. Supper was now ready, and a good appetite caused me to forget, for the moment, the speechless woman in the corner; and when I had finished my meal, I found that she was gone. I conjectured that she had retired to rest, and soon afterward went to bed myself.

On repairing to the boat the next morning I was alarmed by the altered appearance of M. Jules. He set apart and abstracted, his countenance pale and haggard; and when I addressed him, he muttered a few indistinct words, and appeared to wish to be left alone. The night had made a woeful change in him; and, during the remainder of the journey, he continued to be reserved and thoughtful. At parting he pressed my hand, and, in a faint voice exclaimed, "*that awful night.*"

"Sir!" I rejoined.

"I could not pray while *she* stood before me."

"Whom!"

"*She!*" he exclaimed, "with her fire-like eyes glaring upon me, searing my heart and brain."

"What do you mean?" I enquired.

"I had sworn, that when I could possibly come to Chalons again I would make her my wife. And thus I triumphed over her unsuspecting virtue. Then I laughed at the ruin I had made; and" Here his voice became quite indistinct, and he muttered several sentences, among which all that I could distinguish was the name of "Ursula."

I was glad when I parted from this strange man, for he seemed now to be intimately connected with the dumb girl; and I began to have the most painful and terrifying apprehensions.

It was some time before I could shake off the unpleasant emotions which the presence of these individuals had occasioned; but time, which effaces strong impressions, soon caused me almost to forget both Jules and the speechless woman.

Having an engagement with a friend in Paris, about a month after the journey above described, I retraced my steps. The passage boat and the miserable inn at Pomier brought back the traveller's companion to my recollection; and, as I turned my eyes to the corner of the inn-kitchen, where I had last seen the terrible female, I felt anxious to know more concerning her; but all my enquiries were made in vain; and even the conductor of the diligence could only tell me, that whenever he had conveyed the speechless woman, same accident was sure to occur to the vehicle. I determined upon stopping at Autun, and making enquiries for M. Jules. Therefore, ordering my luggage to be conveyed to its destination, I left the diligence, and proceeded toward the chateau of the destined bride.

But I had not advanced more than a hundred paces up the avenue, when I heard a trampling noise behind me, and, turning round, I perceived that a funeral procession was returning to the chateau. I conjectured that one of the parents of Josephine was dead; and, stepping aside, I looked enquiringly for M. Jules in the melancholy group. But he was not there. There were several gentlemen; but all strangers to me, and all appeared in a state of terror and alarm, and all hurried past me into the chateau. I detained one of the domestics, and asked the name of the departed. With a look of fear, and in an indistinct voice, he answered "*M. Jules.*"

The domestic was hurrying away, when I caught him by the sleeve, and asked for more particulars; but he broke from me, and rushed into the house.

I sought the inn where I intended to rest that night, and there discovered the cause of the strange emotion among the funeral group. Jules had returned to Autun in a weak and feeble state; the best medical assistance was obtained; but it was all unavailing.

He became delirious, and was continually shrieking, as if in agony; several times a speechless woman in white had been observed about the chateau, and on the day of his death they found her at his bedside, with her fire-like eyes glaring upon him. They drove her from the room, and she tripped laughingly away.

M. Jules had then called for the priest, to whom it was said he had made confession of some grievous crime, and then, his conscience being relieved, he prayed fervently; and thus he died.

And the consternation among the funeral party had been occasioned by the appearance of the speechless woman at his grave.

She stood among the mourners, looking down upon the remains of Jules. His relatives regarded her with feelings of horror, and shrunk from her. The officiating priest advanced, bearing the sacred symbol of his faith, toward her, when she seemed to glide into the grave.

A shriek from the assemblage rent the air. They looked for the strange female, but all they beheld in the grave was the dark coffin which contained the remains of M. Jules.

List of Stories Considered

Anonymous

William Harrison Ainsworth
    1821 The Spectre Bride
    1823 The Sea Spirit

A. B.
    1818 Story of an Apparition

William Auburn
    1849 The Haunted House. A Legend of Edmonton.

William Austin
    1824-1826 Peter Rugg, the Missing Man

Richard Harris Barham
    1840 The Spectre of Tappington

Charlotte Bronte
    1833 Napoleon and the Spectre

Frederick Chamier
    1844 The Haunted House. A True Ghost Story

Phliarète Chasles
    1832 The Eye with No Lid

Thomas Crofton Croker
    1825 The Confessions of Tom Bourke
    1825 The Haunted Cellar
    1825 The Haunted Castle
    1828 The Headless Horseman of Shanacloch

Catherine Crowe
    1848 Haunted Houses

Alan Cunningham
    1822 The Haunted Ships
    1822 The Ghost with the Golden Casket
    1822 The Haunted House

Charles Dickens
    1836 The Story of the Goblins Who Stole a Sexton
    1837 The Story of the Bagman's Uncle

Benjamin Disraeli
    1820 A True Story

Alexander Dumas
    1849 Solange
    1849 The Slap of Charlotte Corday
    1849 Albert

Rebecca Edridge
    1822 The Haunted Castle

E. F. Ellett
    1846 The Haunted House in Georgia

Baron Friedrich Heinrich Karl De la Motte Fouquâe
    1823 The Collier's Family

J. G.
    1835 The Ghost and the Two Blacksmiths

Theophile Gautier (1811-1872)
    1834 Omphale
    1844 Arria Marcella

Joseph Sheridan le Fanu
    1838 The Ghost and the Bone-Setter
    1839 Strange Event in the Life of Schalken the Painter
    1839 A Chapter in the History of a Tyrone Family
    1839 Jim Sulivan's Adventures in the Great Snow
    1840 The Quare Gander
    1843 Spalatro, from the Notes of San Giacomo

John Galt
    1833 The Black Ferry

Nikolai Gogol
    1832 Ivan Fydorovich Shponka and His Aunt
    1842 The Mantle

S. C. Hall
    1836 The Drowned Fisherman

Wilhelm Hauff
    1828 The Spectral Ship

Nathaniel Hawthorne
      1835 Graves and Goblins
      1835 The Old Maid in the Winding Sheet
      1838 Lady Eleanore's Mantle

Earnest Theodore Hoffmann
      1819 The Mines of Falun
      1819 Automata
      1819 The Spectre Bride
      1819 The Elementary Spirit
      1819 The Adventures of Tragott
      1819 Annunziata

James Hogg (Eldritch Sheppard)
      1811 Adam Bell
      1811 The Wool-Gatherer
      1821 Tibby Johnston's Wraith
      1827 The Brownie of the Black Haggs
      1828 Mary Burnet
      1831 Barber of Duncow
      1832 The Mysterious Bride
      1832 Some Terrible Letters from Scotland [Part III]
      1836 Duncan Campbell
      1837 The Woolgatherer
      1837 The Cameronian Preacher's Tale
      1837 Welldean Hall

John Howison
      1821 Vanderdecken's Message Home; or, the Tenacity
of Natural Affection

W. Hughes
      1847 All Souls' Eve

Leigh Hunt
      1819-1821 A Tale for a Chimney Corner

Douglas Hyde
      1888 Teig O'Kane and the Corpse

Washington Irving
      1819 The Specter Bridegroom
      1820 The Legend of Sleepy Hollow
      1822 The Haunted House
      1822 The Storm Ship

1822 Dolph Heyliger
1824 The Bold Dragoon
1824 The Hunting Dinner
1824 The Adventure of My Uncle
1824 Wolfert Webber or Golden Dreams
1831 The Tale of the German Student

Karl Theodore Körner
1815 The Harp

Francis Lathorn
1800-1830 The Water Spectre

Sir Thomas Dick Lauder
1840 The Vision of Campbell of Inverawe
1840 The Water Kelpie's Bridle and The Mermaid's
Stone

Matthew Gregory 'Monk' Lewis
1808 The Midnight Embrace

Edward Bulwer-Lytton
1830 Monos and Daimonos

L. H. M.
1832 The Visionary

Thomas Miller
1842 The Haunted House

Baron Carl von Miltig
1826 The Twelve Nights

Musäus
1817 The Spectre-Barber

Charles Ollier
1841 The Haunted Manor-House of Paddington

Edgar Allan Poe
1835 Morella
1838 Ligeia
1842 The Mask of the Red Death
1842 The Oval Portrait

Alexander Poushkin
1837 The Queen of Spades

Thomas de Quincey
1845 The Apparition of the Brocken

W. R.
1835 The Haunted Chamber

Jean Paul Richter
1844 The Moon

Emma Roberts
1830 The Haunted House

Mrs. Romer
1849 Story of a Haunted House

W. Rowlinson
1846 The Magician

Sir Walter Scott
1827 The Tapestried Chamber; or, the Lady in the
Sacque

Mary Shelley
1831 The Dream

Caroline Elizabeth Sarah Sheridan
1834 Allan M'tavish

William Gilmore Simms
1849 Murder Will Out

Horace Smith
1820-1838 Sir Guy Eveling's Dream

Joseph Snowe
1839 All Souls' Eve
1839 The Water Spirit
1839 The Dead Bride

George Soane
1843 The Sexton of Cologne
1843 An Adventure Near Granville

1843 Hell-Fire, Dick, the Cambridge Coachman
1843 A Legend of Knole, or Knowle Park
1843 The Deserted Castle
1843 Three Spirits

Ludwig Tieck
      1844 The Klausenburg
      1823 The Enchanted Castle
      1823 Auburn Egbert

J. Wadham
      1836 Lady Eltringham or The Castle of Ratcliffe Cross

Samuel Warren
      1831 (Blackwood's) The Spectre-Smitten
      1831 The Spectral Dog

Sarah Scudgell Wilkinson
      1820 The Mysterious Novice

Index of Real Names

Connect with Andrew Barger Online:

WEBSITE:
AndrewBarger.com

BLOG:
AndrewBarger.blogspot.com

FACEBOOK:
Facebook.com/Andrew-Bargers-Official-Facebook-Page/

GOODREADS:
Goodreads.com/author/show/1362598.Andrew_Barger

TWITTER:
twitter.com/andrewbarger

OTHER TITLES BY ANDREW BARGER

Mailboxes – Mansions – Memphistophels
A Collection of Dark Tales

In his first short story collection award-winning author Andrew Barger has unleashed a blend of character-driven dark tales, which are sure to be remembered.

In "Azra'eil & Fudgie" a little girl visits a team of marines in Afghanistan and they quickly learn she is more than she seems. "The Mailbox War" is a deadly tale of a weekend hobby taken to extremes while "The Brownie of the Alabaster Mansion" sees a Scottish monster of antiquity brought back to life. "Memphistopheles" contains a tale of the devil, Memphis, barbeque and a wannabe poet. "The Serpent and the Sepulcher" is a prose poem that will be cherished by all who experience it. "The Gëbult Mansion" recounts a literary hoax played by Andrew on his unsuspecting social networking friends that involves a female vampire. Last, "Stain" is an unforgettable horror story about a stain that will not go away.

Experience these memorable stories tonight.

The Best Horror Short Stories 1800-1849
A Classic Horror Anthology

The Best Horror Short Stories 1800-1849 is a book for anyone who loves a classic horror story.

Thanks to Edgar Allan Poe, Honoré de Balzac, Nathaniel Hawthorne and others, the first half of the nineteenth century is the cradle of all modern horror short stories. Andrew Barger, the editor, read over 300 horror short stories and compiled the dozen best. A few have never been republished since they were first published in leading periodicals of the day such as *Blackwood's* and *Atkinson's Casket*.

At the back of the book Andrew includes a list of all short stories he considered along with their dates of publication and the author, when available. He even includes background for each of the stories, author photos and annotations for difficult terminology.

'The Best Horror Short Stories 1800-1849' will likely become a best seller . . .What makes this collection (of truly terrifying tales!) so satisfying is the presence of a brief introduction before each story, sharing some comments about the writer and elements of the tale. Barger has once again whetted our appetites for fright, spent countless hours making these twelve stories accessible and available, and has provided in one book the best of the best of horror short stories. It is a winner.
GRADY HARP - AMAZON TOP TEN REVIEWER

Through his introduction and footnotes, Barger aims for readers both scholarly and casual, ensuring that the authors get their due while making the work accessible overall to the mainstream.
BOOKGASM

[a] top to bottom pick for anyone who appreciates where the best of horror came from.
MIDWEST BOOK REVIEW

Coffee with Poe
A Novel of Edgar Allan Poe's Life

Coffee with Poe brings Edgar Allan Poe to life within its pages as never before. The book is filled with actual letters from his many romances and literary contemporaries. Orphaned at the age of two, Poe is raised by John Allan— his abusive foster father—who refuses to adopt him until he becomes straight-laced and businesslike. Poe, however, fancies poetry and young women. The contentious relationship culminates in a violent altercation, which causes Poe to leave his wealthy foster father's home to make it as a writer. Poe tries desperately to get established as a writer but is ridiculed by the "Literati of New York." The Raven subsequently gains Poe renown in America yet he slips deeper into poverty, only making $15 off the poem's entire publication history. Desperate for a motherly figure in his life, Poe marries his first cousin who is only thirteen. Poe lives his last years in abject poverty while suffering through the deaths of his foster mother, grandmother, and young wife. In a cemetery he becomes engaged to Helen Whitman, a dark poet who is addicted to ether, wears a small coffin about her neck, and conducts séances in her home. The engagement is soon broken off because of Poe's drinking. In his final months his health is in a downward spiral. Poe disappears on a trip and is later found delirious and wearing another person's clothes. He dies a few days later, whispering his final words: "God help my poor soul."

To give us a historical fiction look at Edgar Allan Poe is great. The start where we are at his mom's funeral gives a little insight into why he may write the way he does. It is very interesting the ideas the author has put into the story about Poe. I like the idea of detailing the life of Edgar Allan Poe into a historical fiction novel." . . . "A great idea to give us some insight into why Poe may be the way he is.
AMAZON BREAKTHROUGH NOVEL AWARD EXPERT REVIEWER

The Best Werewolf Short Stories 1800-1849
A Classic Werewolf Anthology

Andrew Barger has compiled the best werewolf stories from the period when werewolf short stories were first invented. The stories are "Hugues the Wer-Wolf: A Kentish Legend of the Middle Ages," "The Man-Wolf," "A Story of a Weir-Wolf," "The Wehr-Wolf: A Legend of the Limousin," and "The White Wolf of the Hartz Mountains." It is believed that two of these stories have never been republished in over 150 years since their original printing. Read *The Best Werewolf Short Stories 1800-1849* tonight by the light of a full moon.

Knowledgeably compiled and deftly edited by Andrew Barger, "The Best Werewolf Short Stories 1800-1849: A Classic Werewolf Anthology" is a 170-page literary compendium covering a fifty year span from 1800 to 1849 and identifying famous and not-so-well known authors who wrote werewolf stories . . .. After an informed and informative introduction on the subject by Andrew Barger, five of these stories are presented in full, followed by a listing of short stories considered from 1800 to 1849, along with an index of Real Names. A seminal work of impressive scholarship, "The Best Werewolf Short Stories 1800-1849: A Classic Werewolf Anthology" is highly recommended reading for fantasy fans, and a valued addition to academic library Literary Studies reference collections.
MIDWEST BOOK REVIEW

Edgar Allan Poe
Annotated and Illustrated Entire Stories and Poems

For the first time in one compilation are background information for Poe's stories and poems, annotations, foreign word translations, illustrations, photographs of individuals Poe wrote about, and poetry to Poe from his many romantic interests. Here is a sampling of the tales and poems included: "Annabel Lee," "The Bells," "The Black Cat," "[The Bloodhounds]," "The Cask of Amontillado," "The Conqueror Worm," "A Descent into the Maelstrom," "The Fall of the House of Usher," "The Gold-Bug," "The Haunted Palace," "Lenore," "The Masque of the Red Death," "MS. Found in a Bottle," "Murders in the Rue Morgue," "The Oblong Box," "The Pit and the Pendulum," "The Premature Burial," "The Purloined Letter," "[The Rats of Park Theatre]," "The Raven," "Some Words with a

Mummy," "The Swiss Bell-Ringers," "The System of Doctor Tarr and Professor Fether," "The Tell-Tale Heart," and "Thou Art the Man." The classic illustrations are by Gustave Dore and Harry Clarke, with a great introduction by Andrew Barger.

Andrew Barger opens his hefty book that includes all of the prose and poetry of Edgar Allan Poe with an introduction 'Demystifying Poe', an essay so well written and informative that it sets the tenor for the important collections of his book EDGAR ALLAN POE ANNOTATED & ILLUSTRATED ENTIRE STORIES & POEMS: 'Edgar Allan Poe is arguably our most important original and brilliant author of American letters and most misunderstood. His combination of industriousness, minuteness for detail, originality, and respect for his craft are unparalleled.' Barger then proceeds to offer all of the written works of Poe (many of these will be discoveries to the casual Poe reader), offering annotations to clarify the time and setting and influences on each work. This is an ambitious work and one that immediately becomes the scholar's gold standard for research on this major writer of mystery and thrills.

If for no other reason than to have a solid selection of the works of Poe on the shelf, this beautifully designed and handsomely printed book will serve that intent. But once the reader thumbs through this book, pausing to re-read favorites such as 'The Fall of the House of Usher', 'The Murders in the Rue Morgue', 'The Pit and the Pendulum', and 'The Raven', there are many little known gems of short stories, articles, essays, and poems in addition to the stories that are less familiar to the larger audience to discover.

Barger adds 'guidance' to his method of presenting these works by such devices as listing all of the poems under the subheadings of 'Women in Edgar Allan Poe's Life', 'Miscellaneous Poetry both Before and After Age 25', 'Autobiographical', and 'Men in Edgar Allen Poe's Life.' These may seem like minor adjustments to the collections, but in Barger's hands the divisions add meaning and context to the works.

In addition to all of the written works of Poe, this handsome book contains photographs and many of the famous illustrations for his works - especially those of Harry Clarke and Gustave Dore. The fine art of these two men is also honored with annotations adding to their importance to Poe's popularity as a writer. This is simply a

splendid book, handsomely written and produced, and a fine tribute to the literature of Poe - and to the scholarship of Andrew Barger! Highly Recommended.
AMAZON TOP TEN REVIEWER

Orion
An Epic English Poem

Orion is an epic English poem of love and war. It deserves its place next to *Beowulf* in English literature. Its overtones consist of aesthetically pleasing writing with a Shakespearian tinge, all wrapped in classical Greek mythology. It contains a fine introduction by Andrew Barger, a foreword by the author, Richard Horne, and a fantastic review by Edgar Allan Poe. This is all combined with illustrations and annotations for the first time. As Poe stated, "It is our deliberate opinion that, in all that regards the loftiest and holiest attributes of the true Poetry, 'Orion' has never been excelled. Indeed we feel strongly inclined to say that it has never been equaled." While Charlotte Bronte said, "there are passages I shall recur to again and yet again - passages instinct both with power and beauty." Written in 1843, *Orion* is the greatest epic poem you have never read.

The present edition, which not only reprints the complete text of the poem itself, but also provides a brief introduction, a biographical sketch, illustrations, explanatory footnotes, Horne's Preface to the 1854 Australian edition, and Poe's review, in an attractively prepared volume edited by Andrew Barger, constitutes a determined effort to restore the poem to something approaching its former glory.
PROFESSOR PAUL SCHLICKE
UNIVERSITY OF ABERDEEN

Bottletree®

BottletreeBooks.com

CPSIA information can be obtained at www.ICGtesting.com
Printed in the USA
LVOW08s2203071013

355901LV00001B/113/P